Leto's Journey

Leto's Journey

J.N. Pratley

"The possibility of thinking and the possibility
of existing are in fact the same thing."
—*Proem*, Parmenides

VANTAGE PRESS
New York

This is a work of fiction. Any similarity between the characters appearing herein and any real persons, living or dead, is purely coincidental.

Cover design by Susan Thomas

FIRST EDITION

All rights reserved, including the right of
reproduction in whole or in part in any form.

Copyright © 2002 by J. N. Pratley

Published by Vantage Press, Inc.
516 West 34th Street, New York, New York 10001

Manufactured in the United States of America
ISBN: 0-533-14105-2

Library of Congress Catalog Card No.: 01-129295

0 9 8 7 6 5 4 3 2 1

. . . to Marion and Marilyn for having been . . .

Contents

Acknowledgments ix

1 California 1
2 Piraeus 15
3 Kea 28
4 Ydra 41
5 At Sea 56
6 Paros 70
7 Parian Tales 82
8 Milos 100
9 Ios 114
10 Santorini 127
11 Mykonos 144
12 Delos 157
13 Samos 169
14 Kos 187
15 Patmos 201
16 Nameless Island 224
17 Andros 235
18 Aegina 249
19 California Redux 258

Epilogue 269

Acknowledgments

To the people of the Cyclades, because of their amazing three thousand year culture and *philoxenia,* I acknowledge my inspirations for this tale.

To my dear friend and colleague, Dr. Elsie Leach, for her encouragements and expertise.

To the Greek gods and philosophers, profound humility for this, my tribute to them.

Leto's Journey

1
California

A fog bank poured through the Golden Gate, and in Dr. Theodore Koulokotrou's split level house in the Oakland Hills, six academics sipped jug wine and cracked pistachio nuts. Strangers to each other, their introductions had evoked tepid enthusiasm—their hands offered more to be kissed than shaken—and their conversations between nibbles of Danish feta cheese and Sacramento Valley pitted olives had been muted by westerlies lashing the eucalyptus branches outside the house. The glances they had sneaked at one another hadn't aroused much interest either. They appeared wrinkled and distracted, as if they had just come from lecture halls, the men attired in tweed jackets and Ernst ties, the women in gabardine skirts and mannish blouses.

They felt a little relieved when their hostess, tapping her wine glass with the cheese knife, announced in a piccolo voice, "Welcome, everybody. Perhaps we can get started." They turned to focus on a thirtyish, thin-lipped and pinch-nosed woman with a left eyebrow and upper lip that twitched ever so slightly when she tried to smile.

Then, strangely, she climbed halfway up a stepladder, the kind used to bring down books from higher shelves, and held on to its crossbar, her knuckles white, her voice quivering, her head almost obscured by blue paper streamers dangling from the ceiling.

"This is our first meeting and I hope the beginning of long and beautiful friendships." This was met with wan smiles. She paused, giggled and cleared her throat several times. "Please take a seat. There are some folding chairs in the corner, a sofa over here."

Dubious of their purpose, they had come through heavy freeway traffic from as far as Marin County and San Jose. Up a winding road, they had found their hostess' house hidden in a dank, transplanted Australian forest of burned-out patches. Hanging on a steep hillside, oblivious to threats of mudslides and earthquakes, its style was some kind of a California/Japanese hybrid with thin plywood siding and flimsy shingled overhangs. Inside, orange Greek flokati rugs and plastic reproductions of Hermes and Cycladic fertility goddesses lay about. Table lamps fringed with beige crochet lit the den. Overhead, blue and white crepe paper streamers from San Francisco's Chinatown drooped almost head high, and pink plastic flamingos stood guard outside patio sliding doors. Nothing seemed to fit, and nothing could stifle the guests' thoughts about how they would have preferred having an end-of-the-week cocktails with colleagues—or at least stayed home to catch up with student papers.

At this moment, however, not by any stretch, did they feel sociable. They were not particularly adroit at small talk anyhow, and being of different disciplines, common interests were hard to find. What interests they should share—the turmoils of student unrest and demonstrations on their campuses and Governor Reagan's oppressions—were not convivial topics. Furthermore, though all PhDs, they were prone to the pecking orders of academe, subtle one-upmanships that insinuated superiority of University over Community College faculties, the Natural Sciences over the "Unnatural" ones. Comments such as, "Of course, our main thrust is to feed graduate programs." "Hard data is what we're after." "How much Federal funding does your campus receive?" It was all crap, they knew it, but that was the game they had learned to play, even when gametime hadn't commenced.

But, now, their hostess, waiting for them to settle down, perched with hands folded under her chin, said: "As you know, my name is Theodora, but I want to remind you of its Greek meaning. I'm a gift of god." This begged the question, which god? "But you can just call me Dora," she tittered. Pained smiles. "I've spoken to some of you on the phone and answered some questions about dates. Now you're ready to get the whole scoop. This is to be our organizational meeting, so to speak. I'll try to answer all your questions. Let's relax and get acquainted. I have some special treats to serve later. I'm sure you'll like my cooking. Let's be informal, shall we? We have lots of things to talk about, I've made a list. Like the meeting date in Piraeus, how much luggage to take—thinks like that. And I've got good news for you all. I mailed in your deposits and I'm happy to report that I received a Telex confirming our booking for the the *Leto*. Let's hear it now on the count three: One, two, three, Hurrah!" She threw up her thin arms and clapped.

The stands remained hushed.

Then her audience began to squirm. *Deposits?* They thought the twenty-five dollars were to show good intent, in case they wished to join in Theodora's venture. Now, it seemed as if Theodora thought they all were definitely committed. Could they back out gracefully? What had been the agreement, really? Had anyone signed anything? It was all just oral, wasn't it? But before anyone could comment, Theodora quickly descended from her ladder and walked (limped?) across the room, passing around minty meatballs and some *dolmathes,* then laughing nervously, crumpled down on the sofa between the two larger men, clasping their knees to brace herself.

"Let's start out by going around the room and talk a little about ourselves. I'm a Clinical Psychologist at the University here. My parents are Greek and I know the language. We won't have problems on that account, rest assured." With no makeup and attired in a plain-Jane dress, her smirk was unable to conceal something they had all noticed. Between her feeble attempts at jocularity she wore a hurtful, sad expression, a downturned mouth, rheumy eyes, and a deep furrow between her eyebrows. Because her skin was smooth and her hair greyless, these traits seemed etched too deeply for her years. Did she suffer a physical, neurological impairment? A bitterness that women Ph.D.s faced from sexual discrimination?

Karen, a Dallasite with a slight twang, large and poodle-haired, introduced herself as a Community College Administrator and Speech and Drama instructor who had never traveled abroad (only Mexican resorts) but was usually "open to new experiences." She seemed very robust, big-voiced but guarded, too, posturing like a female lead off stage ready to pounce out for a grand entrance.

Frances, diminutive in rimless glasses, an English professor, had traveled in England and seemed to be very cautious, as if she were opening a book from an unknown publisher. "The issue here, for this summer cruise, it seems to me, is the itinerary," she said.

Paul, a classicist, also in rimless glasses and diminutive, had had a Guggenheim to study Etruscan sites. He talked to the ceiling and avoided contractions. "When one seeks a change in venue, it is always paramount to examine alternatives." He and Frances gazed at each other and nodded synchronously.

Ion, a biochemist, handsome and languorous, had traveled in Greece as a teenager with his parents and spoke in six-word sentences. "I work on enzymatic reactive sites," he said. "That has no relevancy here," he added.

Stan, an anthropologist, had trekked in Bhutan and Zambia. A woolly-booger in full beard and pony tail, he was tall and lanky and talked over everyone's heads. "I study people," he said, shooting a penetrating stare for only a millisecond at Ion.

Despite the fact that they surely knew how to project their voices in classrooms, their tones, either because of shyness, reticence, or distrust, could hardly be heard over the rattling of windows and doors in the Pacific winds raging furiously outside Theodora's house. They had learned long ago how academic proprieties preclude too much personal involvement. The subject matter at hand only was important, and to be objective, revelations about personal traits, interests, opinions, and prejudices had to be minimized. So, they kept their mouths shut.

They didn't know that Theodora could have provided that stuff; however, she wisely kept it to herself. She had unearthed mounds about each one of them: snapshots, portraits, birthplaces, degrees, institutions, areas of interest, marital status, on-campus activities, even lifestyles. She had gleaned methodically all that from college catalogues, undergraduate school yearbooks, *Who's Who in American Higher Education*, and tidbits from college public relation offices. The academic grapevine entwined around the Bay offered interesting tidbits, too. Her richest source was the American Federation of Teachers' Union, which at the time was proselyting college and university faculties. The organization targeted younger faculty for memberships, and Theodora was an officer of the Bay wide organization.

After the introductions, she said, "My, aren't we eclectic. I received such a large response to my notice in your faculty newsletters, so I had to resort to first-come-first-serve for the selection of the lucky six. So, here we are, *Les Six*. Isn't it amazing that we end up with this diversity, yet with a homogeneous spirit of adventure?"

Not a few of those present believed her. Wasn't it unusual that they were all single, the sex ratio was 3:3 and the average age was probably in the late thirties with a standard deviation of no more than three years? And how adventurous were they really? Some looked as if they wouldn't dare stomp a cockroach. She stood up from the sofa to walk jerkily across the room, and the professors noticed her wide fleshy hips, too wide for such a thin torso. Anyone could see that she lacked the vigor, the confident, if slouchy, body language that defined the Californian image.

Furthermore, in the back of all their minds was the big question of why she had taken the organization of this cruise upon herself. Did her motives have to do with some mercenary scheme that she had negotiated with the yacht leasing company in Piraeus? This, she surely must have known, would have been ferreted out and challenged by the picky professors. No, it was more likely that she had deeper ulterior motives.

Though they had known her only briefly, it was obvious, as evidenced by the stacks of journals and monographs in the numerous bookcases, that she was a serious scholar. She was a Clinical Psychologist she had told them, but she hadn't told them exactly her research interests. But her ebullient nature would suggest that she wasn't one of the rat maze type of experimenters. She liked people, that was obvious, and, therefore, was it for the reason of companionship that she had gone out and highly selected companions for her summer vacation?

Not likely, some of them thought. If she was like the rest of them, at this time of their nascent climb to academic fame, every activity had to be directed toward that goal. So why had she spent all this time organizing a three-week cruise of the Aegean?

To Frances and Paul, it had to do with her desire to reconnect to the historical roots of Western Philosophy, which, as everyone should know, formed a cornerstone of so much modern psychological theory. They saw her as seeking inspiration and a quick respite from the dregs of scholarly work. The land of the Asklepeos and Hippocrates could refresh her dedication. Perhaps, she even had some intent to do some research at one of the museums. She was Greek, and presumably could read Greek, perhaps even ancient Greek.

To Stan and Karen, being themselves directed to human behavior and communication, they thought that her motives had to do with her interests in human interaction. In fact, it occurred to them that aboard the *Leto,* with the six of them confined for three weeks like experimental animals in a cage, with almost uninterrupted contact, she would be provided an ideal experimental set-up. But to prove what?

Those thoughts were supported more by their thoughts that she must have known a lot of their backgrounds. No doubt about it. She had selected just them for the only purpose that they made ideal subjects. *Hmm,* they mulled as they unravelled the grape leave wrappings of the *dolmathes.*

Ion figured more simply. She, like himself, was looking for a cheap trip to her ancestral origins. A holiday, that's all. Yet, he thought her efforts seemed rather belabored.

At that time, Theodora was doing her own analyses—of them. She was glad that they had been tight-lipped about themselves in the introductions. She expected it, even welcomed their reluctance, because otherwise she would have had to reveal more of her own vita—a really too boring and humiliating one when compared to her guests sophisticated big city upbringings and prep schools. Her Greek parents, immigrating to frigid Minnesota where Greeks like anemones in cold water are apt to retract into moribund states, owned a small café in a town in the northern part of the state. They had settled there to raise a family only because a cousin who had preceded them to America, the only Greek within a fifty mile radius of the town, had married a Swedish woman and had offered them partnership in his business. Theodora's brother had been killed in Korea, and she had assumed the role of the great consoler to her parents—for the loss of their son, for the loss of their

Greek connections. There was no fame, no money in her background, and her life was loveless, one could even say it was virtually a blah life.

But she had climbed academic ladders like the rest of them, each rung grudgingly gained, and wanted now to change all that. By damn, she had earned the right. She was going to leave behind glacial Minnesota and the foggy San Francisco Bay and open herself to the brilliant Greek Light.

But, ah! Its spectrum was wide. There was to be the illuminating pleasures of a sea voyage and visits to the cradle of civilization, but the invisible range was the crux. In that band, she had perceived a grand experimental design whose ramifications—even if to gain personal ends—were important to the theoretical frameworks under which people in her professional field operated.

Her purposes were crafty, but if achieved, could only be construed by everyone as salubrious. There was no need, at this time, to tell her guests about all this. In fact, to do so now would scuttle the whole cruise. In time, all would be divulged. So, she smiled widely at all of them and proceeded with her evening's agenda.

The last meatball had disappeared from a majolica platter, and she rose from her sofa seat to pick up packets from a side table and passed them around. "I've photocopied for you the details of our yacht, prices, dates, hotel reservations in Piraeus before and after the sail and estimated food costs. And," she squeaked, "I hope you've brought your checkbooks to complete the leasing agreement."

Quick scowls, furtive looks filled the room.

Discussions about the yacht, the *Leto,* followed, Theodora acting like a chairperson at a symposium. But the atmosphere was more like an inquisition, each participant displaying a surprising erudition about yachts and sailing, their questions edgy.

They wanted to know her displacement, number of masts, manufacturer of the diesel engines, two or four stroked, galley equipment, number of reading chairs, deck chairs. Frances wanted to know if the saloon was paneled, if there were writing desks. Was the keel leaded? How many halyards, how many rudders? Stan wanted to know whether the crew were certified by the Greek Maritime Service. Was the boat equipped with radar? Paul espoused the wish that the yacht, their "trireme" he called it, had a glass bottom "to see the marvelous sunken Minoan ruins of Milos." "Can we choose the color of the spinnaker?" Karen said. That was followed by questions about trade winds, gyroscopes, radios, anchors, jibs, ballast, and stabilizers—technical questions that the brochures and Theodora could not answer, questions whose answers might not have been understood anyhow.

When Frances asked whether their private staterooms each had their own bathroom and shower, Theodora lamented that a floor plan of the ship had not been sent to her, though "Certainly, the amenities must be lux and she's certainly seaworthy. I'll prove that in a moment."

Ion, who had done some sailing in San Francisco Bay, remained mum, suspecting that his presumptive crew mates really didn't know the difference between a sailboat and a stink pot. Perhaps didn't know squat about lots of things. Staterooms on a sixty-foot sloop? *These* people sailing? Stan and Karen looked sturdy enough, but Paul, Frances, and Theodora? Ion doubted that they could make a Maypole with those blue and white streamers.

Further questions, as to matters of cost, itinerary, and eating arrangements Theodora deflected with "Oh, those details we can work out later. Don't worry your little heads about all that." The crepe paper rustled.

Then, slowly, an undercurrent began to pull at them. They began to recall what they knew of the Greek islands, of Greek history, of the mythologies and the gods, began to remember the mystique that all scholars have about Classical times. Those "os" sounds—Keos, Delos, Milos, Chios, Naxos, Paros, Rhodos, Mykonos—resonated deep, and all those great "es" names, Demosthenes, Socrates, Thucydides, Sophocles conjured up reminders of their college Western Civilization courses. The classicists, Paul, and Francis, so learned and enthusiastic, piqued them with "And you all remember, of course, that is where . . ." It was not just like going back in time to their memorable college days, nor were they trying to impress each other with their learnedness. It was more like they were wanting to bask in a future they could share, one filled with beauty and idealism in which they could indulge in a dialectic of sheer reason and purity—the alleged Greek wisdom.

At last, after a long evening, they thought they had found the common interest. But time would prove whether their sudden enthusiasm for the trip was founded on that or something else. It would be too hard to rationalize at that moment, and if they had, they'd have disguised it. For none actually would have the guts to admit to themselves or others that their motivation to take this trip might have been something less esoteric. After so many years of dedicated scholarship, they would have been embarrassed to admit to their graduate school professors, colleagues, and chairmen that what they really wanted was just to get away from all the academic bullshit.

Theodora carefully observed them. What she saw unfolding in front of her was exactly what she predicted. If *they* didn't know their exact purpose of the trip, *she* certainly knew hers. There was no self-deception, she plotted everything well and things were on course. It was time to perform the *coup de grace*.

She brought out a large colored photograph of the *Leto* under the full sail, heeling smartly, in a wash of blue ink, a mountainous cliff on her starboard. It was better than anything the Greek tourist office could come up with. Gasps of admiration went all around the room.

Ion immediately noticed that she wasn't a racing boat, her beam was wide and the small squarish sails seemed odd. Still, he was awed with the rest. The thought of sailing in those waters in what certainly looked like a sturdy and comfortable ship gripped him and the others. The symposium came to an end, pretenses dropped, and they felt swept away in a giant wave of excitement, their intellectual modules swamped by all the wine and the photograph's seductions.

Only briefly did they talk of the Greek political situation. They knew little of the ruthless Greek colonels—and how could they with the CIA and state department obfuscating cold war issues? They could only know—and never express overtly—that the supremacy of the American dollar and their high-mindedness (presumed) would carry them through. In fact, as one of them put it, "The dictators are bound to maintain law and order for us."

Paul began to talk of "panegyrics," but before anyone could ask him the meaning of the word—which no one would want to admit ignorance of anyhow—Ion shrugged his shoulders and reached for a checkbook in his leather-elbowed jacket. "What the hell. I'm on. I deserve celebrating getting tenure this year."

"How about the rest of you?" said Theodora.

Out of purses and pockets came pens and checkbooks, and then she turned to Ion and said, "Wonderful! Will you please make a toast, Ion, for us—in Greek?"

"*Yia Mas,*" he said, lifting his glass like a baton of an exhausted athlete.

That was the first Greek expression they learned and Paul, the classicist, tipping his glass to Ion's salutation, added, "My sentiments exactly. Health to us all, yes, indeed. Count me on board. Everyone to the oars! Here's to the Greek Isles and the Greek gods. What a trip this will be!"

"The penultimate apocalyptic voyage! Whoopee!" said Karen in her rich speaker's voice, expanding her chest to reveal big boobs. Stan showed a fist and tugged at his beard, Paul and Francis cooed.

A new jug was opened, drinking continued *ad libitum,* addresses and phone numbers exchanged, and entries made into appointment books. In only six weeks, June 27, 1973, they would forget the problems of Vietnam and meet at the Glaros Hotel in Piraeus.

❉   ❉   ❉

After her guests had departed, Theodora, in her bed, exhausted and exhilarated, thought about pigeons in boxes, B. F. Skinner pigeons. *Well, her guests were not exactly pigeons, but they did behave exactly according to her "stimuli" in predictable ways.* Checks had been written for one thing, but more important was their responsiveness—to each other, and to the plan. Also, she was most pleased by their "in the flesh" appearance. Amazing how photos and snapshots and personal data met all her expectations. Must be a talent. She squirmed under the bedcovers, thinking about how they would look semi-naked in the Aegean, all tanned and bleached out by the sun. Oh, they would be lovely, particularly Ion, who was far more handsome than his photographs. But she expected that.

Sleep didn't come easily, and her mind raced about things she needed to do, such as buying a sturdy zippered notebook to record all the data she would accumulate, not data on pigeon pecking. Oh no, more profound things, such as behavioral nuances, food preferences, mood shifts, libido signs. She'd call it *Addenda,* supportive data for her Human Coercions Theory and its derivative, Personality Profile Projections.

She patted down the comforter. The *Addenda* would have to have a combination lock, too, and not be too large and conspicuous on board the *Leto.* In a gust, the sliding door in her bedroom banged approval, and she nestled down deeper in her bed. *Many other things to do before sailing,* she thought. She had to wrap-up some experiments in the lab, make some wardrobe selections, and start a regime of physical fitness. She'd engage a trainer at the University gym, talk to Marge, the cosmotologist, about sprucing up her looks—a little eye-shadow, mascara, whatever. No more cutting her own hair, let the beautician do it, try a little tinting. For the time being, she'd give up honeyed Greek pastries—or perhaps fast for Holy Week, the way she did growing up in Minnesota, eating no meat or dairy products. Slim down, though it would be such torture. Take communion? Where? She hadn't been in a Greek Orthodox Church in years. She wasn't even sure of the date of Greek Easter, almost always different from normal Easter dates. Business of moon cycles, Julian calendars, how in the hell did that all go? She knew at one time. There must be some Greek churches in the Bay area. Well, she'd give some thought to all that later.

Anyhow, as she cuddled a pillow braced between her legs, she thought about how the venture back to the homeland of her parents had some cogency. Yet, it wasn't paramount, in fact, she wasn't even certain at times that it might invoke too much nostalgia. Well, she wasn't going to get mushy over that. Mama was long gone, and it was in a way sad that she wasn't alive to make the trip with her. Maybe Dad, too? Probably not. He'd have been prone to seasickness. *Oh, how silly, what would the old folks be doing on such a trip?*

Mama would have been proud of her though. She had taught her knitting and didn't the crochet fringes on the lamps look nice? Her guests certainly noticed them. And what about the *baklava* she had served her guests? Why, they wolfed them down. But did they appreciate that the *filo* dough was homemade, stretched and dried laboriously by her own little hands? Yes, Mama would be proud.

Oh, damn, another thing to do tomorrow: clean up the flakes of *filo* on the rugs. Her guests were not so neat, particularly that galumphy Stan. What a bitch of a job. If she didn't do it first thing tomorrow, the buttery flakes would cause oily stains on the *flokatis*.

Now was not the time to think about all this. She remembered what her mother would say to her: *Sichase, chriso mou.* Be quiet, precious.

Then, before turning out her bed lamp, she did something she had never done before . . . she reached across the bed-stand and kissed the small icon her mother had given her so many years ago, one of the parthenic Mary.

2
Piraeus

A sound like a large mound of dough being slammed down on a marble slab resounded through the lobby of the Glaros Hotel. The men of the California group, gathered at seven P.M. for their inaugural dinner in Piraeus, rushed to Theodora's aid. She had slipped on the mezzanine steps, a smile of greeting still on her face as she went down.

"My! You've got to watch these slippery floors in Greece!" Everyone laughed it off, at the same time stunned by what they saw. How could the Greek rays so quickly cause such a lambent transformation? They hardly recognized her. Gone was the homeliness they remembered in Oakland. She was dressed in a beautiful white cotton dress embroidered around the bodice and sleeves in flowered patterns. Her shapely legs were bared, and protruding through new leather sandals, polished toenails gleamed. After her spill, she nevertheless remained composed, even with the pounding her big hips had taken. She smiled broadly, her thin lips painted wide with bright red lipstick, her hair burnished in a new henna. Even her eyebrow tic was gone.

"Let's have a Greek feast," she lilted, kissing everyone on the cheek. When she led the group to the dining room, she found the doors locked. "Oh hell," she said, "we'll get to the bottom of this." At the reception desk, she complained, in her Greek, that they were hungry, but the concierge frowned, then half-smiled and replied, in broken English, "Madam, the restaurant is closed. Eight-thirty it opens. You want your room key? Your name?"

Ion overhead the exchange, and in his Greek, the first time he had spoken it, said to Theodora and the concierge, "Maybe we can find a place nearby on the harbor?"

Theodora led them to a restaurant around the corner past a cooperage and chandlery, all the time ridiculing the crazy eating hours of Greeks. She was speaking Greek to Ion, but it was a funny clipped kind of Greek, a Greek unlike anything he had ever heard in the Greek ghetto of Astoria in NYC where he had grown up. What was it? It was genderless and all the verbs had iota endings, like a child's first language attempts. Or was it Swedish-Minnesota-Greek? Certainly it wasn't Purist formal Greek, or the Greek in the New Testament that Ion knew from his altar boy days. He could barely understand her.

That restaurant was closed, too, but seeing a dim light in the back, she knocked loudly until a man in a dirty white apron smelling of tobacco and old frying oil unlocked the door. "*Peraste,*"—(enter), he growled. Fluorescent lights came up, and the group stood around waiting to be seated, lined up like raw recruits, Theodora tapping her toe, Frances and Paul dressed alike in khaki shorts and white shirts with hands behind their backs, Stan slouching in a safari jacket, and Karen bulging in tight Levi jeans and a San Francisco T-shirt.

Ion, standing tall in the line-up, like a Spartan warrior in a tunic sheathing good pecs, might have been the most hopeful recruit of the lot. That might have been an illusion, however, because his bearing didn't match his manner. There was a demureness in him, a deference to when people addressed him, particularly Theodora. "Yes, perhaps that's so," was his common response. He hesitated to take the initiative or use his Greek to advantage. When three of them had arrived together at the Ellenikon airport in Athens, he had been no help at Passport control, baggage claim, or hiring a taxi. Inclined more to monitor carefully and quietly the recording needle of a spectrophotometer, he was not a bonafide Greek, a take-over type of guy who could make things happen or get service in a Greek restaurant.

Stan, motioning to Ion for help, decided to put formica tables together and gather wicker chairs for their little dinner party in the grungy café. They sat and waited. And waited. Now it was eight o'clock and they were hungry and still jet-lagged. Someone had to take the initiative. Finally, Theodora lifted her pointy chin high and clapped loudly, the sound resonating in the cavernous, terrazzo-floored restaurant.

"Operant conditioning," she said, "that's what we call it in psychology. We demand service, and the waiter responds because he knows we'll reward him with tips. Works every time. Just watch."

A waiter shuffled out of the kitchen, stubbing a cigarette and brushing back his hair. *"Yia soo,"* Theodora said to him.

He did not smile, did not greet them. *"Ti thelete,"* (what do you want) he grunted.

They ordered *souvlakia* kebobs and Greek *choriatiki* salads and toasted each other with ice cold FIX beers. Coping with Greek menus made it apparent that most of the group had no ear for foreign language. "Sewer-lakey" kebobs and "Core-actic" salads was about the best they could manage. Ion tried fruitlessly to teach them "thank you" in Greek, *efcharisto*. Diphthongs tied their tongues, and their PhD degree knowledge of German and French produced something like a biochemical competitive inhibition. He wasn't going to do any teaching on vacation.

So, their first meal together was a quiet recounting of their exhausting trip from California and their first impressions of the Athens chaos, the Acropolis, the Plaka, Lycabettus, and the other tourist sites they visited hurriedly in the days before their rendezvous in Piraeus.

⁂   ⁂   ⁂

Early the next morning, two grey taxis waited for them in front of the hotel for their ride to the *tourkolimani*, the harbor where smaller yachts docked. All a little sleepy-eyed, they began to liven up when they first glimpsed the array of sleek white ships, many with flags and banners fluttering and beautiful tanned people lounging on their decks. The taxi proceeded slowly, Theodora and the rest trying to spot the *Leto*. They found her moored between two magnificent fiberglass yachts. She looked nothing like her pictures. Her hull was dark blue, almost black, and the superstructure and decks were all heavily varnished dark wood. She was all wood, in fact, with a stodgy look, something of a miniaturized QE 1 vintage. Still, she was spiffy, "venerable," Paul said, "tubby," Stan said. On board, Captain Yiorgi and a crewman, Takis, greeted them and helped them and their luggage on the gangway. In the hold, they found two W.C.s and four dark cabins with tiny portholes, each with double berths. Theodora assigned the women to one side of the passageway, the men to the other. Frances and Karen were to bunk together, and Theodora would have her own cabin, and the men were told to divide themselves on the other side as they wished. Paul, quick to react, claimed the single cabin because he "snored outrageously." Ion and Stan did not protest, feeling somehow that they would rather not bunk with the sissified classicist.

The bunking arrangements seemed to please Theodora inordinately, and she said in a loud voice for everyone to hear, "You see how the details work out? Didn't I promise?" But no one was quite sure what she meant, no one commented on the smallness of the "staterooms" or questioned her usurpation of a single cabin.

The captain told Ion, assuming he was the leader of the group because he had greeted him in good Greek, that today they would sail for the island of Kea, off the tip of the Attic coast about thirty miles and tomorrow he would tell them of the "program." He spoke no English and seemed a little officious, "making himself big," as the Greek would say.

"What did he say?" snapped Theodora. Ion translated.

"Well, we'll tell *him* 'the program'. Wait, I'll tell him."

But there was no time. He and Takis were busy with ties and bumpers and revving the rackety diesels.

Before they could unpack, they were knifing through the Saronic Gulf, heading toward Cape Sounion. After exploring the handsomely paneled saloon and galley, they gathered on the poop deck, awed by the blueness of the sea, the freshness of the air, the exhilaration of getting underway. The sound of the diesels and the water slappings on the hull hindered much conversation. Attica slipped by, the crests of Immetus and Parnathi fading in a smoggy veil. When the Temple of Poseidon came into view high on a cliff, they all moved to the port side to take pictures. Frances touched each of her fellow passengers on the shoulder, motioning for them to gather around her as she recited:

Sunium's marbled steep,
Where nothing save the waves and I
May hear our mutual murmur's sweep.

She recited the Byron lines, eyes closed, transfixed as if praying before an altar. Paul looked at her admiringly. The captain at the wheel in the cockpit lifted his bristled chin and pointed toward the columns saying to Ion, "Yes, there it still stands, six centuries before Christ. Tell them."

Paul, almost shouting, related the story of Theseus and the legend of the Minotaur, the black and white sails, mistakenly sighted at the cape by his father in Minoan days, another thousand years BCE. "Oh, so much history right there," Paul gushed, holding Frances arm. "Byron sensed it, Frances, it's why he put his graffiti on the Temple. We must see it when we return to Athens."

He reminded everyone of how Poseidon had thwarted Odysseus' return to his native Ithaca and then he rushed to his cabin to bring out a copy of Homer's *Odyssey*. In theatrical projections, he read the opening lines:

> All the survivors of the war had reached their home by now. . . . Odysseus alone was prevented from returning to the home and wife he longed for . . . and the Nymph Calypso who kept him in her vaulted cave. . . . Yet all the gods were sorry for him, except Poseidon, who pursued the heroic Odysseus with relentless malice. . . . It is Poseidon, the girder of the land, who is ceaselessly enraged because Odysseus blinded the Cyclops, god-like Polyphemus, who of all Cyclops has the greatest power. And since that day the earth-shaking Poseidon does not indeed destroy Odysseus, but ever drives him wandering from his land. . . .

Frances went moony-eyed.

"Oh God," said Karen, "is Poseidon out to get us too?" She brushed back her short hair, frizzed by the salt air. "In the name of Zeus, cloud gatherer, shaker of the earth, save us!" she exclaimed in a booming contralto.

Stan threw up his arms, pleading, "Athena, you bitch. Guide our voyage and we'll sacrifice as many damn lambs as you want."

"We had better make a sacrifice right now to Poseidon," Paul said.

Stan brought out beer and spilled some over the stern as libation. Frances and Paul knelt in prayer, their hands clasped over their hearts.

They're all crazy, Ion thought. Theodora touched his elbow, grinned and nodded her head as if she was in agreement with what he was thinking.

Stan shouted, "Yeah! Let's get lost for ten years!"

Then, like children, they joined hands and skipped around in a circle chanting, "Poseidon, Poseidon," until the *Leto,* tilting in a sudden swell, sent them sprawling.

They grasped for the railings and helped each other up, trying to regain some composure as they heard Theodora say to Paul, "Homer is so much more elegant when recited in the original Greek."

"Do us the honor," Paul said, handing her the Greek text as they gathered around the circular bench in the galley.

She passed it on to Ion. "I don't have my glasses," she said.

Ion looked sharply at Paul. "I don't suppose that the phonetics of ancient Greek are precisely known. You know ancient Greek. You read it."

Paul nodded in agreement and gently guided Frances' arm toward a place closer beside him where he recited as best he could the Greek text. The others could not hear him, but noticed something about the two of them. Ever since Oakland and Piraeus, they had showed a tendency to isolate themselves, as if they belonged to some exclusive society for the study of classical history and literature.

Everyone noticed another remarkable thing about them, sitting there together, in khaki shorts and white shirts, rimless glasses, neither more than five feet five inches, small-boned, fair and thin-haired, they looked like twins. Their bare hairless legs touched, their bodies leaned into each other, like playful children discovering each other, whispering and giggling, their sexes discernible only by Paul's wispy moustache and Frances' nubby little chest.

And out to the open sea the ship plowed, everyone averting their eyes from the too apparent flirtation. The captain shouted raucously to Ion, winking towards the twins, "The sheep that frisk..." then turning to Takis, who laughed and slapped his thigh, continued with, "bring forth the Paschal lamb."

Ion remembered how Greeks liked proverbs and rhymed couplets, but he couldn't think of a retort. There was his grandfather's about donkeys... how did it go? Or his Dad's about "Grab one of them, eat the other one." (He never quite understood the hidden meaning of that one.) He found himself staring at Takis for a moment. What strong dark arms and deep chest. What a handsome face. A cleft chin and what an ingenuous expression, like that of a beautiful adolescent. For only a fleeting moment, their eyes locked and Ion may have blushed.

Theodora turned to Ion, nodding towards the twins with a candid, knowing look. She said to him in her pidgin Greek, "I knew they'd get along."

And Ion thought hard. *Strange she would say that. Did she think she was a matchmaker? What is this trip to be? A fucking voyage for the lovelorn? Paul has a cabin to himself and no doubt will put it to good use. What will Theodora do with hers? Has she planned that, too?* The spectrophotometer needled searched the scale.

Finally, in the open sea, they retired to the saloon. It was getting noisy on deck and the swells were beginning to spray them.

"Oh, my," Frances said. "I didn't realize it was going to be so rough." Her skin, and Paul's, had changed from white jade to grey parchment.

Theodora lay down on a cushioned bench, her olive skin developing kumquat rinds. Karen, her skin blotched salmon, fanned herself and stared out at the horizon.

Oh damn, thought Ion, *is this boat going to become a vomitorium?*

✽ ✽ ✽

Ion sat himself at a desk in the saloon, a carved mahogany piece, slanted with a leathery inlay. *Water, water, everywhere . . .* he thought. Sea voyages can be boring, and they had almost twenty more days of it. He had sailed beyond the Golden Gate and knew also how high seas could be in a small vessel. Twenty years before, he remembered, he had sailed to the island of Tinos with his parents on a large ferryboat. His mother, a strong woman, not the aesthetic types like Theodora, Paul, and Frances, had puked all over the place. And that was on a large ship.

Then, another time, they were on the island of Kerkyra and had visited the reliquary of St. Spyridon. Mother saw the bones in the silver sarcophagus and promptly fainted. He thought he remembered seeing a withered, leathery leg bone. Fresh slices of lemon rubbed under her nose finally revived her. There were other times, too, when the sights required strong stomachs: octopus being banged against rocks then put up to dry in the scorching sun, toilet holes mounted flush on the floor, overloaded septic tanks oozing stench in village streets. There were trying times ahead for these lily-livered Californians.

No, he thought, *the voyage doesn't seem that enticing now.* Despite his initial enthusiasm, he was feeling now that being sequestered with these gushy types would be an ordeal in many other ways. And why, in the first place, did he even want to come back to Greece? He swiveled his chair around to stare across the saloon at the dissipated shipmates. Why was he here, really? Escape? From lab drudgeries? From unmotivated, politicized, graduate students?

He saw Paul and Frances descend to the lower deck holding hands. Amazing that they had gotten to it so soon. As if it had been pre-ordained. But how would those wimps be able to screw in this sea's arrythmic blasts?

A loud splash hit a porthole. Nothing but inky blue, swelling and surging all around. Why was he here? Sonja, that was the probable reason. His shrink argued that that was only part of his consternation. The affair had been over for some time, but there remained, at least in his mind, the quandary of rejection. Why, with everyone it seemed, were people attracted to him and then repelled like a depolarized magnet?

"Broaden your horizons," the shrink advised. "Stand back, get a new perspective of your life. Take that trip to Greece." Far, far away from that scheming, insecure Lithuanian woman and her insatiable cunt-trap.

Was Greece the proper place? With these people? What did they know about what it was like to be the son of a Greek immigrant? They didn't know about Anglo-Saxon slights, about alienation from the mainstream. All they had were silly romantic ideas of the gods and the Greek myths. Didn't they know that whatever the ancient Greeks had contributed had been assimilated long ago, and that the modern Greeks had different agendas?

Such as gouging tourists. He saw it only a few days ago when he had arrived before the rest in Athens and he was walking the streets of the Plaka trying to find his hotel. A Greek pimp encountered him, "Meester, whar yu frum? Come have drink with bouttifull voman." He persisted, Ion refused to reply until finally, in Greek, he told him, "You are annoying me. Go away." Whereupon the Greek started shouting and cursing him in Greek, "You can go eat shit!"

Glories pass, the world moves on. And what was there to learn now from the modern Greeks? About their poverty, their venal nature with tourists, Turks, and with each other?

So, he wasn't a romantic. Sonja had told him that over and over. He knew life could be harsh and science could be very demanding. No purpose was served by wallowing in sappy philosophy about Platonic ideals, the oneness of life, the transmigration of the soul, all those searches for the truth. He rubbed his eyes of the salt that had caked on his eyelids and saw the rest of the passengers go below to their cabins.

What he remembered about Greeks were the encounters with the modern ones, particularly the ones he met twenty years ago with his parents. On that trip, wherever they visited relatives in the Peloponese, the most dominant memory was the smell of goats that resided in the ground floors of their farm houses. That and the incongruous spoonfuls of preserves in cold water glasses that were meant to be welcoming gestures.

He went up to the galley for a Fanta® soft drink, placed it on the desk top and thought more of that trip twenty years ago.

The inquiries: Uncle John in Mystras, "What will you do with your life?" Uncle Petros, "Pray to God to lead your way." All of them asking him, a teenager, heavy questions about the future, as if he could at that moment decide his destiny. It was always that way, the expectations, from everyone, the priests and *thaskali* teachers. His father working him punishing hours in the café, but all the time telling him that education was the only way out of that grueling life.

And when he went off to college to do exactly that, did any of his family ever really know or appreciate his efforts? Did they even ask what he was studying or why? No. There was always some kind of unspoken resentment from a few in the family that he was goofing off, spending his dad's hard-earned money when he should have been home clearing tables and wiping counters.

He swigged on the Fanta. The engines, relics surely, roared like nineteenth-century locomotives. He had hoped for a quiet, gliding, sailing vessel, and what does he get? A stinkpot housing Karen's frizz, Stan's hirsuteness. Theodora's cloyings, and Paul's and Frances' egghead chatters. How could these people in these circumstances possibly help him find, as the shrink had put it, "More meaningful pursuits that would help lead you to 'self-actualization'?" Whatever that meant.

He braced his arms on the desk's edge and ran a hand across the smooth, black leather. He wished his lectern back home had that feel and that patina. Then he realized that the lecture he was giving himself, this self-examination, was leading nowhere. Class was over, so he went below to his bunk.

A small reading lamp hung over his pillow. He had taken the lower bunk under Stan's which had a porthole. Then, another depressing thought passed across his mind, for twenty-some nights he'd have that ugly guy above him, making who knows what kind of creaking, farting noises.

The shrink had given him a couple of books for "light reading" by Russell and Schrodinger. *Light indeed,* he thought as he read the dust jackets. Schrodinger's book was entitled *Nature and the Greeks,* and *Science and Humanism.* These were supposed to give him new perspectives? And what did the shrink know of science and mathematics?

He skimmed Schrodinger and read:

> . . . the scientific world view contains of itself no ethical values, no aesthetical values, not a word about our own ultimate scope or destination, and no God, if you please. Whence came I, whither go I?

Hmmm, he thought. *Nobel laureates are entitled to say anything. And what does he know about my "whither" and what does he know about biochemists' aspirations? I could tell him a thing or so, tell him about why biochemical receptor sites have everything to do with the livingness of things, why molecules interact the way they do to produce muscle contractions, nerve conduction, protein synthesis, everything you please in the whole plethora of living, molecular reactions. Isn't that what we biochemists are about, to understand LIFE? Tell me if that isn't the "ultimate scope," buster.*

But the boat rocked, the book above him kept slipping from his grip. He closed it, began to think of his research, why he really shouldn't be on this trip. He had ideas for some electropheretic experiments, and maybe that new grad student had a good pair of hands.

Anyhow, he was tired, too many things happening at once. Though he knew something of Greece and Greeks, the atmosphere felt exotic. Perhaps it had to do with the deluge of historical references, the technicolor backdrop. Or maybe it was only his dippy fellow passengers, the way they carried on like boobies in a Greek chorus. Whatever, he'd give in to it, loll with the waves, rock from side to side in the bunk, brace his leg against the bulkhead. So what, a wasted three weeks. At least he could enjoy the scenery.

3
Kea

The *Leto,* her sails still furled, approached Kea (ancient Keos) in a golden afternoon sun and brisk air. Not until the engines changed pitch did the torpid passengers notice the mountains looming above the harbor and halfway up a white village, their first of the many cubistic Cycladic villages they would see. Captain Yiori pointed up to it and told them that it would be the best place for them to have dinner.

They boarded a rickety Mercedes bus with tin *filakton* talismans strung across the driver's window, ears, arms, baby figurines. It rumbled up a steep road with villagers, mostly little women in black, carrying plastic sacks of *marithes* (tiny smelt). Karen held her nose. After alighting, they took a brief hike on a rocky trail, Paul and Frances selecting their steps like a game of hopscotch, to see a gargantuan lion carved into the side of a cliff. "It is Helladic, of course," Paul declared. The rest fumbled with their travel guides, walked around it, contemplated it. "Keos," he continued, "one could say, was the crossroad between Helladic, Mycenean, Minoan and Classical periods. Here is the cultural bridge between Attica and the Cyclades. That lion portends it. Ah yes, we are privy to see in front of us the early beginnings of our civilization. It is marvelous!"

But the Letoites were not quite able to comprehend its massive anachronism and placidity. Stan discoursed about animism, a common trait of primitive societies, about dragons and jaguars, but he sounded as if he were talking to himself. For several minutes, they all stood frozen—trying to find "contextual meaning," as they would have put it.

Unfortunately, the day for them had been too filled with a hectic embarkation and rolling seas, too disorienting to lodge anything but awe for the rude, leonine stonework. The damn thing had a haughtiness about it, too, as if it were saying to them, "What are you nincompoops doing here?"

They hiked back to the village to find a small taverna with plastic tablecloths lit with naked light bulbs hanging from the limbs of a giant plane tree. Supper was local sausages, redolent of *thymari* and *rigani*, and retsina wine from a barrel, enjoyed by all except Karen whose tastes she said "ran to plain food," meaning, the rest thought that either she was unsophisticated about ethnic food (something unlikely of a San Francisco Bay resident), that she suffered a picayune gut, or that like most Texans, preferred steaks and Tex-Mex. Theodora had predicted that in the *Addenda,* had noted that she didn't partake of her Oakland buffet. In any case, her finicky tastes bode future problems.

"Well," said Karen, "Anyhow, here we are in Kea. Simonides' home, the Blue Guide says. He's an important guy, you know. He gave us the idea that words are selected to produce certain illusions. In Speech and Drama, that is practiced to the ultimate for desired effects. Metaphor was his invention. Yet, he used language economically, was the originator of epitaphs. Heh, maybe I'll need one. What's in this sausage anyway?"

She grasped her brow, opened her arms, and declared: "I've got it, my epitaph: "

Here lies Karen
of stomach-aching
She 'et some kind of garb-age
in a greasy saus-age

"With some donkey plops thrown in," Stan said.

Theodora became alerted. Something to put in the *Addenda*. Bawdiness. Sexual allusions not funny to Paul and Frances. Ion blank. Noted. Good data. Predictability component a high coefficient.

"Whatever the case, Simonides," said Frances "was economical in another sense. He charged money for his poetry and epitaphs. That was unheard of in those days. He was regarded as a skinflint, but perhaps all of us who teach literature owe him something."

"*Apate*," said Paul, "is what he called his sleight of hand technique in the use of language."

"That means 'cheat' in Greek," said Ion.

"Oh, how interesting," Paul said. "That puts a pejorative slant to literature."

"Language has its pratfalls," said Karen, "one can be sure. But that's my business, you know. To learn to use it, to "twist" meanings—and I wouldn't call that cheating—for a desired effect. It's what makes the world go around. Politicians and leaders in every field subscribe to it."

"Too bad," Ion moaned. "Imprecision leads to confusion. It's why, of course, mathematics and science developed, to avoid misunderstandings."

"Put numbers to it," said Stan. "Yes sir, that'll take the romance and aesthetics out of all of life. You put numbers to an orgasm. I dare you."

Raised eyebrows, all around. Theodora noted. First bit of sexual allusion.

"Is that a challenge?" said Ion. "Well, I can't, but perhaps a neuroscientist can. He can, or in the future, perhaps, put numbers to the volley of electrical impulses in the pleasure centers of the cerebral cortex."

"Should we then count them down as we near climax?" Stan said.

All laughed except Theodora who was too absorbed making mental notes. After a while, she needed to make a prod: "Seriously now, there's a middle ground," she said. "Human behavior is no doubt a complex physio-chemical phenomenon. But that doesn't mean that holistic considerations can be ignored. The effect is more than the sum of the parts. And for that, psychology can introduce certain words to refer to them. Providing, of course, that those psychological terms are carefully defined and understood by everyone."

"Define 'crazy'," said Ion.

"Neurosis."

"Psychosis."

Theodora squeezed Ion's arm. "Oh, you're just teasing me," she said. (Good prod.)

"If you can't, Simonides, right here on this island," said Stan, "could chip it out on stone. For all we know, all around us, are carved stones, buried, with all the definitions of human behavior. Just think, we are surrounded by lies."

"Wittgenstein, where are you when we need you?" said Frances. She sighed. "For myself, nevertheless, I'm enthralled I'm in a place right now when the same ideas were being batted around . . . when was it? Almost twenty-five hundred years ago?"

"Oh, how extraordinary, indeed," said Paul.

"Drink up, then," said Stan, offering the copper carafe to him, but he declined.

In fact, while Paul and Frances enjoyed the food, they drank and ate lightly. But when the *logariazmo*, the reckoning, was calculated by the waiter standing beside Ion scribbling on a tablet, licking his pencil, a problem arose.

"We did not eat or drink as much as the rest of you. It is not quite fair, is it, to split the bill six ways?" Paul said.

Theodora was ready to squelch the expected dissension. "For tonight, let's just settle it that way, and tomorrow morning, we'll discuss it after breakfast in the saloon. OK?"

"Budget committee meeting," Stan said.

"Ugh," Karen said.

"Why don't we all think about it overnight?" Theodora asked. "We can't expect the waiter to tally-up separately every piece of bread and cup of retsina we had, when he doesn't understand English. Anyhow, we'll figure a plan tomorrow. It is kind of funny, isn't it, that the waiter charges us for each piece of bread we eat? I wonder if that's everywhere in the islands. But, oh, isn't it a lovely evening. And the roses, oh my...."

A bank of huge blossoms perfumed the air. Theodora clapped her hands to bring over the waiter and said: "Beautiful! What do you feed them?"

The waiter looked angry that a woman would command his presence, particularly one of those Greek-American women who who spoke rotten Greek. His lips curled, and he answered: "Goat shit, what else."

She smiled, thanked him, but didn't translate for the others. Superfluous data, Greek waiters don't factor in. He shuffled away, and she gaily suggested they head on back down the mountain.

Back at the harbor bus stop, Paul and Frances retired to the *Leto*, but the remaining four decided on a Metaxa brandy at a café by the harbor's edge. Karen and Stan led the way, with Ion and Theodora following.

Ion had been quiet the whole evening, and over the brandies, his focus was on the harbor where caiques and a couple of small freighters lay at anchor. Except for the splash of bilge water from one of them, there were no other extrinsic sounds around the harbor. Stan was talking softly of the fine weather, the low humidity, and the climatic difference from the tropical East and West Indies islands. Karen spoke of how the air felt like west Texas and the Big Bend, and Theodora talked about how she hated the San Francisco bay fog. But their conversations sputtered and at times drifted out to sea, muffled and inane, drowning any camaraderie and cocooning its speakers.

Then, the bilge splashing stopped, somewhere a dome of darkness enveloped them, and the Kea lion brooded.

Chairs squeaked, an uneasiness around the table. Theodora tented her hands (time for a prod) and faced each of the others at the table, one by one. "Do all of you think that after three weeks we'll get to know each other well enough to be comfortable with silence? I've found it a common factor in successful interpersonal relations and my counseling therapy." She turned to look at Ion. "How is it with you chemists? Is silence OK?" Her tone was of an inquisitive child's, an irresistible prod.

He cleared his throat and took a sip of brandy. "Yes, I suppose so. With someone else around, you can analyze data or work at an instrument without saying a word."

"That is communication of a special sort," Theodora replied. "Do you feel afterwards a closeness or warmth for that person?" (Wiggle the prod.)

Ion folded his fingers, contracted them, then opened his palms. "Yeah, like I needed a lay," he wanted to answer but instead bit his lips. He was thinking about Sonja. She had been that way. They had spent graduate student hours working in the lab in silence. In the sack was another kind of non-verbal communication . . . or was it *mis*communication? Finally, he answered Theodora, "I suppose so," but he restrained himself from saying what he really wanted to say to her, that it was none of her damn business.

Theodora didn't press, frowned at first, then smiled and looked at Stan and Karen to pick up the conversation. (Prod re-insertion). They gabbled about nonverbal communication, body language. Stan about primitive cultures use of ritualistic ceremonies, Karen about hand gestures and voice modulations by speech makers. They talked of student facial expressions, how a good lecture can elicit a silent communication with students. "It's so subtle, isn't it," said Theodora. "I see it in the way they record notes, how certain dreamy looks tell me that I've put them into flights of deep thought."

Stan said, "I'm not so skilled at that. I can't be sure that they're not bored or dreaming of lovemaking. Horny little bastards!"

They all laughed, except Ion.

Karen and Stan decided to take a walk off to the beach. Theodora said she'd rather watch the stars and finish her brandy. Ion remained seated watching some fishermen working their nets on the quay.

After a long silence, Theodora said, "How do you feel being back in Greece? Does it seem different?"

"It's been almost twenty years. I've changed. Greece hasn't much."

"How's that?"

Ion put on a pained expression. After a minute, struggling for the words, he said, "I mean this time the parents aren't along."

Theodora said, "I wish I could have traveled here with my folks. Poor things always dreamed of returning, but . . . I was very close to my parents, you know. I guess all us Greeks are. Dad seldom displayed emotions, Mother was the one who laughed and cried with me. And the strange thing to me was that I never knew exactly what *their* relation was. I mean, whether they were really intimate or whether they just got along. I never heard them quarrel, but I never saw any affection between them. Is that Greek? Were your parents that way?" (Strong prod.)

"You weren't around many Greeks?" *Why all these personal questions,* he was thinking to himself.

"Not where we were in Minnesota. We had some relatives in St. Paul. We'd visit them couple of times a year, for Easter usually. They seemed different from my folks. More open, if you know what I mean. They liked to dance. Of course, I . . . " She bowed her head and looked at him with downcast eyes.

Ion immediately thought about Theodora's awkward gait, her clumsiness. It wouldn't be nice for him to ask its cause. She just wanted to talk.

He picked up the conversation with, "I was always around Greeks."

"How's that?" now brightly.

"In Astoria, with lots of family around. The Church, the *thaskali* in Greek school."

"No wonder you feel so comfortable here. It's kind of old hat for you, isn't it?"

"No, not really. I left all that Greek stuff behind me after I entered college."

"Yes, the academic life does confine us some. Do you look back at those early Greek years fondly?"

"No," he said.

She ordered them another brandy, "My treat. So nice to get away, isn't it?"

But she did not relent. "Do you mean you rejected or disliked your Greek background?"

"Not exactly. Just that I didn't want to be a member of sheep herd or another café owner like my dad."

Her shrill laughter echoed around the harbor. "Wanted to be independent, eh? Isn't that how we get our Ph.D.?"

His eyebrows rose. "Well, I think getting a Ph.D. is hardly much different than being a good altar boy. Do as you're told, follow the scientific dogma, don't invent any radical ideas. If you do, they'll smash you, steal your grant money."

"I see what you mean. That's true. But the truly creative scholars aren't good altar boys, are they?"

"The Nobelers, no, the really original thinkers."

"Were you a good altar boy?"

He grimaced. Theodora had a way of digging into one's subconscious. He knew about her prying type. After the break-up with Sonja, the University counselor had put him through his own brand of invasions. He got him to talk of his priapic malfunctions. And he resented very much the guy referring to it as his "Sword of Damocles," as if something about his Greekness were to blame for his poor bedroom performances.

"No, I was not. I'd stuff the censer. Make a smudge pot of it. Put a smoke screen around the whole altar. Congregation couldn't see the iconostassis. Priests and congregation in coughing fits. And you know those big round metal cherubim the acolytes carry in processionals? I liked to bang mine around like a cymbal. Priests always pulled my ears."

Theodora laughed. "Sounds like fun, though. Wish I had those experiences. My folks and my brother and I would fast and pray together in front of the icons in their bedroom. Never made much sense to me. I did it obediently, I suppose."

"I did it disobediently, and I'll burn in hell."

Theodora looked at him, liking his repartee, liking how he said it. Her eyes crinkled, her head bent in shyness, then she pursed her lips and stared at his mouth, as if she might have been thinking to herself. *You devil, I want to kiss your beautiful mouth.* (Subtle prod, so designed, the type that should register subliminally but be encoded more or less permanently.)

He was good looking, he knew it and so did she. Her presumptive analysis had recorded such, but when women would come on to him, she predicted that he was much too proud to let anyone take the initiative from him. He was no narcissist, but he must call the shots and not feel manipulated by females trying to get him to make a pass. She knew the type, the "androgenic imperative" she called it. Laymen called it the "strong, masculine type," but she knew better. They were really imperious pussy cats needing lots of indulgence.

The type, for reasons she couldn't quite rationalize, had some appeal to her. Her father was passive, and her male pals tended towards the effeminate. The nearest she could come to favoring the type was that she simply liked the challenge, like figuring the way to get a maximum yield in a chemical reaction. Play with concentrations, temperature, and most important, flip in a little catalyst. Just a little.

They remained silent awhile. Theodora said, "I suppose if I had learned the difference between the Annunciation and the Assumption I might have developed more respect for the Church. But after a liberal education, how can people like us believe in all those Christian myths? It's so unscientific." (Now, this should surely be a common denominator.)

Ion pinched his nose bridge and said nothing. He was thinking about science and the church and really didn't want to get into a heavy discussion about it. All he knew was that they were not mutually exclusive. In fact, early on in his graduate school days, he began to develop this strange awe for the history and contributions of biochemistry, just as he had, despite his rebellious boyhood, for the "mysteries" of Orthodoxy. It had to do with systematics, the way icons were so neatly lined up in designated spaces on the iconostassis, the rituals so precise, the doxology so repetitive, the Periodic Table so logical, the elegant metabolic pathways of living organisms so universal, the thermodynamic operations so consistent. Now, how could he explain all that to Theodora? She'd want psychological explanations, just as that counselor did, and before he knew it, if she had a Freudian bent, which she might well have, she'd get him onto the sex thing. No thank you, Dr. Koulokotrou.

"I wonder what happened to Stan and Karen?" he said.

Theodora turned her face away. "Oh, who knows?" she said. "Probably off smoking grass." (New tack, blind end required it.)

"Why do you think that?"

"They're the type, don't you think?"

"They're professors, not students. I wouldn't expect that," he said.

She smiled weakly. "Maybe C.P. Snow is right. There are two cultures."

"I don't understand that. I mean, all of us have tried Mary Jane. I had a big stash of Acapulco Gold when I was in grad school. We grow out of it."

"Naw. Some don't. People in the humanities differ from those in science."

He coughed. "*A priori*, I don't see how you can think that Karen and Stan do."

"Hunch, that's all," Theodora said.

No, he didn't believe in hunches. She had some information on them. Where had she gotten it? She acted like she had never known them before the trip. Was she holding out something? And how much did she know about *him*?"

That's paranoia, he thought—that Greek word that's so apt, literally "beyond thinking." That kind of thinking he didn't believe in. It would always get you into trouble. He wanted certainties in his life, no sword of Damocles.

Yet, there was that Greek premonitory way of living. He had been exposed to it all his life. Grandfather, *papou*, calling him "little professor" when he was only six years old, mother always saying, that he would marry a wonderful Greek girl and have the most beautiful, brilliant grandchildren in the world. They were all so naive.

Here's Theodora being Greek. He wasn't going to take her seriously, she was only being reflexively Greek. *We'd be factual,* he thought, and he said to her: "Look, Theodora. We'd better tell them about the Greek hang-up on that. This is a repressive, conservative country. The colonels don't like long-haired hippie types. Did you read that article in the *Chronicle* about the trouble on the island of Los and in the caves on Crete's south shore?"

"I don't think we have to worry about that. They wouldn't dare bother a boatload of what they think are rich Americans. Money—or lack of it, I should say—is the basis for lots of conditioning. But if you think it'll make the rest of us uncomfortable, perhaps you could say something to them."

"Well, I was only theorizing. We don't really know if they are on grass, do we?"

"I know what you can do, Ion. While he's asleep in your cabin, snip off the pony tail."

Ion didn't always know whether to take Theodora seriously. She seemed to be two people really. The one, a rigid academician, the other, a warm friendly person—or at least trying to be.

But he'd play along. "What about the beard?"

"It'd be too hard to shear him. Heh! I know, we'll get him a white shirt with high collar and maybe the Greeks will think he's a *papa*."

Ion didn't like that. Her humor was too broad. A tinge of the sacrilegious, too. No matter, he'd watch Stan a little more carefully, and if he saw a problem developing, he'd talk to Theodora about it. She could handle it, not him. She had that way of managing people, getting them together. Like this "eclectic" group she'd gathered here on the *Leto*, this heterogeneous conglomerate of macromolecular assemblies called professors. *Groan.*

Then he thought of Simonides again, of all the rocky cliffs and hillsides around them, of the buried epitaphs. Karen had made up her inscription. Shouldn't epitaphs summarize a person's life more than what they died of? No, they shouldn't be lies, and they shouldn't be silly. Furthermore, Simonides probably had to use words carefully, he had to cut and pare them to fit the marble, and regardless of what Karen and Stan said about him, he at least aspired to accuracy. It wasn't deceit or "cheating," and considering the times, he was trying to find truth. Paul quoted him correctly when he read to them: "Gold does not become defiled, and truth is totally strong." Bravo for Paul. And bravo for Theodora for at least trying to find precision in her psychological terms. Brandy smooths out things.

By then, the lapping sounds of the sea on the pebble beach began to mesmerize them. The Kea lion purred, guarding their private thoughts. It had been a full day and their initiation to becoming Aegean seafarers had placed them in a new world. They heard the voices of Stan and Karen approaching, and for a moment, between them, they must have felt an indeterminable *sympathia*.

It was nice that the soft air and coruscating stars could not urge, at this moment, its disclosure on buried marble slabs.

4
Ydra

The next morning, the grumpy Letoites, after their first night on hard bunks in stuffy cabins, did not relish Nescafe®, stale bread, and eggs fried in olive oil. But Theodora reminded them of the glorious day ahead—a sail across the wide open Aegean to the island of Paros.

"We'll get our sea legs sooner or later," she brightly said. "*Yia mas!*" she said, lifting her chipped coffee cup.

The "budget committee" meeting, chaired *pro tem*, by Theodora, resolved by vote that there was no alternative to the problem of how to settle up restaurant bills. A protocol had to established, to wit: Ion would negotiate with the waiters the *logariazmo*, the reckoning, since he knew Greek best, and would calculate the individual charges; Theodora would do the banking, dispersing the drachmas; and everyone vowed to always have on hand plenty of drachma change.

All, particularly those not assigned specific duties in the reckonings, would buy palatable provisions on shore that could augment the crews' breakfasts and lunches. This last agreement was to be voluntary, of course, but everyone vouched for fair play in that regard, resenting, nevertheless, that they would incur extra expenses. Theodora had never mentioned anything about that in Oakland.

Ion was skeptical for other reasons. He saw disputes arising, and neither did he like the onerous task of figuring how many pieces of bread Frances consumed and how many thimbles of retsina Paul drank from the carafe. It would be like doing an enzyme kinetic analysis on his calculator, which fortunately he had brought along. He hoped that Theodora would smooth things out.

The more serious problem of itinerary came up next. They brought the captain to the table and he proposed a "program"—a sail to Ydra, Spetses, Kythira and around the Peloponese to the Gulf of Corinth, all the time hugging the coast to avoid the treacherous *meltemi* winds. They could visit Olympia along the way and Nestor's Palace and it would be a comfortable and safe voyage. Ion interpreted it all in English.

Almost en masse, they protested. Ion explained to the captain that they each had their favorite island they wanted to visit, places like Paros, Crete, Patmos, Delos and Samos which were far out in the Aegean.

The captain shrugged but did not argue. "Very well then," he said. "The doctor owner told me to provide you with whatever you want. So, God willing, (he crossed himself) before nightfall, we will reach out for Paros. Takis, get ready, we sail immediately."

They broke anchor and before a motion could be made to adjourn the committee meeting, they headed out into a calm sea. Ribbons on the halyards hardly moved and the Letoites brought out travel books and maps. They circled around Kea's edge on one side, the open, endless blue on the other.

Ion wasn't pleased with developments, particularly with the captain's brusque agreement to their demands. He found him at the wheel on the bridge snorting Papastratos cigarettes and barking commands at Takis, who was busy in the engine room servicing the diesel motors.

"Ach, *Kyrie Ion,* they don't understand," the captain moaned.

"Forgive me," Ion said, "could you explain? I'm a child when it comes to the sea. You can just as well call me *Ion-aki.*"

The captain patted him on the head and smiled.

Ion said, "Tell me the truth, now. Will we be in danger if we go so far out?"

The captain narrowed his eyes and jutted his face to the wind which was beginning to pick up now that they had passed Kea's headlands. He was a handsome man, in a certain way, with a strong profile that reminded Ion of the hood ornament on an old Pontiac car. His torso was almost mammoth, proportioned and lithe for his age, betrayed only by the wrinkles on the back of his neck and crow's feet. From a cupped hand, he threw some sunflower seed into his mouth and then offered the sack to Ion.

They chewed for a while and then the captain began to make circles with a hand, the sides of his mouth curling down. Ion knew the gesture, that it meant something like "what a lot of shit."

"Listen to me, young man. I've traveled the world and I'll tell you this. The sea is a wild woman, and the Aegean is the biggest *poutana* of them all. She's so pretty, very pretty, her blues and greens. The dolphins play with her, the octopus and squid slither all around her like sperm. Then, there's the romance, her history—you know of what I speak. It drives tourists to madness. But what a *stryngla*; what treachery she holds. She can swallow you whole, let her fish eat you or bury your bones in her lightless depths—there, at the bottom, in Poseidon's cemetery with all the other *skata* of the ages. Oh, that temptress! You have no idea. All you see is her beautiful waters and frothy whitecaps and think, 'My, what refreshing breezes.' You become drunk with all that beauty and before you know it, Bah! she annihilates you!"

His hand kept circling, then it grabbed Ion's shoulder. "But it doesn't matter. Do as you wish, tell the rest whatever you want." He grinned and nodded his head. "*Opos thipote* (whatever). I don't care for myself. I'm willing to risk it. Why not have some excitement? I told the owner he should replace the diesel engines, but he thinks only about his *thanato* (death). He says to me, 'Let God put in his hand' and I say to him 'Let God protect us.' But he's too old to connect diesels with our *thanato*."

"Our *thanato*? *Kapitanios,* you must be serious with me. Please don't exaggerate. If there is a real problem here, perhaps I can convince Theodora and the rest of them that your program is safer."

Now the captain laughed and made a bigger arc with his hand. "You take things too seriously, *Ionaki.*" He gave the wheel a good jerk.

What then, Ion thought, *was I to take seriously—the condition of the diesels or the captain's irony*? But then as he carefully scrutinized the captain's facial expressions, he began to realize that regardless of the *Leto's* fate—or his own, in fact—he was intrigued by the Zorba manners of the wily old captain. But he wasn't Zorba, really. He was kind of cavalier in a stiffly starched white shirt, open-collared, its pocket embroidered with a blue anchor. Beneath a high crowned white and gold captain's hat, a furrowed brow and a steady gaze at the horizon, buffoonery did not reside, rather, some kind of hidden truth lurked, rife with contradictions, possibly conspiracies. How many times had Ion seen that trait in the Greeks—that ability to see the conditions of life through prisms that project a distorted image and mock all the human flaws.

Ion stood closer to the wheel, now studying the captain through the corner of his eyes. Unlike analyzing scientific data, this analysis took him into another mode, one requiring speculation, intuition, "behind the mirror" interpretations, like leaning back from the lab table after the numbers have been crunched.

What was this Greek up to? His own father practiced ambiguities, deceptions, implications, non sequiturs. "You cannot be a Greek, my son, unless you learn to be one." But he never told him what that learning process was. Was he to mimic his father? Flaunt his *hubris*? Water the ketchup bottles?

How seriously was he to take the captain? It was a compromising position, and he didn't like it. He wanted to retreat into cognitive science, try to quantify the realities. Yet, the captain had his own cognition, and Ion couldn't be certain that other perspectives lay out there, valid ones perhaps. Why did he stare so much out to the horizon's nothingness—did he possess a meterological clairvoyance? What was he looking for? Were his passengers peripheral to his focus, just objects degrading the final image, his purpose?

On the other hand, maybe all seamen have such peculiarities. Salt air seeps into their brains, sclerifying the membranes of their neurons, making them responsive only to marine stimuli. Still, Ion needed some resolution to the problem. He pursued, "We have sails, don't we, if the engines fail. Isn't that so?"

The captain pursed his lips and in a deep groan, said "*Po, po, po.* Sails, *po, po, po.* Rags. For show, that's what they're for. For an emergency, yes. But if the *meltemi* blow full force, they tear into pieces." He lit another Papastratos, totally ignoring now Ion.

Ion coughed. "But, as I was asking. . . . "

Now the captain, still staring out to the horizon said, "Listen, I do not want to alarm you and the Americans. You convey to them everything I said to you. This is an old boat—that is all there is to it—and whatever you decide, I will provide you with my best effort."

Ion felt dismissed. He went below to the saloon to call a committee meeting. The twins were buried in books. Stan and Karen were playing gin rummy. Theodora, in her cabin, was writing in a zippered notebook but when summoned, she quickly placed it in a combination locked briefcase. Ion caught the *Addenda* label on the notebook. *A strange name for a diary, or whatever kind of journal she was keeping,* he thought.

Ion, trying not to alarm them too much, relayed the captain's concerns, but the Letoites again balked. They wanted to see many islands, that was that. Ion knew that these landlubbers could not be dissuaded, but Theodora, at least, in her usual concessionaire manner said, "We don't want to harass the captain and we don't want to let him off easy. Perhaps we can play it by ear as we go along?"

Stan piped up immediately. "We're not exactly helpless. Takis seems a sturdy crewman, and we have three able-bodied men on board." He paused for a second when he looked at Paul. "I've been in lots of tight places in trips to third world countries. I can't believe we can't muddle through this. Things work out."

"Karen, in her stentorian administrator voice said, "If things get harrowing, we'll know what to do. We'll merely abandon ship and take a ferry boat back to Piraeus. We're educated people. We're not fools or cowards."

Frances joked, "What's a little seasickness?" Paul squeezed her hand and grinned a tight smile.

Takis, in shorts and bare feet, leaned against a bulkhead and watched the foreigners. He whittled a bust of a woman out of olive wood and wondered what the foreigners were so intense about. Karen smiled at him, pumped her arm in a gesture to mean, "Come, join us." Takis swirled both his hands, a Greek gesture Karen interpreted to mean, "Keep going. I'm with you." He approached them with his sculpture, and Karen reached out to examine his carving. She arched her eyebrows and with sign language invited him to pass it to her. Her expression showed a child's delight and he, pointing his index finger at her and then the sculpture, implied that Karen was the model for his sculpture, or so she thought. She guffawed and startled everyone when she lifted her heavy breasts and then pointed to the oversized bust of Takis' sculpture. Takis' eyes sparkled. Theodora tried to look shocked.

The morning passed, and the Cyclades drifted by slowly as floating, tawny masses studded with dark green and silvery green patches. From their maps, the Letoites could not quite identify them. Serifos? Sifnos? Tinos? After a while, it didn't matter. They all had indentations of mountain ranges, swaths of white-washed villages and monasteries. Squinting at them, passing around Stan's binocs, they didn't seem quite real. Hollywood sets? Dufy paintings? No analogy worked, each registered in their brains endless associations, changing ones that ultimately their brains could only interpret as profound abstractions of ethereal beauty.

The winds rose, and they emerged from their trances, lurching around the saloon, bracing each other, laughing. But after a light lunch of cold cuts and cheese, they had to retire to their bunks to protect themselves against the violent surges and listings of the hull. Each secretly wondered if they should have heeded the captain's warnings. Perhaps it was not too late to change course for the Peloponese.

But after a couple of hours, the sea calmed and around three o'clock the *Leto* glided into a snug harbor filled with yachts from around the world. Next to a sleek Swedish one, the *Leto*, half her size, tied up. The Swedes waved glasses at the Letoites and invited them on board.

The harbor was framed by mountains with handsome villas built up their slopes. It didn't appear Cycladic, the buildings were large and Venetian-like, roofs tiled and windows with carved marble lintels, colors ocher and beige.

"Captain Yiorgi," Theodora said, "is this Paros?"

"*Ochi, thespinis,* it is Ydra."

He explained in slow, well-enunciated Greek (so that she would understand) that he had taken a sharp westerly course when the Maritime Band announced the Beaufort number was predicted to rise to eight by late afternoon.

Theodora huffed and turned to Ion, in English, "Weren't we beyond the point of no return? Couldn't we have made Paros anyhow? What's he doing to us?"

Ion shrugged and followed the rest up to the Swedish yacht.

The Swedes were apparently rich industrialists, well-oiled with aquavit and ouzo. Their behavior was manic and suddenly they'd break out into loud folk songs. "Swedes are like that when they get into sunshine," said Stan.

The Letoites, not quite able to catch onto the Swedish frivolity, began to drift down the gangplank and to the harbor front, hungry and curious about the port town.

By an outdoor café with tanks of lobster, they congregated for a meal of fried calamari and tomato and cucumber salads. Karen objected to eating "scavengers of the sea" and had an omelet with bacon.

They ordered another carafe of wine, and as the evening wore on, they went into their silent mode; people casting long shadows browsed gift and pastry shops, their murmurs harmonizing with the squeaks from the straining ties of boats in the harbor. Then from behind them, deep in the town, faint church bells pealed, hushing the air more.

Paul felt a sepulchral mood descending on them, and this time, he decided to break the spell. Brightly, as if giving a morning lecture to a freshman history class, he begin to recite the history of Ydra, about its importance as a maritime power and particularly its role in the war for independence against the Turks in the nineteenth century.

"Now listen to this amazing fact," he said. "The Greeks had this heroinie from that war. Her name was Bouboulina and here is a picture of her."

He dug out a book from his satchel and passed around a daguerrotype copy of a woman in long skirt, boots, daggers around her waist and a large wimple. She leaned on a rifle.

"She was a native of the nearby island of Spétsai, but many of the ships of her fleet were built here in Ydra. The two islands became allies in the war, and the stories about her are incredible, as you can imagine.

"How so?" said Karen.

"She was more than just the Admiral of her rebellious fleet. She was a symbol, a reincarnated Athena. More than that, she was a fierce warrior, killed without a second thought. Went through two husbands and allegedly would command, at sword's point—can you imagine?—that a man make love to her."

"Whooeee," said Stan, "a ball buster."

"And I bet she de-balled plenty of Turks, assuredly," said Frances.

How astonishing of her to say that, Ion thought. *It was out of character.*

"And made a pilaf with them," Stan said. "How about that for supper, Karen?"

Karen sneered. Frances said, "Let's just say that she was a woman of destiny, a Virginia Woolf with real bite. Changing the subject, Paul, didn't Herodotus and Thucydides mention the island? Or maybe Solon?"

"Interesting question, that is. Seems to me, as well as I can remember, its history was rather obscure in classical times."

Stan, turning serious said, "Hard to imagine how such a place with such topography, so rocky and barren, could have had much influence."

Theodora jumped in quickly. "Beautiful, verdant places don't always make for great civilizations. Polynesia and the south Pacific come to mind."

"You may have a prejudice there, Theodora," said Stan. "True, however, other factors enter in. Past history, political economic forces, the things we mouth about today. Heh, Theodora, are you invading my territory? Are you a cultural anthropologist, too?"

Theodora, ingratiating, said, "I'm merely pointing out the obvious complexities of predicting how a people contribute to man's evolutionary advancement. It's easy post facto as we talk here to offer explanations. It's hard enough to understand behavior of single individuals."

"And that's not predictive either, is it?" said Stan.

"The odds are not so bad when all the parameters are considered," she said.

"You'd have to prove that to me," Stan said. "How do you control the variables?"

"You can't completely, but you can approximate."

"Still. You have to control the environment, too, besides taking into account the type and qualities of human behavior. You're not talking about putting a person in a Skinnerian box, are you?" said Stan.

"That's so controversial. Oh Stan, let's not get too serious. We're on holiday. Perhaps I can convince you at the end of the trip by, shall we say, what transpires?"

Stan looked quizzical, but before he could pursue the topic further, the waiter brought the reckoning to Ion, and the odious task began.

One by one, everybody recited what they ate, how many pieces of bread; then Ion translated to the waiter; the waiter penciled the cost of each item; Ion, then ... *Oh, skata*, he thought, every night they would go through this, even multiplying in the proportionality factor for the tip, which for god's sake, had to be agreed upon each meal depending on how satisfied the group was with the food and service. The calculator screen was dim after a few glasses of wine, and Theodora, with her bag of drachmas, still had to give change and with Ion's assistance on the calculator, they had to do an accounting of accounts received and payable.

Finally, one by one, they pushed away from the table, and Stan, sensing the group's restlessness, suggested a stroll up the promontory above the harbor. They proceeded, two by two—Frances and Paul, Karen and Stan, and Theodora and Ion—a pairing, that seemed natural—midgets, extroverts and Greeks together. On the road to Mandraki, high above the harbor, they made a turn away from the port to the dark, unpopulated rocky and mountainous coastline, scented with wild sage and myrtle. After about twenty minutes, they gathered at a ledge along the road to take in the view towards the Peloponese mainland and what they thought were the dim lights of the island of Spetses.

"Bouboulina fascinates me," Frances said, as if whispering to herself, "Out there, doing battle. A woman warrior."

For minutes, the rest, lost in pitch darkness, could hardly register her words. The sea's lappings against the rocks made deep kettledrum sounds. Far out at sea, dim sparkles danced on the horizon, fishing boats probably.

Finally, Karen, trying to capture Frances' sense of the melodrama, muttered, "Amazing, indeed. Perhaps she was a Sappho's disciple."

Stan cleared his throat. "Nah. Paul said she had male lovers."

Theodora, sitting on the ledge, leaned her elbows on her knees and speaking with hands under her jaw said, "Strange we should be talking of such things here. Nevertheless, aggression—if that's what we're talking about—has many forms. In females, that behavior might appear masculinized. But when—oh, God—when will we ever recognize that women of intelligence can act with strong convictions and actions? Well, I don't mean to be argumentative, but Bouboulina, obviously, was a woman of destiny, motivated by patriotism and who knows what altruisms. Women are just as capable of achieving goals like that, with sharp insights, incisive deeds, with pistols and daggers if necessary. History has many of that type. Ancient Greeks had many examples of such women, some were goddesses."

As she spoke, the Letoites began to gather around her, the rocks and pebbles on the roadway snapping under their crushing steps.

"Let us gather on the Pnyx at the feet of Socrates," said Paul.

"Oh, knock it off, Paul," said Stan.

"They were mythological figures, goddesses," Ion said. "Women in Greek society, to this day, take submissive roles to men." His tone was acerbic, as if he were answering a student's stupid question.

Theodora did not rebut. Instead, she turned to Paul. "You've been reading about the Greek Revolt against the Turks, I see. Were these battles around here?"

"The Greeks had fireboats with which they rammed Turkish cruisers. Blew them out of the water with their smaller kamikaze boats stuffed with tar, sulfur and gunpowder. Bouboulina, no doubt, had a hand in that."

"Whew," said Stan. "Boom-boom Lena! Don't mess with that hyena!"

Theodora rose quickly. "You make her into some kind of savage. She must have been a very clever woman to have commanded a naval fleet. She'd have had to gain the confidence of lots of men."

"How was she clever?" said Stan. "By gentle persuasion, or by seduction?"

"Oh, kerfuffle," said Frances. "You are all speculating. The fact is that she's considered a heroine. How are we to psychoanalyze her? There are books about Joan of Arc's character, and yet, who can be sure?"

Theodora clapped her hands. "So true, dear Frances. Figuring motivations of historical people is even worse than trying to figure living ones. I'm a psychologist, and it's what I deal with all the time. I can only say this: It's hard enough figuring our own, personal motivations."

"So you keep telling us. But can you?" said Karen, "I mean, can one—speaking rhetorically, of course—manipulate other people's motivations?"

"To a large extent, yes. I believe so."

Ion threw a rock as far as he could. They waited to hear its plunk in the sea, but there was none. He turned to Theodora, "We always are trying to do that with scientific experimentation, aren't we? We are motivated to find an answer to a problem and we design accordingly."

"Ha!" said Stan. "Let's put Theodora's thesis to test. The captain here, I hypothesize, is trying to manipulate, motivate, us to *his* 'plan.' He doesn't want to go far off into the Aegean. He's given all this bogus about the diesels. And here we are in the lair of Bouboulina, way off course from what we wanted to do, but right on course with the Captain's circumnavigation of the Peloponese."

"You bet," said Karen. "We need someone to motivate that codger to *our* ways."

"Absolutely," said Frances. "I simply must see Delos. Seasickness or whatever. But we can't convince the captain of that with muskets. We need gentle persuasion, right?"

"I say, we need our very own Bouboulina," said Paul. "A smart, modern sophisticated one."

"Ah . . ." the Letoites declared in unison. They all turned to Theodora. "Admiral Bouboulina," said Stan, "proceed to your command post."

They all laughed, except Theodora. She didn't want to be a Bouboulina. Her ways of making a man do her bidding were more subtle than they could manage. Furthermore, the idea simply was not consistent with the protocols in the Addenda. No, she must be careful to dispel these notions, even if made in jest.

❖   ❖   ❖

That night in her cabin, she sat on the edge of her bunk and wrote in the Addenda. Things had gone out of whack, momentarily she hoped. Bouboulina, in any guise, with or without muskets, was the antithesis of her role model. The mere word "persuasion" was offensive. It connoted an active input, whereas her operating principles relied on action to proceed from the subjects alone, without any intervention of the therapist.

Now, *that* she knew needed clarification, that word *intervention*. It wasn't a mere matter of semantics, it had to do with being certain in her own mind that she was in no way being willful with her subjects. She'd have rather called it a "passive" acknowledgment and support for her subjects' innate desires and subconscious needs. To be passive was the clue, to be the backboard (a tennis prof patient had given her that metaphor) and recipricator for what were the subject's aspirations.

Her only "role" was to bring out and enhance those intentions. She wasn't to pull the strings of the marionettes. They were self-propelled. All she was to do was to set the stage. Then they would perform accordingly . . . and in the way that she would have predicted and, well, the way she wanted them to.

Careful, though, she must be very careful with that last thing. Her desires were not the ultimate goal. If they were in fact achieved, they would have been achieved by not her own active interventions, but rather by the preliminary screening of possibilities and the selection of people and events to bring out the natural outcome—one that she condoned from the very start, in fact, embraced as her own motivation to be the "enhancer," "facilitator." Yes, her role was to be, must be, passive. Otherwise, the whole thing is a ruse.

Bouboulina, indeed. Then, she took her hair brush, and looking in the small mirror tacked on the cabin door, she began lifting locks of her henna hair. The hairdresser had done a nice job. The luster was still there, but suddenly she startled. After three weeks, would it stay that? Would the black roots began to show and what would the harsh sun and sea air do to the sheen? Oh my, she hadn't thought of that.

5
At Sea

Without any machinations, coercions, or pleas from Theodora, the captain embarked early the next morning for Paros, and Theodora, after breakfast with the Letoites, staying in her cabin and removed from her self-appointed duties of keeping things on board the *Leto* shipshape, decided to work more on her Addenda. She was trying to relate recent happenings to her monograph back home entitled: *Human Coercions: Their Limits and Potentials*.

Before writing anything new in the Addenda, she instead reviewed some background. The data in the *Coercion* paper came from tightly constructed experimental conditions. The data she was accumulating now was rather haphazard, spotty, buckshotted. But data can often be that way at first, the synthesis comes later. In fact, in its scattered notations—funny the similarities—were not unlike the diary that she begin keeping while in third grade. Her teacher urged her to record what she had done during that day, what she wanted to happen the next day, and what she wished for her life in the distant future. Lot of those thoughts were superfluous, as they turned out, but *in toto* they gave some definition to who she was and what she wanted to be. Composed in solitude, through so many years, that diary also formed some of the basic tenets by which she operated in her professional life. Hard to explain that, but her ruminations in the diary were more than daydreams, they were in fact some rather deep insights about human motivations and ambitions, her own most of all. Retrospections and introspections evolved with her intellectual life, and they blended all her world views into some coherent manifesto by which she lived and, one would hope, by which she achieved something in her life.

Thus, she kept that diary going through undergraduate years at McAllister where, majoring in chemistry, she augmented them with entries about the use of Grignard reagents in her organic chemistry lab. However, she continued her wish lists from third grade, juxtaposing personal items (whose confidentiality she guarded assiduously). In her junior year, she recorded the details of her crush for a classmate, a handsome, strapping Norwegian boy from Hibbing—about the color of his socks, the blond fuzz on his nape of his neck, and the cuticles of his big thumbs. Was there a correlation between the size of thumb and penis? Do rosy cheeks connote shapely buttocks? Between the condensers and reflux columns of the chemistry lab, she stole glances of him, embarrassed by her brazen thoughts, humiliated by the knowledge that her sexual attractiveness had almost zero energy of activation. None of those feelings, however, prevented her adulation of his shiny golden hair and the luster of his blue eyes. Somehow, all his hues she came to associate with her chromatographic columns, all the colors stirring in her secret, unfulfilled passions.

The most despairing aspect of all that was that even if she had been able to make a connection with the boy, her Greek parents would have thwarted her. She had to marry a Greek, and they had prospects lined up in Minneapolis. They talked to her incessantly about those boys, and what she knew of them, compared to her golden boy, they were sheer abominations, nothing more than bus boys.

Clearly, she had to plot ways of finding a man *she* wanted, something approximating that Norwegian boy. She reasoned that was not so difficult a task, what with her keen analytical mind to guide her. All she had to do was to mesh her personal sexual desires with her academic pursuits. Like planning an experiment to provide the maximal reaction product, all could be attained by the simple expediency of placing herself in an advantageous position; to wit, she'd convince her parents that the very best proxenia, matchmaking, could be achieved by meeting a very bright young man in Graduate School. And surely, there were some smart Greek boys floating around there (and maybe a rare blond one).

Furthermore—and this was the clincher—she told them "Psychology is about how humans behave, how people can learn to get along with each other. That's what I'll study," she told them. "And I'll use that know-how to find a mate—a smart Greek one at the University with richer prospects than any bus boy." They'd be proud of her. She invoked the goddess Athena and St. Helen as role models, she declared to them, and her parents finally acceded, wanting to believe that their daughter had rare gifts they must financially indulge. Papa would keep the café open on Sunday.

She had taken a couple of classes in Psychology, and the State University was eager to give her a graduate scholarship in the Psychology Department, which wanted "cross-disciplinary" inputs, such as from a Phi Beta Kappa in chemistry. So far, so good.

She miscalculated on one thing, however. She hadn't realized how engrossing, or how competitive, the graduate work would be. The nature of her new field of psychology put her more in contact with living things, not burettes and flasks. The amazing thing was that her clear-thinking scientific mind could find a niche for itself in the halls of Behaviorists' theories. Testing human subjects found a parallel to devising synthetic pathways for organic chemicals, and her colleagues admired her. Her diary began to fill with her achievements of the day and the goals for tomorrow. She didn't have time to think of Norwegian boys.

Still, her parents, no grandchildren in sight, did not desist, and from time to time they'd harangue her about finding a Greek husband. They knew she wanted someone with a brain so they presented her with a fat-cheeked Greek engineer from Minneapolis with a personality something less than that of an experimental rat.

It was hard to put them off, and Papa was beginning to tire of the long hours in the café. She dodged dates with that engineer valiantly, but an unfortunate event solved her dilemma; her beloved brother, Sammy was killed in Korea, all because of MacArthur's ego. Her parents went into depressions, forgetting everything about grandchildren. How she hated male aggressiveness! Fat Greek ones were the worst. She agonized, thought hard, and designed experiments on how to deflate aggressive behaviour in her subjects. Electroshock might work nicely, but she'd have to watch the amperage. She fried some mice testing that hypothesis.

With her parents' miseries and her own grief, she buried more and more of herself in academic life. Not until, two years later, when her father died, and her mother was relegated to a rest home, did she begin to think again of her sexual needs, her needs for affection, and as she wrote in her diary, "The emotional needs of a young professional woman." Yet, she couldn't quite shake the wishes of her parents. They haunted her, and she had to admit that, yes, it would be nice if she could marry someone of the same background—not that she thought Greeks were superior—but knowing that she wasn't a good-looker, she rationalized that it might be more expeditious to find someone out there who might appreciate her genes—such as another Greek.

Serendipidity came to her rescue, a way to sublimate her

grief with professional pursuits. Her research on operant conditioning in children, which got her a nice appointment in her California university, and behavior modification with biofeedback techniques led her to promulgate her Coercion Theory—a spin-off of the old F. O. Skinner ideals. She had gained some recognition in professional circles by claiming that people put in conflicting situations will always choose the easy, most rewarding solution. All subjects (pubertal males worked best) could be made to eat their first oyster if they were promised big colored pictures of lubricious genitals. Carefully designed experiments with subjects sitting behind one-way glass could be coerced in many different ways, even to choosing options that were contrary to their normal customary desires, even to the point of abuse of other test subjects.

From these self-enhancing potentiations in her subjects, which recorded all kinds of physiological measurements such as muscle tension, skin conductivity, pupillary size, pulse and ventilatory rates and blood pressure, she began to extrapolate her ideas to nonlaboratory conditions. In day-to-day life, she argued, human beings perform in exactly the same way, only instead of an experimenter selecting choices, a complex "social order" proffers them. If the "social order" could be manipulated, then in the manner some desired outcome could be achieved. Such manipulations could be constructed at the very personal level—not in the political, grand scale of fascist or communist propaganda—and if carefully selected, those could lead to "personal fulfillment" of specific goals for the subjects.

It would be up to a trained, behavioral psychologist, such as herself, to select appropriate subjects (by her Personality Profile Projections technique), to interpret the subject's needs, and she would be the one to position all elements of the subject's environment to consummate his desires. Such gambits could have wide applications, ranging from achieving career goals, investment strategies or, even to finding a mate.

Many problems with her theories remained, however, the most important being that the "social order" to be selected had not only to be selected (not an easy task) but it had to be cloaked, otherwise subjects would sense a "deceit" (a word her professional antagonists used). More than that, subjects must believe that the choices they made were wholly theirs, and no one else's. In other words, the psychologist's identity had to be completely concealed.

Now, to the issue at hand. She opened the Addenda and thought about how here on the *Leto*, all the pieces of her plan, the execution of the gambit and the juxtapositions of events and people were "in progress," the modus operandi in place, all for the purpose of 1. enabling a *proxenia* and 2. lending support to her Coercion Theory.

As a consequence, the Addenda was beginning to fill up with she hoped some confirmatory detail of the voyage: dialogues were entered, every mannerism, every circumstance of the trip. Examples of Karen's hoyden nature. Stan's insouciance. Paul's pedantry. Frances' parabases. Ion's *faux* detachments. The grand scheme unfolded, day by day, and she felt confident that that things were pretty much on course, all elements performing according to plan. Only one parameter had to be attended to: the budding animosity of the Letoites for the captain. He and Takis from the beginning were variables that she could not account for into the original Oakland idea, yet she had to be sure they didn't undermine the experimental plan.

So, she wrote, the only thing to do was to make sure that the crew created no dissension. They must be staged as background, neutral, or, if possible, as enhancing elements to the "social order" she was constructing.

✿ ✿ ✿

She zippered up her notebook, and ascended to the wheel

house. Everything sparkled, the sea, sun, and sky, blinding her. Her pupils finally adapted, and she saw the captain talking with Ion. "*Ella, ella,* come come, *thespinis,* join us," he said pulling out a stool for her. She almost fell, but the captain's strong arms caught her. She had never felt such hard forearms.

"I was telling your friend here of my tanker trips in the Orient," he said.

"I'd like to hear of them, too, Captain. But my Greek is not as good as Ion's. Can you talk slowly *siga, siga?* I understand Greek better than I can speak it."

The captain nodded with a graceful diagonal tilt of his head.

"What part of Greece are you from?" Theodora said.

"Arakhova, in Boetia, on the way to Delphi. You know?"

She didn't, but Ion explained its location. He and his parents had bought some goat rugs there. Conversation among the three of them followed the usual Greek pattern. The captain quickly found out that both were Assistant Professors, unmarried, their ages, and where their parents came from.

"Let me tell you of Arakhova," the captain said. He related how he had been fighting the Italians in the snowy mountains of Albania. "We were punishing them for trying to invade us and like fools thought of pushing them back all the way to their own soil. The Italians were smart. They knew the stupidity of war, hardly put up a fight. And we were so gallant. Ha! How could we have known that the Germans were about to outflank us from Yugoslavia and drive straight for Athens. How bitter the lessons of life. The occupation was the worst. They made a slave of me—I was only sixteen—and they put me to work in the factories of the Ruhr. How I hated those Germans. They treated us like *skata,* like Jews. But the worse was what happened back in Arakhova. I knew my people would not tolerate an occupation. Of course, they rebelled, what else could they do? And what could the Germans do but retaliate? They massacred more than a hundred of the townspeople, my father and uncles."

After the war, he returned to marry a local girl and then shipped off on a Greek oil tanker to the Pacific for six years. "Horrible, lonely years. Typhoons, the bitch seas."

His wife died and he returned to Athens, despondent. Fortune smiled when the Athenian anesthesiologist wanted a captain for his yacht. For the last twelve years, he had been so employed on the *Leto*.

"And now life is beautiful again, not so?" said Theodora.

"Hmmm . . ." He lit another cigarette and asked Ion to hold the wheel while he checked the diesels. Takis was snoozing in his bunk beneath the wheel house.

"Now let me tell you of this," he said, leaning hard against the wheel. He offered them some fresh melon. "On this very day, five years ago, the doctor leased the yacht to two German couples. I was the captain, of course. The men, oxen with blond hair on their backs, and their wives, if they were wives, wore tight shorts and *boustakia* with ropes to hold up their utters. What disgusting people! They drank beer day and night and ate nothing but boiled potatoes and sausages dripping fat.

"Five years ago it was, yes. We were in the Dodecanese, near Kos. Many little island around there. We had left Kos and they wanted to take a midday swim and a picnic on one of those islands.

"Those islands are under watch all the time by the Turks. I don't know why. There is nothing on them, nothing. But the Turks . . ." He lost his train of thought, but Ion brought him back.

"About the German, *Kapitanios* . . .

"We were in those waters when the one ox started bragging of the 'good days' during the war when he was stationed in Greece. He said, 'Only trouble we had was in a town called

Arakhova. There was a rebellion. Those peasants dared to oppose us.' Then he boasted of all that to the others, but I understood what he said, I knew German, though he thought because my accent was poor, that I didn't. I had good ears. Listen to me, *Thespinis, Kyrie Ion,* understand how I felt. The very *teras* (beast) could have gunned down my father. You understand my rage? I had had enough of those bastards and their filthy ways. They threw beer bottles and food scraps everywhere. Even the dolphins would have nothing to do with them."

His eyes widened, then suddenly gleamed with delight. "Well, then, you ask, what do I do? I packed them a lunch and told them I would take them to an undiscovered beach whose waters were pure emerald, sands of gold. 'No other like it in the world,' I told them. We circled the little island and found a deep cove—I had discovered it by accident years before because a French deep sea diver wanted to explore it. I launched the skiff and with the outboard motor took them ashore. I told them I would be back for them after lunch and their swim, about two hours. Everyone agreed."

The captain adjusted his hat, stroked his chin, then turned to look Theodora and Ion in the eye. "Now, my fellow Greeks, what do you think? What would you do with such an opportunity?"

Theodora and Ion looked straight at each other in astonishment, thinking, no doubt, the same evil thought; then they turned towards the captain expecting him to allay their terrible suspicion.

He immediately supplied the answer. He continued, "I had two hours to think about it, two hours to resolve a guilt for the plan that was in my mind. I thought hard." He touched his temple, then very deliberately, made a big sign of the cross from forehead to navel and to the tips of his scapulae.

Oh God, thought Theodora and Ion. *Expiations!* The blue sky took on grey tones, and the sea started to boil. A storm was brewing.

"Think of it," the captain continued. "No water, blistering sun. Deep in that cove, hidden from passing fishing boats, which probably would not have passed anyhow. And by the remotest chance, a fisherman did find them, do you think any Greek would rescue them? Remember, it was not long after the war. The hatred remained."

"But the authorities . . ." Ion said.

"If they came around asking I would tell them that they disembarked in Rhodes. They had been seasick, I'd tell them, and they didn't want to continue sailing."

"But if they did disembark, wouldn't you have to report that to the Harbor Police?" said Theodora.

"What Harbor Police? They were a joke. Before the colonels everyone did whatever they wished. No one cared much about anything."

"Wouldn't the Germans' families make inquiries in Piraeus? Surely there would be records of their boarding the *Leto*. You'd have to account for them when you returned to Piraeus," said Ion.

"No, as I said, no records. There were no records of their boarding the *Leto*."

"They may have told their German friends in a post card."

"Eh . . . all I could say was that they disembarked in Rhodes. What happened afterwards, how would I know?"

"Sooner or later, their remains would be found,' said Theodora.

"So, next season I go back to bury the bones at sea. If they find them before that—not much chance—the wild goats would have picked them over. And how could anyone prove that I left them there? I tell you the truth. The Greek authorities would turn their backs on such things."

The three looked at each other quizzically, trying to find who or what really to believe. Then they stared out to the sea which had turned into a calm lake smoothness. One of the diesels sputtered and quickly the captain went below to the check the oil pressure.

Theodora's face squinched and she said to Ion, "God, we're at his mercy. He's like a character out of Melville. He's vicious. He's a sea monster. He has power over us. He could poison our water supply. If he wanted to scuttle the *Leto* he could. He could dump any of us overboard if he didn't like us. At night while we're sleeping. Oh, Ion . . ." She rested her head on Ion's chest and Ion, for a second, raised a hand as if to console her, but he instead froze, shocked and embarassed.

The captain returned quickly, bouncing up the stairs to the wheel house, and almost shouting, "Ha! Have I frightened you?" He guffawed. "You know about sea tales. I have many of them. The sea makes you lonely. We seamen make up these fantasies. It is a nice story I tell you, no?"

"Then they didn't perish?" said Theodora.

"Oh, *Thespinis*, of course not. How could you think that of me? I'm civilized. Thoughts crossed my mind, that's all. Anyone would have had the same ones. The fact is the *antithesis*. I don't think I was afraid of being caught. I think that those oxen may have good, beautiful children back in Germany. No matter how disgusting *they* were. But every time this year, I think of them. If, if . . ."

✿   ✿   ✿

Theodora went below, stumbling on the ladder down to the hold of the cabins, shaken. The captain was a much more powerful man than she reckoned. She didn't want to fear him, yet she felt a certain awe. He was, or at least she wanted to believe that he was, a kind, decent man, but there was something else about him that she really didn't like. In her grand scheme, she could not picture him now as a neutral backdrop. She'd have to involve him into the scheme in another way, as a contributing partner in the "social order" perhaps.

She opened up the Addenda again and began to think of alternatives, new avenues to pursue. All was not lost. In fact, if she played her cards right, he might fall nicely into a more refined means of reaching her goal. For example, with his sea skills and worldliness he might help in the selection of the most idyllic sites.

Oh Lord, what idyllic sites? No, no, he was really an unknown influence to her plans. She'd watch him very carefully. Like it or not, she'd have to befriend him, if nothing else but to circumscribe any mischievous force. She scribbled possibilities: talk more Greek with him, tell him of her father, what a wonderful sweet man he was, a true Greek, talk to him about Minnesota Greeks and how they got there, what they were like, how wonderful Greek people can be, so adventurous and honest, etc.

Then, she reviewed her encounter with him, listening to him tell her about that horrible German fantasy. What did she get so emotional about it? Wasn't it really girlish for her to lean her head on Ion's shoulder? What must he have thought?

She gritted her teeth and began to brush her hair vigorously. *Get hold of yourself,* she thought.

❖ ❖ ❖

Meanwhile, back up on deck, the captain held Ion back with more questions about his passengers. "All American, eh? How did you meet? Who planned this trip? I like Americans, they are innocent, like children. Why are all of them not married? The two little love birds, I like. They wink and smile at me. That bearded one you say studies *anthropoi?* Why is he so dirty? Why doesn't he shave and make himself respectable? He's not one of those 'hippy' types they have on Ios and Mykonos? They are all *poustis,* you know."

He translated for Ion the Greek word for "fuckee" by gesturing a goose in his butt.

"That woman with the frizzy hair and big breasts, the Jewish one, do you think she wants to fuck Takis? Takis is a good boy, let him have some fun."

The sex talk was too bold for Ion. He never liked locker room talk, and he didn't expect it in Greece, yet, here he was just now learning the Greek "f" word.

The captain brought out a cold *glyko* from the galley, a fillo wrapped custard. 'Yes," he said, just barely catching the custard spilling out the side of his mouth, "we have a good group. *Thespinis* Theodora is a fine woman. She needs to be more Greek, that's all."

❊   ❊   ❊

After a lunch of cheese and cold cuts on board while the *Leto* quietly sliced through a giant vitrine, the passengers lolled around the outer deck, exquisite zephyrs brushing their sun-warmed skins. Paul, his arms crossed on his chest, said, "It is not real, you know."

Hardly anyone paid attention, except Stan. "Now what are you up to, Socrates?"

"I was thinking of Parmenides, the Eleatics, and ontogeny."

"Get you. Are you going to demolish our serenity with more pedantry?"

"Quite the opposite, I was going to enhance it." He pouted for a few minutes.

Theodora rose to the rescue. "Parmenides was the Father of Western Philosophy, wasn't he?"

"Indeed. In his poem, 'his ideas of Being,' oneness, virtually negated all of what our senses perceive. The thing that *is* is the True Reality, and everything that *is not* is an illusion."

"All this beauty that surrounds us, at this moment, you are saying is only an illusion?" said Karen.

"Precisely, not in the context of the real meaning of life."

"I'll be damned," said Stan. "You've taken away my pleasures."

"I'm not, of course. I'm only saying that you cannot assign purpose or meaning to your pleasure. I give you permission to go ahead and enjoy it nevertheless."

Theodora hunched her shoulders. "You mean that this whole trip has no purpose? I don't accept that. I know for myself what purpose this trip serves."

"You think you do. I dare say that you may later find that your purposes were flawed. They are not the true reality."

Theodora frowned. How to confront this philosophical impasse?

Frances came to her rescue. "Protagoras would dispute you. Our senses are everything. 'Man is the measure' as is commonly stated."

Ion jumped in. "Besides, do you say that all our scientific theories, abstractions, quantum mechanics, the arts are illusions?" (He'd been reading his Schrodinger.)

"We can never separate the duality of man, his rationality and sensate perceptions. But from the standpoint of logic, his 'Oneness' must be acknowledged. Whether you want to make anything of your other—your thing, Theodora—that's up to you. I cannot deny you that."

"Thanks," said Theodora. "May I ask you this . . . why did you come on this trip in the first place?"

The Letoites hurrumphed. Their conversation stopped with a thud when the hull skimmed a ripple.

6
Paros

At the harbor of Paros, the mid-afternoon sun blazing, the Letoites craved cooling. Clothing needed shedding, skins needed refreshing. Oh, how many nights had Theodora dreamed of seeing them semi-naked in the Aegean! But there was a little problem she had neglected to take into consideration. After three days of close quarters, they hadn't really seen much of each other's bodies (perhaps Paul and Frances had, or so she hoped). She now realized how averse she would be to reveal hers, but she had to accept the reality: Greece is warm in the summers, that was one of the stimulatory agents in all her calculations, she must fully utilize it. What she had to relinquish were feelings of shame or embarassment. *Hell,* she thought, *with appropriate discretion, my own exposure did not have to erode my stratagems.* A little panache, that's all, a little stylish modesty. Besides, body awareness of each other should heighten mutual understandings. These people were not just animals in heat, and showing some flesh should improve mutual acceptances of each other. Yes, that was the proper way to amend her "social order."

Besides, as recorded in her Addenda, the physical aspects of human attraction are only transitory. Enduring relationships are not always initiated by libido flare-ups but rather evolve through time when people began to explore a meeting of minds. Then, providing there is no deep physical revulsions, erogenous elements slowly conjoin and seal mutual, permanent commitments. Blah, blah, she wrote. It was too obvious. She underlined her conclusion: *she didn't have to be a knock-out, she had only to make herself presentable.*

Therefore, to her fellow passengers, she ordained a swim and she carefully prepared herself.

Her swimsuit, a two-piece affair, with a flared skirt bottom and a padded halter with frilled edges, was, in her mind, dressy, yet circumspect of her anatomical flaws. She had brought along a silk kimono from San Francisco's Chinatown and from a tourist shop in Athens had purchased a wide straw hat with bright red ribbon on its brim. Thus attired, she and the rest of the Letoites, in conservative beach garb, appropriate for cold, foggy northern California beaches, walked beyond the harbor to a beach lined with tamarisk trees and laid out their newly bought beach mats.

Very soon, though, on the beach, they found themselves in an altogether unfamiliar, very foreign environment. Scattered around the sand were men in g-string jockey briefs edged with pubic hairs. The women wore panties no less scanty, and, most shocking, they were all topless, except for the flaccid Greek grandmothers.

They stood gaping for awhile, wondering whether they shouldn't find a more secluded beach. Karen, however, seized the initiative and said, "Hey, gang, when in Paros . . . She craned her head to the sky, reached behind her halter and with a tug flung free her top. Her jugs bobbled free in the sunlight, and she, unabashed, turned to the Letoites with her upturned hands, fingers waving, saying, "Come on gals, let's not be prudish."

Frances had no qualms, she even admired Karen's spirit, and feeling that with or without a top, she wouldn't look that much different. Theodora's olive skin actually bleached, her face looked mortified. But what could she do? She fumbled in her plastic bag for a towel. She pressed her sunglasses to her nose bridge. Then draping the towel across the shoulders, she turned her back and loosened her halter. The rest turned their attention to spreading their mats, aware of her shyness.

There they were, the Letoites on the beach. Ion, gym-fit except that his oversized boxer trunks made him look middle-aged; Stan with so many beads of sweat on his hirsute body that he looked like a Neanderthal emerging from a prehistoric sea; Paul and Frances like little sand pipers; and Theodora with her arms crossed on her chest like an obeisant vestal virgin.

They plunged into the cool sea, Ion and Stan breaking out quickly for the deep, Paul and Frances splashing in the shallow, and Theodora and Karen walking cautiously out to the surf. Karen rinsed her armpits with the cool sea water and then herself plunged in all the way and thrashed her way out to Ion and Stan. Theodora stumbled and plopped down in the water up to her waist. There she remained.

Back on their mats, Theodora, on her back, finally unclasped her arms and closed her eyes. She clinched her lips and hoped no one was looking at her. But she kept reassuring herself; she was far from the most unattractive on the beach, and Ion and Stan, trying to be discreet, seemed to actually notice "something" on her chest. How did she know that? Well, their heads swiveled all up and down the beach, and wasn't that just a guise to sneak a glance at her? No question about it, it was the manifestation of a common displacement activity of mammalian subjects under duress or excitement.

After sunbathing awhile, Stan became restless and went walking down the beach towards a group of husky young men playing paddle ball. Big bosomed Karen sat with her arms stretched behind her as if waiting for a milking machine. And the sun blazed.

Refreshed, after a couple of hours on the beach, they returned to the *Leto* for a change of clothes and then wandered through the town. Buildings resembling giant marshmallows tinged with bright colors and white chapels with blue mushroom tops dotted the labyrinth byways. Everywhere bougainvillea, hibiscus, roses, and jasmine spilled across their paths. They climbed the *kastro,* a hillock that was the remains of a Venetian fortress built on top of an ancient temple and found a bar playing Handel's Water Music. They ordered the fruit punches, special of the house, dynamited with Metaxa Seven Star brandy.

As was becoming their style in late afternoon, they lapsed into silence. Below on the *parelia* they could hear faint disco music and see a slow moving crowd performing the ritual *volta.* The murmuring sea and sky changed color every second, and they became transfixed by the sight of a sun slowly funneling down between two giant rock outcroppings in the bay.

They was no "clunk" when it finally sank, only a silent "whiff" that triggered ethereal projections, now yellow, then orange, pale green, and deep mauve, each chromatic shift so gradual that their "ahs" became almost audible. Still, no one spoke.

Abruptly, Paul said, "Damn! That's it. Evenus is the name of this bar. You know who Evenus was?" No one answered. "Plato mentions him in the *Dialogues,* in *Phaedrus* if memory serves. He was a friend of Socrates and he was from Paros. Imagine!"

Frances: "How wonderful. What does Plato say about him?"

Paul: "Not much. Only that he was a philosopher, the 'inventor of covert allusion and indirect compliment,' that's about all."

Stan (groaning): "Now, how in the hell would you remember something like that?"

Karen: "I agree. With all the erudition in the *Dialogues,* all the philosophies and profundities, you remember *that?*"

Paul: "Well, pardon me, hoity-toity. What do you think classicists do? We have to know about all that trivia, or what you *think* is trivia. There are dozens of such characters in the *Dialogues*. It is where scholarship begins, don't you know?"

Stan: "In a bar named Evenus on the island Paros, 1973. I get it. Proceed."

These little rifts among the Letoites, which of the WCs on the *Leto* were for men or women, seats up or down, were becoming too prevalent. Theodora knew she had to intervene, make peace among them again. "Now, we'll all agree that it is interesting, a coincidence, perhaps, that after so many centuries, someone would think of naming a bar after him. I want to know, Paul, what you make of his epithet. Does it have any philosophical implication?"

Paul: "In Plato's context, I suppose it is relevant to his long discourses on the nature of reality—that perceived by the senses, and that by the more lofty cerebral. You know, the stuff about forms and ideas. Evenus—and I'm only speculating—may have been one of those 'other' guys who looked for 'truths' by artifice. Allusions and indirect compliments may be presumed to be his tools."

Frances: "Literature is full of that approach. Allusions, symbols, metaphors. Folklore in primitive societies, too, isn't that so Stan? Think *Beowulf*, Wagner."

Stan: "Well, Paul, you're only speculating as you say about Evenus. But it's certainly true. *Anthropoi*—get my Greek, Paul—have been doing that for eons to cushion the harshness of life. We invent gods, myths, symbols. So, what's new?"

Theodora, to the rescue again: "You're all right, of course. What's interesting to me is the historical evolution of, what shall we call them, devices we use to learn more of human nature. I was thinking of Freud, with his metaphors of Id, Superego and Ego. Their existence is not necessary to prove and he certainly couldn't. But they were useful concepts of the time. We do that all the time, and perhaps, as you might be suggesting, Paul, we should reexamine the old ones for new insights."

Paul: "Hmmm."

Then Theodora caught Ion staring out to sea, detached as usual when conversations got heavy, and she tried to imagine what his scientific mind was thinking. Remembering her scientific training, a B.S. in Analytical Chemistry no less, probably it was about how you don't need gods and myths and Icarus plunging into the sea to explain realities. You only have to know about the physics of light, that's all.

Theodora: "Science has its devices, too. You can call them paradigms that we use for awhile until something better comes along. Ion, isn't that so?"

Ion, rubbing his chin: "Of course. You don't need all the words, you need only experimental observations."

The conversation plunked into dead silence again. They finished their drinks and decided on another round of punches. The terrace with awnings caught a gentle breeze to soothe their sunburns. Many languages from adjacent tables surrounded them and a young English barmaid brought out roses for each table to go along with small votive candles that would be lit later.

Paul finally resumed: "Theodora, if what you say is true, our 'devices' can change. If your Freudian devices are no longer applicable, what are the new ones?"

Theodora: "They may not be so new, but they're updates. We call them 'conditioning.' They're based on what we know about neural pathways and reflex arcs, repetitive stimuli and learning theory. Actually, they are rather old concepts, but we've given them a scientific basis."

Stan: "Brainwashing? Political propaganda? Are they what you call conditioning?"

Theodora: "An aspect. But you can apply them to all social sciences, including your own. Frances, maybe you can to the Arts, too. What do you think?

Frances: "Tastes in Arts are conditioned?"

Theodora: "Well, don't critics determine what is good or bad. By their preconceptions they presume to influence and condition us into their own views."

Paul: "I'm not following this. If what you say is true, free will has no application. We're nothing but victims of all these conditioners, 'devisers,' or what in the old classical period we might call 'sophists.' "

Frances: "Certainly. We're talking of tastes here. They change. Charles Dickens had his day and was immensely popular. That had nothing to do with what critics said. People just liked his serialized stories. Today, whether people like him or not is still a matter of individual taste. Some people still adore him, despite the fact that some critics knock him for his extreme use of coincidence. Conditioning, if it exists in the first place, is short-lived. If it's long-lived it would have to have relevance to deep urges in us, deep yearnings of the soul—not to what some critic tells us or tries to condition us to believe."

Paul: "And isn't it true, Frances, that such literature, great literature I mean, cannot find an explanation as to its origin? Later, it may be shown to possess the qualities you mention. But at the moment of inception, it can arise as a fresh, new idea, not all contrived by any critic, psychologist, or conditioner."

Theodora: "I disagree. Everything comes from something. If you think it's *de novo,* you admit to not knowing all the facts. Hard to find all of them, certainly. But when you do, you can use them as conditioning agents. Soul? What is that? Yes, dear Letoites, it's conditioning all the way down."

She tried to laugh it all off.

Around the table, icy dissent weighed down further comments.

Stan, watching the crowd below: "Here we go again into a seminar mode." He yawned big. "Tell us, Paul, more about this island."

Paul: "This island is fascinating. I suggest we spend a couple of days here. There's a fine museum, a cathedral, quarries, and classical sites. And don't forget that this is the island of Archilochus."

"Who?" said Theodora.

"I am surprised, and you a Greek. He can be regarded as the first humanistic poet. He writes about the beauties of nature, war, and love."

"Love poetry back then?" said Theodora.

Frances: "You bet. Sensuous poetry. He and Sappho were the preeminent early poets. He comes between Homer and Sophocles, seventh century BCE."

Stan: "I want to hear that. Give us an example."

Frances: "Well, you surely have heard the story of Romeo and Juliet. Archilochus and Neobule's romance was just as hot."

Paul: "Goodness, it is porno actually. Such detail."

Frances: "Here's one I remember: after Neobule's father breaks off her engagement to Archilochus, Archilochus writes scathing iambic pentameter denunciations of her and her father. He says 'he would as soon hump her as kiss a goat's butt.' Other fragments are equally delicious. Such invective. I'll get them out for breakfast tomorrow."

Ion, once again amazed that from such little bodies could come such saltiness, announced that he was getting hungry, and Theodora suggested he go scout for a restaurant while they finished up their drinks. (She was going to suggest that anyhow, part of her protocol to break down his passivity and involve him more with the group.)

He left, and now Theodora felt free to continue their discussion. "Why did the father break off the engagement? Conditions were not right?"

"Why, who knows?" said Frances. "It could have been that the old man just didn't think Archilochus worthy."

"But there are no historical facts to confirm that?"

Paul: "Ipso facto? You seem to think everything has a reason, a fact. It could have been no more than the old man's whim. Spontaneous decisions like that have no *raison d'etre*. In fact, in this case, his whim was so unreasonable that his public derisions of the family led ultimately to the suicides of the old man and Neobule. The point is, that many things we humans do have no rhyme or reason—illusions, as Parmenides would have us believe."

Theodora would not relent. She argued that without historical facts, the whole issue was *reductio ad absurdum*. She finished her punch with a big gulp, then surprised herself and everyone else with a belch. She apologized and said something silly about it wasn't worth arguing about bits of poetic fragments from 750 BCE.

Then they all lapsed into inner thoughts, and Theodora began to compose in her mind items for her Addenda. Three things: 1. their recent discussion, 2. their afternoon on the beach and 3. Ion's remoteness.

In regards to the first, she had to ponder awhile its usefulness. The sky was darkening and around the table, a lit small votive candle barely made faces visible. She was thinking about the Archilochus-Neobule romance story when it hit her. Why not dwell more on it, tickle the libido with the poetry? A little porno talk might get juices flowing. How fortuitous. It hadn't been in her plan, but why not be flexible? Paul and Frances' free will, or whatever they wanted to call it, wasn't necessarily antithetical to conditioning theories.

She smiled to herself and then squeezed the arms of Paul and Frances. They looked puzzled.

Faint stars began to appear high in the sky. About "2," the beach, that too had some encouraging aspects. Her unveiling was not so traumatic. She, olive-skinned, looked lots better than some of those splotchy pink girls from northern Europe. She belonged in the Greek sun, they did not. She had no cellulite.

She had bilaterally-symmetrical breasts, not too smallish. She had wide hips, but they didn't bobble like others. She had taut skin, firm little muscles, thanks to the isometric exercises her physical therapists had prescribed before the cruise. And she was a virgin. Some of those broads on the beach looked pretty worn.

She pulled back her shoulders and smiled around the table, evoking weak smiles and quick sips of punch.

As for "3" she concluded that she should engage Ion more, particularly with non-controversial subjects, ones that they could share, for example, things Greek. And she would study hard her Greek, and try to speak it exclusively with him and the captain.

Yes, she was feeling good about herself, and not all of it was because of the Metaxa. Wasn't it true that Ion seemed always to sit beside her whenever the group went out? And he showed no revulsion to her nudity, and, though she couldn't be absolutely sure, she sensed that he was looking at her on the beach through the corners of his eyes. She couldn't substantiate it, of course, but it might have been about 80 percent of the time. Promising, presumptive data she could call it.

And wasn't he handsome? Such muscle definition. Modest chest hair, and thank goodness, no hair on his back. In swim trunks or fully dressed, he impressed her with, what was it? Consistency? Yes, that was it. He was quite predictable in his movements, attitudes, expression, though he seemed to lack a certain amount of initiative; therefore, it was very appropriate for her to send him out to scout for a restaurant. It would bolster his confidence, make him more responsive.

Some stars began to twinkle. The two remaining couples small talked about music, commenting on the Beethoven string quartet cassettes emanating from behind the bar. Theodora preferred Addenda preludes, such as thinking about how Ion was stoic like her father, not at all like Sammy. How she missed her big brother, his sparkle, his *joie de vive*. The way he tried to make a tomboy of her, how he dragged her everywhere on her sled, how he taught her chess and let her help him with his airplane model building. Her mother called her the *athinati, to kakomiro* (the weak, poor thing) behind her back, but Sammy never acknowledged that. He shared everything in life with her, his crushes on girls, his hatred of things Greek, particularly the insane forty-day fasts of Easter time. And she shared with him. She taught him about priorities, about mowing the grass before going off to basketball practice, how to keep on the good side of the parents. He was too young to die and she was too young to be so deprived. There could never be a replacement.

But why was she thinking of Sammy now? Would she have wanted him by her side, here on Paros? How different would be his responses. They'd be spontaneous, unpredictable. He'd have been the leader of the group, not the follower like—oh, she didn't want to admit it—like Ion. They were so dissimilar. But that didn't mean that she couldn't try to bring a little more life into Ion. He only needed the right woman for that, and wasn't that the original premise?

The Beethoven ended, replaced by the modern Greek composer, Theodorakis, songs with a *rebitiko* beat. The Letoites fingers tapped their glasses, their eyes brightened, and a get-up-and-go spirit seized them. And their stomachs grumbled. Where was Ion?

A chill ran up Theodora's spine. The evening was cooling fast, the way it does in the desert. She thought about how Ion'd be returning with the results of his exhaustive, scientific search and no doubt he'd be recommending some outrageously expensive, dull restaurant where she'd have the endless banking routine to perform. Surely, after a long day and all the drinks, a simple grill would suffice.

He, in fact, did return to lead them off to a restaurant he said was deep in the town, a 'garden restaurant' where the owner promised to arrange a table with flowers. *Oh no,* thought Theodora, *the Letoites were not up to it,* she was certain. But as they walked along the *parelia,* they passed a *psisiterio* with meats and organs being grilled on the spit. The patrons on the edge of the water were lively, wine and beer was flowing.

"Oh," she said, "this place looks like fun. What about it, gang?"

Ion: "But they've set up a special table in the garden. Flowers and a real table cloth. What can I say to those people?"

No one listened. They were all punched out and agreed with Theodora. They found a table, "Apologize tomorrow," Stan said.

And Theodora, biting her tongue, suddenly realized that she had just fouled up her protocols. Damn the Metaxa!

7
Parian Tales

The next morning at the galley table, Paul, playing the imp, recited fragments of Archilochus from Frances' book:

> His penis, as big as that
> of a Prienian ass, a
> stallion fed on corn, spurted. . . .

    The Letoites, hearing that while breakfasting on rock-hard sesame bread and feta cheese, closed their eyes and chewed hard. Impassive and speechless, except for Frances' giggles, they slowly began to notice fishing boats unloading their catches at a nearby dock. Villagers began to gather and haggle over the price of the *bourbinakia* and *lithrina*.
    "Enough of this. Let's haul our asses to see something of this place," Stan blared.
    Off they traipsed across the town's garden and schoolhouse up a slope to the Archeological museum, a blinding white building sheltering blinding white relics—remnants of the Sixth Century BCE Archilochelon temple, fourth century Asclepeion, twenty-second century Proto-cycladic Kandili, tenth to the fifth century shards. Almost all the objects—including the sarcophagi and funereal steles lying about and the famous Parian Chronicle, its other half in the Ashmoleon in England, Paul was quick to point out—were sculpted and carved in luminous quartz-rich Parian marble.

And there was the headless Nike, leaning forward. "Just look at her," said Karen to Stan. "She's alive under all that marble. Her folded garments are so real. You just know underneath is a gorgeous lithe female. Wow."

"What about those beautiful *kouri* on the mosaics," said Stan to Karen.

"And the archaic *kore*. She's as pretty as those boys," Karen said. Then she whirled around to say in an affected stentorian British accent, "And isn't it extraordinary that we admire most the objects d'art of our own gender? Queer, don't you think?"

Stan grinned and said, "Quite."

They and the rest of Letoites had wandered around the museum separately, but then by some kind of herding instinct, together they began their descent back down the slope, this time along a shaded path of high pines that led by a large sunken Byzantine Cathedral.

Karen to Stan: "I need darker sun glasses. The glare up there was too much. Notice how faces look so dark? Theodora and Ion most. They're Mediterranean. Stan, you look just hairier."

Stan to Karen, walking slowly behind the rest of the Letoites: "You and I have something in common. I'm trying to figure."

"We must have met. Yes. There's something."

And they ran through their college affiliations, their activities around the Bay area, it came out. They had met only casually, when they were in adjacent marching contingents in the Gay Pride march in San Francisco, 1972.

"You?" said Karen. "In the 'Mormon Gays'? I was in the 'Thespian Lesbians,' remember?"

And then they came out to each other. They stopped at a coffee shop while the rest went on ahead towards the Cathedral. Stan related how he had been excommunicated for espousing gay rights. "Didn't matter. I never believed Joseph Smith's hallucinations. I wanted to make a simple protest about all the phoniness of the world. At State it was a pretty fashionable thing to do. And you?"

"I told you I had been married. Now the details. Are you listening? He was my Speech and Drama Instructor back at my Eastern University. A hunk, or so I thought. But it was all voice and gestures, if you understand what I mean. It wasn't until we married that I realized that all those elocutions and posturings were not just displays. They were *him*. I mean, his real, unadulterated bare bone exhibitionism. He wanted the lights on in the bedroom and wanted me to keep my eyes open, focused on him. All of him. Archilochus could do a number on him. It was all for him, never for me. So what happened next? I divorce, come out to the Bay area and meet this sweet, charming, caring, affectionate woman. I was starved for attention."

Stan sat with his fist under his bearded chin, enthralled by her story. She continued about the four-year affair with her fluff, art professor dyke who painted dozens of water colors of Karen in fields of lupines and California poppies.

"Then I began to feel smothered. She worshiped me like I was some kind of bleeding Madonna. I was her 'Life,' her 'inspiration,' her 'one and only.' Me? An overweight, frizzy-haired Ashkenazi Jew? Couldn't take it. Couldn't be that responsible for anyone. I split. Period."

She clapped her hands, pretended to wash them, then grabbed Stan's. 'You don't know me that well, but I'm not a callous person. It hurt me to do that, but I just couldn't take it. We went through her suicidal attempts—trying to knock herself out sniffing turpentine and acetone. Whew. Then the therapy with a fine, wonderful lesbian Jungian. That may have done the trick to free me. The transference, I mean. Maybe. Anyhow, I snuck away and here I am. You?"

"That all happened just months ago? How is she doing now?"

She shrugged. The debris would be waiting for her when she returned. "Hope that therapist beds her. What about your love tragedies?"

"Mine's mundane," he said. He told her how he came out, how he had circle-jerked in the Boy Scouts, did the gay bars and bathhouses in San Francisco but had never established a long-lasting relationship.

"Why?" Karen said. "You didn't want one?"

"Not quite that. I guess I preferred to play the field."

"Yeah, it's the promiscuity thing, isn't it? I understand that. It may be the more normal biological way. They say hetero men are jealous of gay guys for it. Women's lib may bring us to admit that sexuality is multifarious. But do you ever think of settling down? You seem to be sensitive person who could relate to some nice boy."

Stan frowned. "Maybe I haven't come to grips with it. All these anthropological things I do are really a subterfuge, you understand. Like I'm thinking that in studying more primitive cultures I might find basic causes of gayness and ways to deal with it at some primordial level. There may be something to all that. Borneo and New Guinea aborigines may harbor that secret. We don't know that much about human sexuality, Kinsey or Mead notwithstanding. It's selfish, I admit, but isn't self-discovery what life's about?"

"A life left unexamined. . . . What a better time and place to remember that, here," she blew up her chest to pontificate, "here in the cradle of human knowledge, here in Golden Greece." Her arms flung open histrionically.

"Shit," he said.

And they both guffawed, the strains of their confessions relieved.

And they agreed particularly on one thing: that it was a good thing to be living in the Bay Area where sexual 'deviance' was tolerated, at least in academic environments. They were missionaries of the great sexual revolution, proud of it, glad to have escaped all the witch hunts of their college days.

"We've got a long way to go," Stan said, "and we can go too far. I don't think we should mess with students, that gets fascistic. Turns the Ivory Towers into seraglios. But, Lord, have I been tempted. There lots of horny boys out there, and it's hard to resist."

"Best that you do," Karen said. "Women don't have that itch so bad. Seems like Lesbians develop emotional attachments more than carnal ones. They are satisfactory ones for awhile, at least. Maybe female P.E. majors have different game plans. Women's P.E. departments may be more promiscuous. I'm not sure I wouldn't prefer it myself. But poor you. In the your discipline, the pickings must be relatively slim."

"A few. But I teach a general course where I get the whole gemisch."

"Then couldn't you select one, 'bring him along' as they say, gently guide him *à la Grecque,* to become a companion to for you? I've heard of such long-developing, long-standing relationships between men."

Stan didn't speak for awhile. She turned to her Michelin guide. He was finding it astonishing that with this woman he had bared so much of himself. He hardly ever talked to anyone so frankly. With his queen friends, the talk was about cruising and camping, and a lot of that he didn't believe and really didn't like. In comparison to their "talk," he was virtually chaste. Still, he felt sexually deprived. Low libido? Low self-esteem? Lack of guts to risk 'trade'?

But why was all this coming up? It was the god-damn Greek light, he decided. He was spotlighted, no escape, and Karen was right there with him. They had until the last few days been a little stiff with each other, not sure where or whether to draw any lines. Now both were thinking to themselves that these three weeks were supposed to be free of personal attachments. That was the purpose of the trip, for the both of them. Subconsciously, they wanted simply to escape, go into limbo about sexual concerns and their professions. And look what happened? Here the two of them, without wanting to, without really asking anything of each other, were being sucked back into talking of the revolutions back home.

And then he finally got back Karen's attention. She had strayed from her perusal of her Michelin guide's description of the Cathedral and had looked up from the pages with a blank expression.

"I don't know how much we should get into all this," he said. "We're supposed to forget about that nonsense back home. But let me say this. What I told you is not wholly true. It's all a rationalization, I suppose. What I said about anthropology as my camouflage. What I said about my alleged promiscuity. Do you mind hearing my big confession?"

Karen closed her green book, took a sip of water, gave him undivided attention. "Shoot."

"It's not that I don't want a relationship. It's because I know I'm ugly. You have to know this: The Gay Life has to do with a mad search for the 'ideal' human form. Like the ancient Greeks, sculpting those *kouroi* and discus throwers and what have you with such perfect physiques. That's what all gays want. But where does that put me? Where's my market? With the scraps, that's what. And why not settle for the 'less than perfect'? Because, they want the ideal as badly as I. Where does that get us? We keep dreaming, like fools, that he will fall in our laps."

Karen sighed, nodded in agreement. "We gotta talk more about this. It's deeper than you think, this thing about the 'ideal.' There are many aspects to it. I don't know all of them myself. But I do know this: You're on the right track by being honest with yourself. You're ahead of me on that score. Meanwhile, we'd better join the rest in the Cathedral. We should see it."

As they settled up the bill, Karen touched Stan's elbow. "Hold it for a minute. Last thirty minutes have been really nice. Thank you. Something has just struck me. Isn't it odd that we find each other simpatico? I'm glad, of course, but what are the odds that two people like us, out of how many that tried to make this trip, end up on the *Leto*?"

Stan stood up, frowned. "Yes, you're right. We never believed Theodora's assertion that 'Les six' were chosen randomly, first come, first served, as she said. Societal groupings are never random. No, there's a highly selective process going on here. Indeed. Gotta think more about that."

They slung their satchels with tour books and cameras over their shoulders and proceeded toward the Cathedral. On the way, they stopped at a small chapel, a Catholic one almost hidden by the pines, Latin inscriptions on its lintel.

"What the hell is *that* doing here," Karen said.

"A remnant of Venetian occupation probably," Stan said.

"It's not accident then, OK," said Karen. "Like it's no accident either that we're here, you and I. Think of this: We're gay and Paul and Francis are not. I mean, they seem naturally to go together. It's like a matchmaker got to them. And who's left? Two Greeks, both unmarried, same age, academic, etc. Get it?"

"Why . . . that scheming bitch," Stan said. "I get it all now. All that b.s. about conditioning. She's selected a boat full of people that provide her a perfect foil for any competition. You a lesbian. Me ugly. Paul and Francis 'taken.' She's got a clear field to seduce that poor, innocent Ion. And what a set-up. The Aegean, the isolation, all the time in the world for her to work her wiles."

Then, he paused. "Aha, but does she have Ion figured?"

Karen fumbled with her camera as they approached the entrance to the Cathedral's courtyard. "Yeah. Just a minute. Yeah. Ion is a strange duck. He's not quite 'there' is he? And how do we know he isn't gay, Stan? And he's so good looking. I have this prejudice that all gay men are good looking. I wonder what you'd look like if you shaved off that hair?"

"That's another confession. Another camouflage," Stan said. "We'll talk about that later. But as for Ion, your speculations don't sound right. I change my mind. He has to be straight. She wouldn't fuck up on that."

"Now really, Stan, how can her formulations be so perfect? How does she know, really, that we're gay, and he's not? How does she know that I wouldn't put a move on Ion? Does she have some magic pipeline to our inner psyches?"

"Good question. Maybe she's more clever than we think. Maybe she knew your Jungian therapist. Shrinks network a lot. Maybe she knows somebody on my campus who knows me. Got the scoop on Ion, too, somehow. Who knows? This requires some detective work."

"We haven't seen the half of it, my dear," Karen said.

"Bet your bottom on that," Stan said. "Groupings of people, no matter how highly selected, are not so predictable. If she catches Ion, I'd be surprised. Things will pop up to thwart the bitch, just watch."

They stopped at the entrance to the cathedral's courtyard. Before them stood a large brick and stone concretion, a domed Byzantine church with side chapels, all with heavy tiles, all slightly askew from centuries of earthquakes. It looked very ancient, partially sunken into its site and surrounded by white washed buildings, a monastery perhaps.

Karen began focusing her camera. As an aside, she said to Stan, "Takis could screw up her whole plan. Isn't he a kouros, or what?"

"A verisimilitude, oh yeah. But how does that alter her plan of attack?" Stan said.

"Why, for one thing, there's the unknown in her calculations, Takis, I mean. He has a soft quality about him, do you see that? Even with no English, his body language, his high-pitched voice, says to me that he might be gay. Of course your radar is better than mine. As for Ion—we can't be sure he is straight. I've seen no indication whatsoever of any wolf quality in him. He's got a soft manner, too. Didn't you see him at the beach? He hardly noticed all the life around. Get it? The two of them, Ion and Takis. So maybe Theodora's sources are wrong about Ion being straight."

"And what if I lust for Takis? Does that put me in competition with Ion? What have we got here? A three way, but I'm not a player? Is that what you're saying to me?"

"Oh, I'm so sorry I didn't mean that at all, Stan. I was thinking that those two beauts might make out. Yes, because they both speak Greek. That's the only reason I said that."

Stan stepped into the courtyard, confused, hardly able to grasp all the implications of what Karen had said.

Neither had she. She kept the camera across her brow, unable to click the shutter. She was thinking about how Takis liked to tease her with sign language, with his flashing smile, the way he'd bring her, special, while she sat in the saloon, some fresh, cold melon from the galley. He didn't do that for anyone else. He'd whittle his olive wood and look at her. And they touched, he always helping her across the gangplank, she always, unnecessarily, grasping his sinewy forearm for balance.

What kind of man is this Takis, she thought. She clicked. Advanced the film. He wasn't like other men, wanting to be admired, kowtowed to, told how brilliant they were. Macho shits. Takis was a gentle, sweet, affectionate lamb. A different kind of man. And so pretty, the little darling kouros.

❖   ❖   ❖

Approaching the *Ekatontapiliani,* the church of a hundred gates, the Letoites had come through a large courtyard with bells dangling from cypress trees and had come to a sunken arched atrium, the obvious remains of an ancient temple. Paul and Francis purchased a guide book and led the way into the narthex and the main temple. Pink and green limestone vaultings and a dome with archangel frescoes glowed pastel, iridescent like the nacreous interior of a giant sea shell. Dim frescoes and gold and silver encased icons loomed all around, the whole atmosphere of the complex laden with venerable architectural motifs from pagan and Byzantine times.

A small chapel off the nave contained the tomb of Osia Theoktisti and a magnificent icon. Paul read the story of the saint, how, as a nun from the island of Lesbos in the ninth century she had escaped her Arab corsair captors on the island of Paros, at that time deserted because of frequent pirate raids, and lived for thirty-five years in the abandoned temple. Paul read about her legend, how she had perished only a year after she had been rescued and how her severed hand remained encased in a chest beside her tomb.

The icon moved them all. The saint holding a silver cross was dressed in a dark shroud, and she wore a silver crown and an expression of complete supplication and beatitude.

"She seems so soft and pretty, so confident of her devotion," said Theodora.

The rest began to wander around the church, examining the colossal ciborium and synthronon behind the iconostassis, but Theodora remained frozen in front of the icon. She had never been moved by iconography, in fact, by any Orthodox beliefs or rituals. Here, though, was something else. Its portrayal of belief was uncanny. She wanted to think of it as an abstraction, not a testament to Christian theology but an assertion of how a woman's profound belief can produce not just sainthood, but something much larger: a belief in self.

Yes, Theodora, was thinking, *I'd like to have that self-assurance about myself. I'd like to be like Theoktisti and feel so dedicated to a purpose in life. I know my goals, I seem to have the intellectual apparatus to achieve them, but am I sure unequivocally that they really are my goals? How did Theoktisti know? Was she forced to by the exigencies of her life, the urgency for survival? If she was so "conditioned," happenstance would seem to have been the shaping force. But in my case, what are the "conditioning" elements? My intellectual drive, my humdrum life? Are these what point me in the direction I follow? Fate or Free Will, conscious or unconscious conditioning?* Oh, she was so tired of all the soul searchings, the Evenus Bar conundrums. Why couldn't she just go ahead and follow her instincts?

Where was Ion? She turned to look up at the dome where light streamed down through small windows, their shafts piercing the enormous chandeliers and marble reliefs on columns and arches. Ion was nowhere in sight, and as she wandered about, she found a door that led to the narthex of another basilica, smaller than the main temple but with its own dome. The Baptistery. There, in lemony light streaming around the pastel vaultings she found him sitting on the edge of a large font, a marble cross shaped pool with a pedestal at its center with stairs leading down to it.

He seemed so engrossed that she approached him gradually, not wishing to disturb his reveries. When he finally noticed her, he said:

"It's fifth century, the guidebook says," he said, peering into the dry font.

"I've never seen anything like this in any other Orthodox church," Theodora said.

"Back then lots of adults converted. Nowadays, they use only those baptismal tubs for the babies."

"It's so, huh? We Orthodox believe in total immersion?"

"You've been to a Greek baptism, haven't you?"

"One."

"They dunk the naked babies then anoint them with holy oil. Babies scream like crazy if the water's cold."

Theodora noticed Ion's sandaled foot dangling over the ledge of the font. Handsome foot, defined ankle, smooth with faint articulations and long, straight toes. "If you were going to be baptized back home as an adult, how do they do it? Do you strip?"

"Interesting question. I think they put them in swimming suits and dunk them in bath tubs. Not sure."

"What about then? Were they naked or clothed?"

"How the hell would I know?"

It was a non-sequitur, so she tried to make amends. "Adult conversion must have been profoundly meaningful, don't you think?"

"How? Why?"

"Well, the adult knows what he's being converted to. Babies can't, right?"

"Whatever. I was just imagining the ritual. The priest stands with his vestments in the middle on that pedestal and pronounces the hocus-pocus stuff, then the converts descend down these steps, splash around, then come up the steps on the other side. They got oiled down, probably, then swaddle themselves in white clothes, the way they wrap the babies today."

"Amazing transformation, don't you think, Ion? Go in as sinners, come out drenched in piety. Wish we could transform other aspects of life so easily."

"That's the party line. Baptism is supposed to free you to reach higher ideals, finding God, and all that kind of thing," he said.

"Or find ways to overcome our shortfalls. Such as insecurities, shyness, insensitivities to others," she said. "Find love."

"Not that easy with only a slosh of water," he said.

"You mean that psychologically something else happens? What would that be?"

Ion dangled his feet, looked up at some faded frescos in an aisle of the nave. He was thinking again of how annoying Theodora could be. She always seemed to be trying to scratch under his skin, trying to get too personal. Then a faint smile crossed his mouth.

"I know what the baptismal immersion is more like. It's more like phosphorylation."

"What's that?"

"Phosphorylation is the means by which biochemical molecules are energized for metabolic reactions. You were a chemist. You remember free energy concepts and energy rich bonds. So, the holy water phosphorylates, the font's a virtual cesspool of phosphates. Makes the converts feel good." He snickered.

Theodora frowned and turned away. As she walked back into the main temple she was thinking that the others might think of her as Bouboulina, but she'd rather be a Theoktisti. She'd have faith in herself and not have to suffer the intransigencies of others and the hard shells of handsome Greek men.

✿ ✿ ✿

Afternoon was to be filled with a visit to the ancient quarries of Paros. They boarded a crowded bus filled with tourists bound for the "golden" beaches on the east side of the island, but halfway there they got off on a sunburned mountainside surrounded by fertile fields of barley and grapes. From there, they hiked along a dirt road, their sandals trapping rocky slivers and Theodora shouting at them to slow up. Her voice was shrill, and she was angry that none of the men, not even Ion, gave her a helping hand. Finally, in a hidden ravine of scrub cedars and thorny bushes, they reached the three ancient shafts, each about one hundred meters deep. Not a guide or soul was in sight, not even a shepherd.

Theodora scrambled, almost tumbled, down the ravine scratching her ankles on wild thyme and thistles. She grabbed Ion's arm and he tried to steady her. She was angry not only for her own discomfort but angry, too, that she had even come along. So what if these were the quarries from which the marble for Napoleon's tomb and the Venus de Milo had been mined? They were abandoned now. What could they expect to see except mere holes in the earth of unpolished marble walls.

At the entrance to the middle shaft were some marble reliefs, NYMPHAIS they spelled out. Paul theorized they were depictions of the auctioning of women slaves in the fourth century BCE. Karen took exception to such a wild speculation. The girls were too pretty to be slaves. Theodora disagreed, saying that Greek men even back then treated their women badly and Frances mumbled some things about the role of women in Classical times.

Irrelevant patter like that was becoming customary for the Letoites, much to Ion's disgust. He was thinking only of the possible fun of spelunking and asked if anyone had a flashlight. Stan had a small one on his key ring and he led the way down the rubbled opening which, as they descended farther, became mossy and cold.

The Letoites slipped around, holding onto each other for balance. Theodora felt marble chips catching in her sandaled toes and all sensed a frigid claustrophobia. Stan cast his flashlight around the walls and behind them, the light from the shaft opening by then had all but disappeared. In darkness there was nothing to see of the world's most finest, most translucent marble. He turned off his flashlight and said, "Let's sing 'Rock of Ages'."

They were not in the mood. Paul said, "Let's get out of here. It's too eerie."

In complete darkness and dead silence, they waited for Stan to turn on his flashlight. They heard some clicks, then Stan saying, "Oh shit, my batteries are gone."

But they knew the opening was above them. All they had to do was walk up the shaft and sooner or later they would find the dim light of the shaft's entrance.

Groans, profanities, and huffings and puffings. Then the remarkable thing happened to Ion. He was sure it wasn't his shorts cutting into his groin, his scrotum retracting in the cold, or a testicular itch. It was real. Someone, in that complete darkness, had fondled, for only a millisecond, his cock.

He didn't protest, didn't grope around him to find the culprit. It had happened so suddenly that he had no time to react. As they approached the light of the opening, he scanned the others to see any telltale signs of—remorse? Mischievousness? Pleasure?

Nothing.

Emerging at last into a blinding light, they laughed at their adventure and joked about what would have happened if they hadn't found the shaft's opening. Headlines in the *International Herald Tribune:* CALIFORNIA TOURISTS FOUND CRYOGENICALLY PRESERVED IN MARBLE CAVES. ACADEMIC SPELUNKERS IMMORTALIZED. MISSING TOURISTS INHUMED IN MARBLED CHIPS.

Ion was not so exhilarated. Whether it was Theodora or Karen (more likely because of her bold manner), he felt insulted, demeaned by the prospects of having to beat off lecherous women. He never liked the idea of being surrounded by horny women. Some of them were not subtle. Sonja wasn't either, the way she could unzip his pants with a feathery touch and engorge its contents with guzzling lips. (But why did he have to think of her now?)

At last, somewhat rested after the bus ride back to the Paroikia, they talked of a hike up to the hill of the Delion where the temple of Apollo formed a nexus with the temples of Apollo in the nearby islands of Delos and Naxos in the fourth century BCE. Foundations only remained, but in late afternoon the view to Naxos and Delos would be dazzling. There would be time before the sun went down and dinner time. Theodora declined. Stan saw her limping as they walked from the bus and asked if she'd like him to help her back to the boat. He, at least, she thought, was solicitous but she told him that she could make it back. She wanted to rest up, that's all, she told him.

❊   ❊   ❊

Just as she started across the gangplank, the captain emerged from the cabin. *"Po, po, po,"* he said, "what has happened to the *thespinis*?" He extended his hand to guide her across then led her to a deck chair. Quickly, he brought her cushions and told Takis to bring a damp towel for her face.

He told her to refresh herself while he went below to bring up a foot bath. "You shouldn't walk in this heat, *Thespinis Theodora*. You all are not donkeys, you know."

He lifted one foot gently—Theodora stiffened, surprised with his familiarity—then removed the straps of her sandal. *"Po, po, po,* this is not good. We must take care of it."

She looked at him under the towel hood, relieved to find someone who recognized her predicament. She unstrapped the other sandal, wiped the coolness of the towel across her arms and bare legs, and submitted. Succor was deserved.

He immersed one foot in soapy warm water. He rubbed her ankle first, then her foot. She saw his huge hairy paw of a hand. She didn't care. She was grateful. She was Fay Wray, he was Kong. She closed her eyes.

She thought of Ion hiking on the road to the quarry, his cotton shirt clinging to his sweaty back, his so proud bearing, his helping arm on the ravine, wet and cold with perspiration, the fine velvet feel of the hairs of his arms, and that damnable aloofness. If only she could get his undivided attention!

She felt the captain's rough fingers between her toes, lathering them, massaging them, rinsing and lathering over and over again. She would have liked to baptize Ion, get between his thighs in the font, oil them, bless them, kiss them.

Her eyes remained closed. A lightness filled her, as if someone had pumped helium in her and she would at any moment float away. Up to the Delion, "Hello, down there, Letoites, look at me. Don't you wish you were with me? I can't give you a helping hand up here. You'll have to manage by yourselves. 'Bye. Up, up and away."

She smelled something medicinal. The captain was doctoring her scratches. She felt anesthetized, as when she had her uterine fibroids removed. She had dreaded it so, the first time anyone had entered her, yet the anesthetic and pain killers were so pleasant. As then, she knew now everything would be OK.

Then, barely opening her eyes, she saw the captain smearing olive oil on her feet. She was being anointed, how nice. "Why?" she whispered.

"We use olive oil for everything, *thespinis*. It preserves our food. In the old days, we didn't have refrigeration, our food was cooked in communal ovens. The food remained clean for a long time with the oil protection. It's good for the skin. It will soften the skin of your feet, protect them. Stops the rotting."

And he massaged the oil in, and she felt sanctified. All she wanted now was a huge white sheet to swaddle herself in, Ion, too. To sleep.

"I'll fix you a cheese omelet for supper," the Captain said. "You will stay off your feet. Walking in the countryside with sandals. *Po, po, po.* Use your kernel." He tapped his temple with a forefinger.

She didn't like the way Greek men command. She had a brain, not a kernel. Her father had been that way sometimes, and it took him a long time to realize that his daughter could disobey. She didn't quite trust this captain and his itineraries, no matter that he obliged the passengers. Furthermore, as she had recorded in her Addenda, she wasn't really sure that he hadn't abandoned those Germans to their deaths on that islet.

8
Milos

It had to be Milos next, Paul insisted. It was the most westerly of the Cyclades and from there the *Leto* could wing back to Ios and Santorini and other islands. At breakfast, his arguments were persuasive, that after the quarries of Paros it was only logical to visit the site of the Venus de Milo (more correctly, the Aphrodite of Milos he insisted).

Theodora, ensconced in pillows and cushions beneath the awning with her olive-oiled toes protruding into the sunlight with a strange green opalescence, turned to Ion and asked, in Greek, his approval of Paul's plan. "Makes no difference," he said, "if the captain thinks it's OK." Not OK for Theodora, however. Why couldn't she engage Ion? Why did he always defer to someone else? They could talk pros and cons, at least get some kind of dialogue going. Not since Kea had they tete-teted, if that's what you could call it. Surely, she wasn't intrusive, was she? Was he that lacking in self-confidence? Or did he simply wish to detach himself from her? Well, that couldn't be. Everyone else related easily with her, there was nothing actually repulsive about her.

Nevertheless, Ion went up to the bridge to propose Milos. The captain shrugged, *"oposthipote,"* whatever, he said, offering him some pistachios.

At sea, the meltemi jostled them, but Theodora sat queenly and munched on Parian plums the captain had brought her.

They were the color of the sea, purple blue. Ion stood at the wheel, watching the compass and studying maps. Down below, in the engine room, Stan was following Takis around while he monitored the rpms, petcocks, gauges, pumps, and storage batteries. The two diesels were like prototypes of Stan's old Mercedes back home, except these diesels were all brass fitted without an inch of plastic. Both men had their shirts off, but the oil fumes masked the odors of their perspiring armpits. From time to time, Stan lingered a touch on Taki's shoulder, pointing to a mechanical part and asking its Greek name, *"elleniko?"*

Karen came down to see them, watching them intensely. "How you two getting along?" she asked Stan. Stan winked.

Stan said, "Guess what the Greek word for 'gauge' is? *Manometron*. I could have guessed that."

Karen smiled and left them for a while only to descend later with wet, cool towels. She gave one to Stan and with the other, she wiped the back, forehead and neck of Takis but was a little too coy to ruffle his pecs. Yet, the boy seemed so docile, so willing to let her clean him, even raising his arms like a child in its bath. Finished, he gave her the sideway nod of the head the Greeks use to show appreciation and then flashed the Archaic Smile of a *kouros*.

Stan frowned, was about to rebuke her when shrugging she said, "What's wrong with coping a feel?"

Disgusting, he thought, *the blatancy of dykes.*

Frances and Paul in their khaki shorts were doing less well. Frances lay stretched on a bench in the saloon, and Paul sat beside her reading and talking with her. Their rimless glasses were thinly coated with sea spray.

"Sea voyages are pukey," Frances said. "Melville didn't know the half of it."

"How did the ancients do it?" Paul said. "They were always flitting around the Aegean. Good Zeus, what stomachs they must have had. But do not worry yourself, we will be in Milos in a few hours. The meltemi are blowing us a good clip westward."

"Talk to me of Milos. Get my mind off all this bouncing. I've had Erskine Caldwell on my mind, don't know why. Maybe it's all those Papastratos cigarettes of the captain's and Takis'. Paul, why didn't we just stay in Paros? Such a lovely place and we saw only a bit of it."

"Don't fret, darling. We'll suffer only a few hours and we'll find Milos equally beautiful. Listen, and imagine what it will be like. It is a volcanic island, like Santorini, beautiful rock formations and caves and Ah! the history."

"Oh Paul, you're a hopeless romantic. Worse than me." She put a Kleenex to her mouth. "So what does it mean to be on a spot where something big happened in history. 'This is where Pythagoras took a dump on his way from Samos.' You just tell me what's so great about that. And don't give me any *longueur.*"

Paul cleared his throat, brushed his hand across her forehead. "You're feverish, relax, forget Caldwell."

They sat for a while in silence. Paul provided cold compresses.

"Forgive me, *Pavlo,* I didn't mean to be so peevish. Tell me of Milos."

"I have been thinking about what you said. There is, you're quite right, something silly in getting gushy about historical places. But it is not the place, you understand, it is what it evokes. Places where those events that shaped man's future are meaningless per se. But, were you not moved on the Delion to be in the place where twenty-three hundred years ago the ancients celebrated the rites of Apollo? I mean to know, actually know, that those people of the Delian League had such high ideals? That they gave us high art literature, and democratic principles?"

Frances moaned. "Oh, you can read about it."

"But the site, don't you see? It is part of the whole drama. The setting. All part and parcel."

"Yes, it was pretty. Big Sur is, too."

"Come now. They are not at all comparable. Scenically they are different, but that's not the point. Don't you 'feel' the difference?"

Frances sighed. "Big Sur has no significant history, that's so. But in both places, one wrong step on those cliffs, and you're dead. Both give you a sense of mortality. Both give 'pause.' So what else?"

"The Delion does much more than that, come on, Frances. If you were some addle-brained, uneducated person, I could not argue with you. But you know literature, art, history. You know that the evocations are not comparable."

She folded her hands on her little chest, then reached for Paul's hand. "I know, I know, what you are saying. I'm not emotive right now. Sorry. I feel like I do after I leave your bunk. Spent." She giggled for a moment. "Do you think anybody knows?"

"Who cares? The guys next door snore and the panel between the cabins is thick. What about Karen?"

"She is out cold as soon as she hits the bunk. All night, she sounds like a cow chewing its cud. She could not care less."

Frances sat up and the two stood up to look through the portholes to a passing island. Sifnos, they thought, but weren't sure. They saw mostly undulating blueness and when the foamy sea splattered the glass, they imaged sloshing digestive juices.

"Uhuh, *Pavlo*. I think I'm going to heave." He brought her a plastic barf bag, but she only coughed a little.

"I know what I can do for you, I shall read you Thucydides' *Milesian Dialogue*."

"You brought so many books," she said. "You should have brought more medicines. Read to me."

He read about how the Athenians had come to Milos in the fourth century BCE and demanded their surrender. Milos had been loyal to the Spartans during the Peloponnesian Wars and were reticent about joining the Athenian League of city states. Refusing, the Athenians laid siege and eventually slaughtered the male population of Milos and took the women and children into slavery.

"Brutal, brutal." Frances said. "Read again the passage of the law of nature."

... it is a general and necessary law of nature to rule whatever one can ...

"Athenians were into power politics. It was 'us' or 'them.'" Paul said.

"And what was that part about hope?" Frances said.

... hope is an expensive commodity ...

"Athenian pragmatism," he said. "Notice. Forget about the gods and hope. The Athenians depended on their own resources, no one else. Smart cookies."

"Really?" said Frances. Then, she filled the barf bag.

* * *

Approaching Milos from the north in quiet waters, the *Leto* passed the volcanic islets of Glaronissa with their towering sixty feet basalt pillars rising from the sea.

"No, it's nothing like Big Sur," Frances said. The captain slowed the engines so the Letoites could absorb the wonder.

"Poseidon's triumphal steles. Glorious," said Paul.

Then they sailed into the roadstead of the irregular round island. The harbor was actually the crater of an ancient volcano and around it stood hills and a towering Profitis Ilias mountain, the name of high mountains on many Cycladic islands.

They dropped anchor and discussed the afternoon activities. Karen, Stan and Ion would take the dinghy and an outboard motor with Takis and explore the marine caves of Papafranga, Sikia, and Kleftiko. Perhaps they'd find some obsidian. Paul and Frances would disembark at the main port, Adamas, and from there by bus make their way up to Plaka, the site of the ancient Acropolis. Then they'd hike south to the hamlet of Klima near where the Aphrodite statue was discovered by the French.

Theodora said she'd stay another day off her feet and play cards with the captain. *Kolotsina* was the game, the Greek canasta that Theodora's parents played their entire life. "We play for money, *Kapitanios,* a drachma a point. And beware. My father before he died owed my mother 3,487 dollars."

※   ※   ※

The views from the Acropolis site were spectacular, but Paul's and Frances' hike down to the road towards Klima was hot and monotonous, the volcanic eruptions giving the whole landscape a look of petrified vomits. There were some ancient polygonal walls farther down and beneath a cypress tree, they rested and drank bottled water.

"Reminds me some of the Morgantina site in Sicily," Paul said.

"What were you doing there?"

"Important excavations there. Princeton archaeologists back in 1955. Still going on. I was there trying to date some of the silver coins. Ancient Syracuse was there, next in importance to Athens and Alexandria. The coins were minted to record historical events, like the dedication of a ruler, or to commemorate the end of a plague. Tells us classicists about the commercial and political ties of the ancients."

"What great thing did you discover?"

"Nothing. It's piece meal work. We learn that the Ancients were fairly adroit about managing their affairs. But day by day, for six months, it was exceedingly boring. I can tell you that."

"What did you find to do in your spare time?"

"There were other workers. Learned some Italian."

"Graduate student types?" Frances said.

Paul nodded.

"Female?"

"Actually, yes. Oh, I don't need to hide things from you, Frances. We seem to have good liaison. You will understand. I had a little *affaire de coeur* with this girl named Pia. Passionate Italian type, not really my type. Hippy and brunette. Not petite like you, my darling. But it happened. I was only twenty-five."

"What did you do together?"

"Ate pasta and grapes. Baby talk. She knew some English and we could shop-talk about the work."

"Do you ever see her? Write her?"

Paul grimaced, picked up Frances' hand and in a low voice said. "There was a baby. She wrote me two years later in the States. She finished her philology degree in Florence, went on to teach at Bologna. She never asked for support. Simply wanted to inform me."

Frances tightened. "You didn't offer?"

"Oh, Frances, it simply was not feasible. We came from two different worlds. She was so Italian. Mushy. And her politics so screwed. She had been an anarchist, for goodness sake."

"And you're so Greek." There was mockery in her tone.

"Now, what is bothering you? Out with it," he said.

"Oh, you were so pragmatic, like those Athenians in the Milesian Dialogue. You had a right to take. It was either you or some wop that would seduce the poor girl."

"That is not fair. I send money and gifts to her from time

to time. It is not that I am heartless. She has never given a hint about marriage. She knows we are incompatible."

"And the child? Do you feel anything about the child? Do you even know its sex?"

"It was a girl. It was unfortunate. Pia has means, comes from a wealthy family. I would not fit into her future. Old noble Italian families have strong traditions. I would be an outsider, no matter. And besides . . ."

"Besides what?"

"I do not live in the future. And I am a Platonist. There exists in this world concepts which humans have access to by intuition. Simple logic fails sometimes. I had an intuition that Pia and I could not make a life, no matter about my moral responsibilities to the child. I could surely intuit that there was no future for us—I mean, Pia and that child. I am equally certain that the past should be my concern. It is what I am, a classicist. *There* I will make my mark in this world."

"So here we are trying to relive the past in Milos. Where great art was created. Right where Venus squatted."

" 'Aphrodite', I keep telling you."

They sank into deep silence.

Finally, Paul softly said. "We have known each other intimately for five days. Yet, I feel I have known you for a long, long time. Amazing what is happening to us. The magic of the Greek Islands. It's so, isn't it? Do not think me crass, though. I have depths that you may not have seen. I do not think of my personal life as important. I do not have to explain to you the values of studying the classics, do I? My professional work is what does count. Everything is subservient to that. Screwing is irrelevant, in that sense."

"Oh, really?" said Frances. "Why, you're the best of satyrs. You put your heart and soul into it."

"You are teasing. That is not what our relationship is about. Is it not about understanding each other? Is it not about how we can enhance each other?"

"And how do you think you can enhance me?"

"Why, I hope that in sharing what I see all around us with you, you might be inspired to a deeper understanding of human endeavors. I do not know for sure. Maybe I can inspire you to write the great novel. Be a Mary Renault, or someone better than her."

"Open new horizons?"

"Yes, like that. Why not? Am I not useful that way?"

Frances lapsed again into deep silence. He didn't have a inkling as to her aspirations. He had no idea, whatsoever, what it was to be woman, to be a mother. Should she tell him that all her life, with her sexless body, she'd felt deprived of a consummate love? All the books and poems could not replace that void and when she finally could find intimacy, it was always with the hope that . . .

And now? What was it to be with Paul? Another imbroglio? Should she tell him about Vic, her graduate student, who clung to her as a mother, burrowing all his insecurities in her hot little titties? Hot sex, that was all it could be. Soon enough, she realized their future was bare. She pushed him out into the world, into journalism where he might find himself and a woman his age. That was three years ago and here she was now approaching middle age wondering if she would ever have a chance again. Was she coming to realize that men, at least the ones she knew, no longer cared for women? What was so wrong about her?

What was wrong—and now at last she was beginning to see it—was that she had come out into the brilliant Aegean light, away from the myopia of scholarly work and the dusty carrels of University Libraries. How could she have spent so much of her life becoming an encyclopedia of literature, a repository (a suppository?) of authors, book titles, dates, and subject matter? Those endless preparations for the Ph.D. exam, the minutia, the chagrin of not knowing who Robert Mannying of Brunne was, the fearful days waiting for a verdict, the anxieties of finally getting an academic job. To teach illiterate students the basics of English composition, the grueling repetition, the realization that her knowledge had no application. To know that any original, creative ideas she may have had about writing had been systematically bred out of her. She could only be a "critic," and how many people would ever pay much attention to her for that? Obscure scholars, a dozen or so scattered around the globe?

She blamed the Light, now she was beginning to see clearly. That, and the way it opened her to any and all licentiousness with Paul whose libido knew no bounds. With Vic, she was the passive recipient, but with this new partner she had found new expressions, ones that really had not so much to do with him and sex, but with her own desires that now, at last, were becoming unlocked.

Could she tell Paul all that? Tell him what her real aspirations were? Damn his Platonism and the Classics. She didn't want to be a creative writer or scholar, couldn't be. The unlocked desire glistened now in the Light. It had taken her whole life to see it. She wanted to nurture. Give. Actively, to another being. That was her biological destiny. Could he understand that that was a higher ideal than deciphering Linear A or dating silver coins?

She took a deep breath. "There's no telling about human ambitions. You have yours and I, mine. We, at least, seem to have no problem butting right in. Now as for me . . ." Suddenly the words wouldn't come. There was a crevasse in their relationship that they could not negotiate yet. It was too soon. If there was to be any chance . . . So she veered away, spoke up brightly. "Now, take Karen and Stan. What's with them?"

Paul lifted his shoulders, glad to have the subject off him. "Stan is an enigma. Everything with him seems 'off the cuff.' Either he is more sophisticated than we give credit, or he is hiding something. Karen? She is a party girl, I think. Lots of chutzpah. You mean, the two of them? Together? Really, I do not much care one way or the other."

"You wouldn't. Let's go look for the Aphrodite's arms."

Paul laughed. "We do not need to find them really. They might spoil the composition. How in the world the sculptor managed those gentle curve of her torso! The ogee epitome of female pulchritude. That is all. Who knows what the hands were doing. Whatever, they might have detracted from the marvel of the composition."

"Maybe she had been fingering herself," Frances said.

Paul screeched. He smacked her hard on the mouth. "You *are* an absolute delight, you are!"

✿   ✿   ✿

The marine caves and volcanic outcroppings off shore provided Stan, Karen, and Ion with stunning views of Poseidon's handiwork. They spoke little, holding tight to the gunnels of Taki's little putt-putter. Stan, however, with dark sunglasses, was secretly taking it an even more intriguing sight: Takis. At first, he fixated on the way his muscular bare legs contracted isometrically, standing there braced against the tiller, showing fine definition and a fine white margin where his shorts ended and the deep tan of his thighs met. His calf muscles contracted and relaxed, pulsating like orgasmic surges, and his groin seemed overstuffed, like a basket of delicious, ripe fruit. The boy's shoulders, covered by a transparent tank-top, arced in perfect symmetry, the voluptuous pecs and deltoids straining against currents and waves splashing against the little boat's hull. There was no self-consciousness, it was as if he were a male model from *GQ*, all he needed was an Italian logo on a piece of his apparel. Maybe a mini-tunic, nothing underneath.

Gawking, Stan felt a hardness in his swim trunks, and his tumescence grew even more when the dinghy rocked back and forth, subsiding only when the rocking threatened to dump passengers over the edges of the dinghy. Then, Takis would flash the brilliant whiteness of his teeth, and shake off ocean spray from his curly black hair like some exquisite show-dog. He'd then raise a fist, point at each of his passengers, and shout, *"Ompah."* Everyone shouted back "Whoopee!"

What fun, Stan thought. Better than any show of go-go boys at a San Francisco gay bar, better because of the stage set, the magnificent scenery all around. There was hardly a momentary repose from his trunk's pinching.

Then he noticed another drama on the dinghy. He began to watch Ion, to see if any of his beauty could be revealed. But Ion was dressed in long pants and long sleeved shirt, for Christ's sake, and a baseball cap that covered his thick, wavy hair. No excitement there, though there could have been. *Too bad,* thought Stan. He kept watching, however, and then he began to catch something else: Ion too was eye-balling Takis. He jerked his head in Takis' direction every time the dinghy leaned heavily, but then he'd also do it occasionally even when they were in calm waters. It was a quick gesture, followed quickly by a jerk in the head in the opposite direction, as if he were avoiding some objectionable sight. *Puzzling,* Stan thought. *Was he embarrassed? Ashamed of his voyeurism? Or was it only that he was expecting Takis to pay closer attention to his boating?*

He tried to catch Ion's attention, took off his glasses and smiled at Ion. Ion ignored him, kept his attention on the scenery and his little secret peeks at Takis. *Hmmm.*

Drifting around the cliffs, marveling at the caves and the remarkable crystalline rocks, Stan edged closer to the stern, almost feeling the boy's warmth and odors. Still, the boy's attention was riveted on the boat, hardly ever looking at his passengers.

Except—now he saw it. Karen had all along been eyeballing Takis, too. Perhaps not with his own intensity, but with looks that were more than checking on Takis' handling of the outboard and the tiller. No doubt about it. And she slouched, her bare legs spread a little too openly, her cotton blouse pulled down on one side to almost her nipples.

Returning to the harbor and the *Leto*, Stan caught Takis shooting quick glances at Karen. Brazenly, she smiled back at him! Although whipped by the sea and wind, Karen looked sexy, and her ingenuous manner, Stan observed, could not help but tantalize Takis. Shame on her for teasing Takis. He'd have to talk to her about it. What was she up to anyhow? Wasn't she a dyke?

※ ※ ※

When the Letoites returned on board, Theodora greeted them as long lost friends returning to the fold. Her day of playing cards and chatting with the captain had not been exactly wasted. He was beginning to come around, she thought, no longer a haughty threat to the wishes of his passengers. Also, he was helpful in improving her Greek. "*Thespinis*, put in the *tonos*, hard. We Greeks accent, so don't slur your words like a French whore."

His brusque manner and questions of her at first were annoying. She had known from back in Minnesota how Greeks can be, how they get personal too quick. "Why are you not married, *thespinis*?" to which she replied, thinking she was choosing the right words. "I try, I try." That answer only promoted other ones, like "What kind of man do you want?" "How old?" "What nationality?"

She deflected them all, smiling only and fortunately finding the right Greek phrase to respond with: "Whatever God chooses." To which, he replied each time, "You're a good woman, *thespinis*. May you have good luck."

That night, as they all supped on board, talking of their day's excursions, Theodora, for the first time, felt left out. Poor

Takis, exhausted by his hard day had retired to his bunk in the engine room. It wasn't that she regretted seeing the sights. It was that she had missed out a day of data collecting. Her precious subjects weren't in her "cubicles," they had reacted and responded to each other without her observations. Not good. She must keep tabs, avoid any future injuries.

So, she sat back and listened to their conversation, trying to pick up any new developments. Paul and Frances dominated, leading discussions about the importance of Milos to early Minoan civilizations. They didn't seem quite as intimate as before, she noticed, but that might have been natural. And Ion did not sit next to her.

"Minoans were such a gay people," said Paul. "Frescoes and vase paintings showed them dancing and bull vaulting. Adorning themselves with flowers and snakes and cavorting with dolphins. Happy, happy people. So gay."

"Gives me ideas," said Stan. "Ready, gang?"

"Neither were they obsessed with death, like the Egyptians," said Karen. "Live for the day. You're right, Stan. Let's have some fun!"

They spent a jolly late evening drinking from skins of wine that Takis had brought on board. The Cycladic Minoan spirit lived on, they decided, and they talked about whether they would be able to get as far as Crete to visit Knossos and other sites. Probably unlikely, too far for this trip. A future trip? They drank to it, and Theodora laughed, silently congratulating herself.

She kept her antennae out, took in everything. Only one blip on her screen. Karen every now and then seemed disengaged. She kept looking down into the engine room. Curious.

9
Ios

The silvery bay of Milos the next morning cradled the *Leto* in a mirrored reflection. Under the awnings of her rear deck, dishes and cups tinkled and echoed off the nearby cliffs. The Letoites sat in deep silence, oblivious of each other, barely aware that they were floating atop a volcanic cenotaph filled with liquified cobalt.

Frances was the least aroused. Vaguely, she remembered the previous evening in Paul's cabin hearing his whispers, "Oh, oh, my Aphrodite." They had spoken little and had muffled their climactic groans for the sake of their fellow passengers' sleep. Their lovemaking had passed like a dream, yet Frances knew that that evening had made things between them different.

For the first time, she took her coffee "Greek," in a demitasse cup with fine grounds on the bottom. She drained the cup with one gulp and started examining Paul sitting across the table from her. She saw him in the morning light as a frail, winsome little guy, a thin gold bracelet on his bony wrist, a napkin draped across his shoulder like a *tivenos*. There he sat, chin held high, eyes peering beyond everyone to the horizon as he began talking, almost lecturing, to the others about why the island of Ios was important for them to visit on their next stop, but there was nothing of *him* in what he said, about what he felt about the importance of Ios, about why exactly he wanted them to go there. He recited the historian's suppositions about Homer and how, allegedly, he had died on Ios. But what he said was not meaningful, not to Frances at least. He always seemed to be escaping the present, using whatever artifice—history, the classics, mythology—to gain attention, to drench himself in feyness. Was she nothing but part of his allusions? How could she be Aphrodite? She was Frances, that's all, an Assistant Professor of English trying to vivify herself, shake off the numbness of English Lit freshman classes by whatever means—by spiritual, esthetical, or genital.

Why could he not stop and listen to her or at least to the others? Why couldn't he respond to Karen's, Stan's, and Ion's talk of their adventures in the Marine caves of Milos, the beautiful green colors of the recesses, without bringing up Plato and his Legend of the Caves and the Sirens of Odysseus. *For God's sake,* she thought, *why couldn't he just experience the moment, accept the others' rapture on their terms without bringing up all his classics claptrap?*

And for that matter, how did this person named "Pia" fit into all his fantasies and delusions? Did she really exist, an Italian with the name "Pia"? Or was she just a romantic invention, a specter of an inflated ego?

Then, Frances thought, how did *she* fit into all his fantasies? Aphrodite, indeed!

Then she studied the others' faces. The coffee had brought them to life, and they seemed interested in his discourses. It was as if their own identities had become swamped by Paul's erudition. What was going on? Had Paul seduced them into his way of life? Were the Letoites turning into antiquarians reveling in the glories of the past, escaping the travails of modern life and their middle-aged disenchantments?

She didn't want a part of that. She wanted to be here and now, jump into that limpid sea and let her body, not her mind, soak up the beauty. Their journey otherwise was meaningless, and they might as well have stayed home in their books and laboratories. But there they were, motionless, only occasionally crunching on their dry toast and hanging on Paul's words.

But were they really that engrossed? Perhaps something was registering deep in them, apart from Paul's propaganda. Perhaps they were only being polite. Were Karen and Stan with narrowed eyes really paying attention to Paul or were they recounting the details of their previous day's coupling?—if there had been one. It seemed probable or was she just making assumptions that because she and Paul were, everybody on board was screwing someone or the other? Stan and Karen, obviously, had a cozy relationship . . . of some sort.

Then there was Ion, the Euripides protagonist in the play by the same name. Did he know where his Greek name came from? She'd have to ask, to tell him that Ion was the bastard son of Apollo, a beleaguered guy in the play with two fathers. He always wore that stoic mask, but his eyes were always riveted on whoever spoke, whether Paul or Theodora, particularly Theodora. There was a blankness in that stare, however. Was he really listening to them or just tuning them out? Like the original Ion, was he obliging a *dea ex machina,* Theodora, an Athena reincarnation, ministering to him in not too obvious ways? What was going on inside him? Was he actually put-off by Theodora, merely being polite? So handsome, he was, how much a better lover he probably would be than Paul, Paul with his sweetness and gentleness and his prolonged oscillations. Ion, she imagined, would be strong and silent. He would take her, not woo her, force her to his will, whatever it would be—a spontaneous act of procreation maybe, the way Nature intended. No cerebral rationalizations, no intellectual abrasions, just raw sex. He would be a real man, in control of his destiny, ready to oppose the gods. Wham, Bang!

Then she bit hard on her *friganes,* its crumbs sprinkling her lap, and saw Theodora emerging from the hold. Strangely, only then did she realize her absence. With her feet still healing, she seemed to be only a disinterested observer. Even at last night's dinner on board with cold cuts, cheeses, and fruits she had taken only one glass of retsina and retired early. But she did relate with gusto her card games with the captain. He had forked up about four thousand drachmas, and the competition would continue, she cackled.

Frances noticed another strange thing about Theodora, she shined. Not only her face, devoid of make up, but her shoulders and legs, and most of all, her hair, too.

Frances sniffed and said, "Did you pour a bottle of olive oil on yourself?"

Her hair was slicked back, as if she had just emerged from a swim. Yet, it all gave her, with her deepening tan, a bronzed look like some polished statue excavated from the deep. "Why?" Frances said. But her tone was a loving enquiry, for Frances, like the rest had noticed every day a transformation in Theodora. She was metamorphosing, day by day, from an Oakland shriveled spinster into something regal, a Nike, a refined Bouboulina.

Theodora smiled wanly, but it was Ion who supplied the answer. "The captain may be right about olive oil's panacea qualities. It softens the keratin proteins, probably helps break some of the hydrogen and disulfide bonds. A medicinal compound in a way." Theodora nodded appreciation to Ion and she stroked her slippery arms and swept back her hennaed mane.

Takis began to clear the table and soon enough, they broke anchor and headed to the open sea. Frances laid out cushions in the saloon, in the corner where it would be difficult for Paul to attend her. She'd face the sea ordeal by herself with a copy of Papadiamandis' collections of short stories, some Seferis and Cavafy's poems. They, she would want to answer Paul, were about the real, modern Greece, about the peasant life on islands today, not about epic legends two to three thousand years ago.

❖ ❖ ❖

On Ios, that afternoon, they all went to the beach, the captain and Takis, too, with umbrellas, mats, baskets of fruits and snacks. The long white beach of Milopotamos, different from the Parian one, was dotted with nude young bathers. They found a deserted spot near *kalami* canes and oleander trees and prepared themselves for a leisurely day of bathing and lounging. Paul, of course, had a basket of books, and Theodora wore canvas shoes and her large, ribboned straw hat.

Takis showed Ion and Stan how to play paddle ball. The lady Letoites sipped Fanta lemon sodas, admiring the dark tanned bodies of the Greeks, Takis and Ion, like paintings of athletic silhouettes on white backgrounds of kratera or amphora. Stan roamed in the background like a lost giant goat.

Paul read to Frances, but his cuddly touches went unnoticed. A strange repulsion filled Frances, as if she wanted to tear free of his unctuousness, cleanse herself of his goody-goodness, wallow maybe in some debauchery. She wanted to run to those dark Greeks, leap on their brawny shoulders, straddle their haunches, caress their pecs and deltoids. Oh, won't Paul ever shut up about Homer!

The captain hadn't disrobed. He sat cross-legged with Theodora under an umbrella, his shirt opened and his hat off. Theodora wrote in her Addenda, but seemed easily diverted by things around her, by the lapping surf, the sea birds, and the manly graces of mobile Ion. But she, too, like Frances, felt a detachment. Watching Ion was vicarious pleasure, no more, and she felt restless, impatient. The man simply was not paying her any attention. It was if an invisible wall had descended between them, and it was insurmountable, yet there had to be some way to scale it, make a breach, or something. Maybe she could recruit the captain, maybe he could be her champion, yes, her Trojan Horse, to circumvent Ion's defenses. Oh, won't Ion ever open up?

As the day wore on, a languorous mood began to enclose the Letoites in a vacuum. The captain saw it coming. They were too self-absorbed, too much wine from the previous evening, they needed rejuvenation, so as the sun rays slanted behind the peaks of Megalo Vouni and Pirgos, he rose to holler at them, "*Ella, ella, pame,*" come, come, we go. He motioned them back to the harbor and told Ion of his plan. Tell them, he said, they should change clothes, have a drink on board, and at dusk begin a slow twenty minute climb up to the town of Ios. There are beautiful marble steps all the way up, and even Theodora could make the climb. Along the way, they could admire the many white chapels, something Ios is famous for. Then, dinner near the windmills higher up and an evening of dancing. "Yes, we'll dance at a disco," the captain ordered and the Letoites would surely want to obey.

So, that night, dodging donkeys and excrements on the way up, they arrived at a *psisitirio* to order baby lamb chops, fries and carafes of retsina. There were mostly young people around, dressed in scanty, torn clothes. One girl with stringy blonde hair passed by them with a large swatch sewn on the front of her abbreviated shorts. "Kiss my patch," it said. Others wore beads and floppy hats with plastic flowers. The narrow street had few Greeks, mostly merchants delivering goods to the cafes and tourist shops.

"The Haight Ashbury transported to the Cyclades, sans fog, sans real flowers," said Paul. He spoke in a sneering tone, but Frances gave no support. The others were too busy devouring the delicious baby lamb chops smothered in oregano and lemon.

The night air was cooling fast, and above the moonless black sky was quickly being perforated with white sparkles. The crowds grew, the noisy, dusty and smoky street began to fill with what looked like refugees from a desert. They seemed tired, burned by the sun, an empty, abandoned look on their faces.

"It's early yet," said Stan. "These young people are just waking up from a long day's siesta on the beach. They'll come alive, you watch."

"Hmm," said Paul. "I could have stayed home to see this hippie event."

Theodora made her move. "Ion, have you seen anything like this back home?"

"In the Golden Gate panhandle once. Just in passing. Drop outs don't interest me much."

"Me neither, but they must be acknowledged. They're symptomatic of our times," said Theodora.

"Why?" Ion said. He turned to Stan and said, "You explain it. That's an anthropologist's job."

"Rites of passage," he said. "Does that satisfy you, Theodora? No more than that. Mardi Gras, Bohemian Life, what's the difference?"

Frances perked up, turned to Paul and said, "Dionysian rites, OK?"

"Hmm . . ." Paul curled his lips. "But these kids are not Greek. What in the world are they?"

"What does it matter?" asked Frances. "Greeks do it somewhere else, these foreigners do it here. Mykonos is where the Greek kids go, I hear. We'll see. We're going to Mykonos, right?"

Paul didn't respond.

Karen said, "You don't mean to say, Paul, that Greeks today don't let their hair down?"

"I'm talking about ancient times. Sure, they did. But not with the hedonistic abandonment of these kids. They celebrated in the name of the gods. They had their entourage of satyrs, sileni, maenads, and nymphs. It was a religious ritual, you understand, with purpose."

"Oh, knock it off," said Stan. "What purpose? What the hell is wrong blowing off your lid for the sheer pleasure of it without having to justify it in the names of mythical gods? Anyway you look at it, it was a way to get plastered and have an orgy."

"The gods may have been mythical, but their celebrations had a higher purpose. They wanted to please their gods, not only themselves."

"Horse shit," Stan and Karen said in unison.

Theodora's back straightened, and like an Empress suppressing Byzantine squabbles among her keep, said, "Indeterminate data, let's say. We ought to go meet some of these young people and let them talk for themselves. Shall we? Captain, where's that disco?"

The reckoning of the bill was complicated and by the time they were ready to climb the hill where the windmills and discos were, a new moon had risen. They marched towards it through rows of eucalyptus and gnarled old fig trees, upwards to an rising cacophony of amplified music. But after marine quiet, the Letoites, braced by good food and wine, anticipated the adventure. Who knew what kind of new Cycladic excitement?

The "Boo-Boo" disco, open to the sky, built of cinder blocks with sheds on its margins and bamboo roofs, lay on a mountainside crowned with a black panoplied sky and a windmill with tattered vanes. As soon as they entered the place, waiters scampered to pull together tables and chairs for them. Very soon, they realized they had entered a bizarre strobe-lit arena. The crowd was young enough to be their children almost, but they looked dead, zombie-like. The air smelled heavily of jasmine and marijuana, the combination almost putrid. Few were on the dance floor. The ear-splitting rock music sounded like crashing boulders, and the slow-motion of pelvises on the dance floor and quivering jaws trying to be heard at the tables presented a surreal scene.

The Letoites could not talk, they could barely hear patrons in nearby tables giving each other a perfunctory *abend*. The crowd was mostly European, mostly German, with some pink Brits and dark Italians and French thrown in. The patrons paid no attention to the Letoites, paid little attention, in fact, to each other. They were transformed into a super-conscious world of rock and its pounding, fucking tempo, in a world of infinity, in the smallest possible space, in the largest imaginable time frame.

A soft air and a few plants in painted oil cans surrounded them. The decibels, notwithstanding, made only a slight dent in a general ambience, one that the Letoites had experienced indefinably elsewhere—perhaps in funeral parlors back home where the stiffs lay out in little mourning parlors filled with anonymous people drifting around. Animations lay suspended, mourners and patrons suspended in caskets of sadness and dopiness.

The blare went on and on, but as the evening passed, as if church bells were beginning to sound at midnight, the patrons, like ghosts arising from their graves, slowly one by one, two by two, began to gyrate on the dance floor to acid rock and Joplin. Eyelids notched up a few millimeters and awareness began to creep in between the billowing cigarette and maryjane clouds. Pelvic tilts, bobbing tits, and spreading crotches, more and more, filled the place, and ear drums vibrated in spasms of syncopation.

The Letoites' eyes widened, they looked askance at each other, their own bodies began to weave to the one-two beat. They couldn't talk, they could only holler unintelligible sounds. Their identities shrunk, they felt they were sucked down into a quick sands of sensuality, yet they didn't rebel, couldn't. They gawked at the groping hands slithering over breasts and groins. They marveled at buttocks swollen by libidos straining to coordinate thrusts and parries. Then, in their wicker chairs, they felt pinches on their rears and they could not but rise and join in.

Even Ion got caught up, his hands motioning small claps. He looked around to see the other's reactions, but they were all focused on the dance floor. But then he noticed Stan with his back partially turned from him, who shouted in the ear of German boy at the next table. The boy was tall, thin, emaciated, bearded, pigtailed—a blonde, young Aryan version of Stan himself. They tried to converse, but couldn't. Ion heard only one word in exchange, *wissenschaft,* that Stan shouted with cupped hands into the boy's ear. After awhile, they stopped trying to speak and instead, to Ion's shock, began to hold hands. The boy wore torn jeans, and Stan had inserted his hand through a hole on the boy's knee!

Ion numbed. The music, like a giant discordant pipe organ, resounded a fortissimo cipher, blasting him to the realization of what had happened in the Parian quarry. It was Stan who had groped him, now there was no doubt. Stan's a fruitcake, how would he ever had known? How could he be sharing a cabin with him?

He turned to the other Letoites for support, for verification, but some of them, too, were engaged in their own self-gratifications. Paul was kneading Frances' breasts like a kitten, and she, delicate Frances, with a wild animal look, was massaging Paul's thighs. Karen, who had touched Ion several times on the arm, had pulled his head towards her mouth, and shouted in his ear, licking it: "I'm going back to the boat, Takis is alone. See you later." What? She and Takis? And the licking for whose benefit? His? Hers? She departed. Libertines all.

He saw only Theodora and the captain maintaining their dignity. They smiled at the goings on, occasionally sipping the tall glasses of fruit juice spiked with *raki.* The "boo-boo" was the house drink, and it was driving everyone to madness.

Ion had wanted to leave, but not with Karen. He didn't want to be witness to *her* seductions (how horny can a woman get?), and he wasn't sure that he was steady enough to descend those marble steps alone. Anyhow, he was still in shock with all the new revelations. Stan a fruitcake, Karen leching for Takis (or him). How had this all happened so quickly?

Suddenly, the music stopped. The audience froze and waiters in black pants and short-sleeved shirts and bow ties lined up on the dance floor. They raised high their heads, arched their backs, raised their arms and began to snap their fingers. Then a band started, the *bouzoukia* and *clarinos* screaming the *ribetiko* beat. They pranced, they swung off each other's handkerchiefs in acrobatic flips, slapped the bottoms of their shoes, shouted *ompah,* and paraded around the dance floor like conquering heroes. The crowd roared and joined in.

Before Ion knew what had happened, he was dragged off to the floor by the captain and Theodora. They danced the *sourto,* round and round, arms clutched on each other's shoulders. Theodora, with a silly smile on her face, began to dig deep into his shoulder, not just holding on to him for balance, but more like she was clinging to him in rapture. Her fingers twitched, trilled, and caressed. *Christ*, he thought. He knew it would come sooner or later . . . the overt pass. All her subtle ingratiations and ministrations of the last few days were too transparent. He knew that game. He tried loosening his grip on her shoulder, hoping she'd get the idea and reciprocate. It didn't work, he was feeling trapped, as when Sonja cornered him in the dark of a movie house or the photo lab.

But his deliverance was not long in coming. Plates began to crash on the dance floor. Patrons threw them wildly at the feet of the *palikari* dancers. Splinters flew and the hysteria mounted. The captain sensed the danger and grabbed Theodora's waist to lead her off the dance floor. The evening was late, the climax passed. It was time to retreat to the safety of the *Leto,* and gathering his passengers, the captain slowly led their descent down the marbled path to the harbor. Stan, however, remained at the Boo-Boo with the German. Frances and Paul weaved but braced each other with laughter. Theodora kept upright with the captain and Ion on each side of her.

❊   ❊   ❊

Theodora felt no pain. She didn't care. For once in her adult life, couldn't she just rely on someone else? Such as these two men—the one her dream boat, the other, the epitome of stalwart, if not devious manliness . . . yes . . . surrender. She had forgotten what it felt like. She stumbled down the stairs and remembered when Sammy pulled her on the sled, how terrified she was of falling off, how she might go tumbling out of control down the hillside, her feet sliced off by the sled's blades. What terror, she felt then, she remembered so well. But she remembered, too, that Sammy loved her, knew he couldn't do anything that would put her into jeopardy. It was so natural, then, to surrender, confident of his love. Of her love. So why she could surrender now to these two men? It was easy, just to let go of all the restraints, of all those self-guards she had encumbered herself with, like a shield protecting her from life's pleasures. It was like that, wasn't it, this moment of descent from the ancient site of Ios?

She began to hum the disco song, *Yiorgi o poneros*. She remembered the lines:

George, you sly one,
how clever of you,
in the middle of night,
to find the way,
to where you want to be,
George, you're so . . .

Over and over she sang it, and the Captain, in a deep husky voice joined in. Her head tilted back to laugh at the heavens, she grasped the shoulders on each side of her, lifted herself from the ground and kicked her feet to take wing. They caught her as she began to fall on the marble steps, and the next moment, she found herself piggy-back on the captain. She clasped her arms around his thick neck, locked her hands under his bearded chin. She nuzzled into his wiry black hair, the smell of the Papastratos cigarettes like perfume. Security. Surrender. Sanctuary. His back a bunker to defend her. His arms secured her legs, and straddled, she sensed an unknown pleasure. They bumped all the way down, but, almost asleep, she wasn't sure that she wasn't straddled to a horse or donkey. But whose hair was she nuzzling? It didn't matter whether it was the captain or Ion or a hippie. In one little corner of her consciousness some cortical neurones continued to fire, telling her only that operant conditioning lay suspended and neural arcs of unknown origin were bombarding her.

So what? she giggled. I'm a Minoan tonight!

10
Santorini

Stan straggled on board the next morning at breakfast. No one questioned, Stan did not volunteer.

"Where next?" he said.

The captain, seeing that his passengers needed to recuperate from their Iosian escapades, suggested a brief sail down the island to Milopotamos, one of the most beautiful beaches of the Cyclades. There, he would have them relax and dine on fish at a taverna.

"So nice, isn't it, gang, to have someone who knows the territory," said Theodora. She was shining, but a little perturbed, too, at Karen's appearance. Early in the morning, she had seen her on the deck with a entranced expression, starring out to the sea, closing her eyes dreamily. Takis sat on a stool nearby, like a puppy dog waiting for a feeding. They touched hands.

Oh my, Theodora thought. *It wasn't in the plan.* Karen was supposed to be a Lesbian, her Bay Area contacts guaranteed it. But now, there could be no question, some kind of a budding romance between the two was unfolding. How could it be? In the Addenda she had made notes of what she called "innocent flirtations" between the two—the little attentions Takis paid her, the whittlings and fruit. But she had no idea that it would be going this far. Perhaps her calculations were wrong. It simply didn't fit into her personality profile projections.

Damn. Furthermore, Takis is crew—so is the captain for that matter—and now the both of them were disturbing the order of things. They were supposed to be only providers of service. Now, the Letoites were becoming too dependent on them, even emotionally in Karen's case. And how could Karen and Takis find a way to communicate in any sort of meaningful way with no common language? For God's sake, Karen was supposed to be a Professor of Speech and Drama and an Administrator and she surely knew the importance of language. And here she was, devoid of the her principal means of communication. What can sign language accomplish other than relate necessities, like food, glee—and sex? And what kind of sex would that be if the organs were not compatible, if Karen had come to realize that the penis was nothing but an engorged clitoris?

Her mind fogged. Was it kinky sex? She'd read of all the bizarre forms of sexual inversions. And she had no data whatsoever on "sweet" Takis. No telling what kind of "queer" Greek he was, and you know what they say about Greek men. Oh, no. It was horrific. That beautiful boy with that corpulent . . . Oh, she didn't want to think of it. Karen, everything about her, was going off the chart.

Theodora needed to talk to her. She waited until Karen was alone on the foredeck, and brought her some fresh figs, smiled at her and said, "What an evening, huh?"

Karen remained mum. She only narrowed her eyes and half-smiled as she peeled and slurped the fig lovingly.

Theodora turned toward Stan. Maybe he could help her to bring Karen to her senses. With him, she was pleased. He was following the plan, indulging himself predictably in sexual matters. Good. She had to reward him, that was an operant conditioning axiom. "Why don't you ask your German friend to join us at Milopotamos?"

Despite the enigmas of Karen and Takis and a hangover, Theodora almost shined that morning for reasons other than smeared olive oil. She had to admit that after last night's caravan down the hillside, Ion might, with the Captain's help, be opening up. They had danced together, held each other's shoulders. He supported her coming down. One step at a time, that was a logical progression in the scheme. That little piggy-back ride last night (whether on the captain's or Ion's back) should have told Ion something else, too, that she had a playful nature. The message: Play with me, Ion. Good probe.

The day at Milopotamos, Theodora realized, was the correct prescription. There was time to assimilate the events of the last few days, write postcards, nap, do nothing really and give Stan a chance to make contact again with the German boy, which he did, inviting him to spear fish for octopus. The boy, though knowing some English, showed no interest in the Letoites and they had none in him.

She made notes of Ion's reactions, especially. He was detached, as usual, sitting away from everyone else on a towel staring out to the horizon again. She occasionally saw him looking at Stan and the boy, almost with a contemptuous look. She expected that, but she couldn't gauge really what Ion was thinking. He was, in fact, wondering why they needed all that superfluous hair. The contemptuous look Theodora saw might have been a misinterpretation of what was in reality his more circumspect anatomical observations of the two men. His brow always furrowed a little when he was in deep thought, this time about whether he really thought hairiness was really unattractive. Their bodies, particularly, the boy's, weren't exactly unattractive, from a locker room point of view, of course, if one liked hairy jocks. Theodora, clairvoyant as she thought she was, could not discern what Ion thought, nor could she have yet recorded in her Addenda the Parian quarry incident. What she saw, what she thought she saw, was rather a confirmation of Ion's vigorous normal heterosexual drives. She was happy for it, happy that Ion, having lived long enough in the San Francisco Bay area to have observed the fluttering gay ways, like most super-males, disapproved of type. Of course, she herself was disapproving of that attitude, being herself, like most psychologists, tolerant of different life styles. She couldn't expect him to be that sophisticated. Later, she could educate him on those matters. Every day, regardless, the field seemed to clear.

She turned, then, her psychological telescope on Paul and Frances. They weren't buried in books, for a change; instead, though they still fondly smeared sun-tan oil of each other's bodies, they seemed not their usual, emotionally intense selves. She wondered whether their love-making had reached a plateau and needed now a little augmentation towards its final fulfilllment.

She laid her towel beside them, and began talking about the children playing in the sand several yards from them. "What delightful little creatures," she said. "I love to work with them in the lab. So fresh, so inventive. My colleagues have delightful children. I enjoy them so much." She turned to them and asked, "Do you have colleagues with children?"

"I love them," said Frances. "Wish I had some myself."

"And what about you, Paul?" Theodora said.

"Well, to be truthful, I don't know about the personal lives of my colleagues. Isn't that the most typical situation with us academics?"

Frances and Theodora could do nothing but agree, with some few exceptions.

The big question, I suppose," said Theodora, "is whether children enhance academic careers. Or is it only that couples must endure them? I would rather think, even when both partners are academic, that it should be a positive thing."

"Well, what I know is that some of my colleagues, without academic wives and with children, seem hardly aware of their children. At least, they never talk of them."

"What about academic couples?" Theodora said.

"No knowledge of that species," said Paul.

"I do," said Frances. "And they are ecstatically happy. Their children bind them more and give them relief from all the academic concerns."

"Splendid for them," said Paul. "I simply have no foreknowledge. Seems to me that children would only be an enormous impediment to their scholarly work."

All three then entered into a prolonged discussion of the matter. The sun burned, their brains simmered in heated pros and cons. They could not resolve anything, but when Theodora withdrew, she felt her seeds planted.

However, she should have asked Frances, because she was the only one to fully comprehend Paul's implacable nature. And she knew what to do about it.

✿ ✿ ✿

At dawn, the *Leto* set sail for Santorini (Thera, its ancient name), out to the open sea at the southern edge of the Cyclades. Everyone looked forward to what was supposed to be the most stunning sight of the entire Mediterranean. They talked about it, compared travel guide information, looked at photos of the famous Akroteri frescoes in the Athens museum and anticipated almost a full day of sightseeing.

The sight was stupefying when they entered the calders of the volcano with high cliffs and white cubes of villages at the top, much more dramatic than the gentle volcanic setting of Milos. There was something awesome about it, too, a landscape painting of no known earthly locus. Beautiful? Theodora didn't think so. The whole scene looked burned out, pulverized, buried in pumice and schist, and the pozzuolana mines reminded her too much of the mines of Minnesota. The barges loading the stuff to be made into cement were rusted old vessels that spoiled the picture of the deep blue circular bay. And the heat off the stony cliffs made the caldera an insufferable cauldron.

They docked and looked up the steep winding path up the cliff to the town of Pheira, where they would begin their sightseeing. There was no funicular. The only way up was by foot or donkeys. Theodora saw the tourists pitching and tossing upwards on those donkeys and decided that no way would she participate in *that*. Unfortunately, she'd have to lose another day of data collecting. She bade the rest goodbye, told them she would rest quietly and help Takis with the provisions he would bring on board later.

She asked the captain to position, as best as possible, the *Leto* so she'd have some shade and breeze.

"*Pos, thespinis*? How in midday in this volcano can you expect that?"

This was to be the low point of the trip, she admitted to that. She would have liked to have seen the site of Minoan digs at Akroteri, but the pictures in travel guides weren't exactly exciting. Mostly stone house debris covered with pumice and ash. Ancient Thera might have been more interesting, but again, that required a long hike. No, the only thing was for her to sweat it out.

She decided not to go on shore with Takis for shopping and instead made herself some cold tea and waited for suppertime when things would cool and the landing party might bring down some of that famous Santorini white wine.

"Cards?" the captain asked. "Well, of course," she agreed. There wasn't much else to do.

They played for about thirty minutes and the captain had begun to win. The way he slung his cards down was aggressive, almost belligerent, and whether it was directed at the cards, her, or whether he too, was bored with their circumstances in the hot harbor, she couldn't be sure. But he snatched winning stacks and slammed them down on the table, and twice she caught him miscounting card values.

"Careful, now," she said in her best, careful Greek. She had her dictionary nearby, knowing that if disputes would arise, she'd have to look up words like "miscalculation," "errors," "additions."

Their communications in Greek, nevertheless, had improved since Piraeus, or at least, he was beginning to understand her idiosyncratic pronunciations. He had begun to talk slowly to her, and in a way, she resented it. It sounded like he was talking down to her, like a child.

He continued to win, his score up several thousand drachmas. Theodora began to squirm, asked for a recess.

"You don't like to lose, do you?" the captain said.

"Well, you need to improve your arithmetic."

"Cards can't do what you want, *thespinis*. They have their own ways."

"What?"

"I mean, that you must reckon the chances. You can't make the cards fall just by will. You understand?"

"Look, Captain, I am a professor. I know—(she had to look it up in her dictionary)—about probabilities."

"Yes, I can tell. You are an educated woman. Probabilities work out over many hours, days, years of playing cards."

How smart of him, she thought. That's in the books, too, but experience could teach one that, also.

She hesitated dealing and looked at him. He always wore a starched white shirt. Who did the ironing? Takis? *Impractical,* she thought, *in this heat.* His shirt was wringing wet and she could see the outlines of dark hair on his chest. She wore only a halter. She wondered what he would say if she suggested he remove his shirt? Would he take it as an overture?

They continued to play. His manner began to soften, perhaps because he became accustomed to winning, and now instead of swooping up the stack, he rather gently tapped them together, sliding them slowly out in deals. Then he'd smile a little and nod that Greek smile of appreciation at her for letting him win, or was it pity for her?

His manner was fawning. "Do you want to quit?" he asked.

"No, absolutely not."

They played in silence, the cards began to even out. But that didn't soothe Theodora enough. "What a horrid place," she said. "Why do people come here?"

"No place else like it in the world. You know about Plato and Atlantis? Marinatos, the famous Greek archaeologist? It has a *psyche* (soul)."

"*Psyche?* You mean good publicity."

"And big history, you know, *thespinis*."

"I know. I read. But why would people want to live in this place God has cursed? It blows up all the time."

"They know that, and that's exactly why. *Ti na kanoume?*"

Theodora frowned. She hated that expression "What can they do?" Her parents used it all the time. She took it always as a surrender to bad luck, to the "fates." No such thing. No sir. We can master our fates, plan, avoid misfortunes. That Greek expression transliterated as a stupidity.

She had to educate this Greek and she said, "Human beings are smart animals. They can reason They know when *physis* is against them. Catastrophes are recorded in history books. So they must adjust. Live elsewhere."

"You think that you can avoid *physis*?" he said. "Perhaps you even think that you can control *physis*?"

Odd that she didn't know the word for science. She had to look it up, found it was the root of the English word, epistemology. But that was more a philosophical term and for a fleeting second she wondered if the Greek word for science had quite the same connotation as the English one. Linguistics so complicated, she had to clarify her meaning.

"That's what we hope to do with science. We measure, plan. That's our only recourse."

The captain loosened another button on his shirt. "Pity. There's no excitement in life that way."

"Why would anyone want to risk being buried by a volcano?"

"Don't laugh at me. I talk of another thing. I talk of how sad life would be if you tried to plan everything. You will be disappointed."

"Perhaps not. I will have security, instead."

The captain rose to raise his arms for the little breeze that was beginning to stir.

"I see what kind of woman you are. You want to calculate everything. But what if by chance, like the probabilities of cards, things cannot be planned."

"I don't try to plan those things," she said.

"Exactly, then, what *do* you plan?"

"Life. My life, it's going according to plan."

He lit a Papastratos, blew the smoke above her head. "You had a brother, Ion told me. He died in the war. How can you plan that?"

"Don't ridicule me."

"Listen, *thespinis,* I say to you, this: If you think you plan everything, you leave out possibilities of chances."

"What chances?"

"Chances you may not ever know about because they are not in your plan."

"Such as?"

"This trip. I told you about my story of the sea and the Germans and war. How could I have survived if I wept and beat my chest every time things did not go to plan?"

"What's that to do with this trip?"

"You don't know what will happen tomorrow. None of us do. But when something suddenly happens, not your plan, how do you know that you should not seize it. Enjoy it, the miracle of it."

"Miracle? I don't believe in miracles. I don't believe in God, if you must know, *Kapitanios.*"

"Pity."

He rose to go ashore. A donkey with melons trotted by the quay. He bought some and a few cold drinks from a vendor.

They played more cards.

The captain had another streak.

"Tell me, *thespinis,* what is your real plan for this trip? Are you only entertaining yourself or do you have a grand *programma?*"

She said nothing.

"You write so much in your black book. What is in it?" he said.

"Science. You would not understand."

"No, *thespinis,* you lie. It is not science. It is your *'ph'antasies.* Science is back there in your university. Here, that black book is a *'ph'antasia.*"

"*Oposthipote,* as you would say, *Kapitanios.* But the *phantasia* as you call it may be my ingenious plan. And it is probable, I assure you."

"Let us make a bet here, and now," he pounded the table with his fist. "That by the time we return to Piraeus you will *not* make your *phantasia.* I will win. 25,000 drachmas, *en taxi?*"

"*En taxi,* OK, careful. I could lie. I'm a liar, like you say. I will declare my *phantasia* realized. How would you know when you don't know the *phantasia?*"

"I know. You cannot hide that from me."

What gall, she thought. *He acts like he can read my mind. If the man would take his shirt off, I'd pinch his tits, pull the hairs on his chest. He lets me piggy-back him, fool around with my feet, I have a right to touch him. I could douse him all over with oil, see how he likes it.*

Then, suddenly, a thought crossed her mind. Why does he hide his chest? It's burlier than Ion's. He may not be educated, but he knows about cards and probability.

※　※　※

The Letoites returned at sundown, bubbling over their sightseeing and sky's ethereal displays.

"Magnificent down here, too, scorching though," Theodora said. "The sights up at Oia must have been spectacular. Did you get any pictures, Ion?"

Their supper onboard was enormous vermilion tomatoes, Santorini wine, and some fried eggplant and squash from a shop in Phaera. The sea was a silvery slate and all around them kaleidoscopic colors flared from the cliffs of the caldera. They absorbed, they reflected, they became charged. Even Ion seemed almost animated talking of the black sand beaches of Perissa, and it bothered Theodora for a fleeting moment to think that it was because she had not been there with him.

Sitting around the table with Takis standing behind them at the door to the galley, Karen, hardly ever keeping Takis out of sight, said, "Gang, I don't know about you, but today has put me in a very strange mood. I've found a new identity. Do you know what I mean?" She rose and filled everyone's glass with cold white wine.

"It's a strange place, I agree," said Stan. "In the Himalayas, I felt my identity change. Those Buddhist mystics ignored me, made me feel that I didn't belong there, that I had no identity whatsoever. I feel here another kind of identity effect." He shuffled his feet and pulled on his beard. "There. I didn't seem to care. Do you know what I mean? I mean, acceptance by a people whose culture does not impact on mine simply has no relevance. I could just as well been observing an insect colony or a penguin rookery. Intellectual interests solely. Nothing that rings in my soul."

"Soul?" said Theodora. "Strange you, a scientist, talking about that. You'll have to elaborate."

"I'll try. Listen, I passed by the sight near Sumatra where Krakatoa erupted. Nearby are interesting Indonesian settlements that have survived. But they didn't touch me, shall I say?"

"I think I know where you are heading," said Paul. "Keep plowing ahead."

"I mean that here—another place that has survived such a volcanic cataclysm—I feel that the event has relevance, to me, personally, I mean."

"Ah," said Paul. "Go on. How?"

"We got the Atlantis pitch. We were talking about it after the guided tour of Akrotiri. It doesn't seem to matter, does it, that this island was really part of the Atlantis myth. It is important only that it evokes Timaeus and Critias and the great Platonic dialogues. There can be no question in my mind that this place was an important site of early Western history. Minoan relics everywhere. There it is, and it was from here that our civilization—*our* civilization, was launched. So . . . can we not feel a profound feeling of identity with the place. It 'rings in the soul,' what else can you expect?"

"Let's define that 'ring,' if you please," said Theodora.

Stan scrunched up his lips. Said nothing. The Letoites stared at him.

Frances said, "Scratch your heads, gang. Little help. What is Stan getting at?"

Ion, almost whispering, said,. "Stan implies there is such a thing as a historical, cultural, racial, memory. A residual strip of DNA that encodes human values. Whatever that is."

"Human values?" said Theodora. "You mean a predisposition towards certain stimuli? And what would be those stimuli?"

As usual, Ion didn't take her bait.

"I'll make a stab," said Paul. "You see a house in rubble at Akrotiri—my God! almost four thousand years old—or a Classical period ruin at ancient Thera, and it impinges on the DNA memory bank and it says to us: Ah, that's familiar. And you lock onto it, identifying your 'soul' to it. It rings, don't you see?"

"And why wouldn't an Indonesian site, or a Bhutan temple, cause you to respond the same way?" said Theodora.

"Simple, Watson," said Ion. 'The Asiatic brain and his progeny were fried by that volcanic blast of Krakatoa, leaving a different mutation than what the Minoan eruption on Atlantis caused. And we are more descendents of the Minoans than Indonesian."

"I've read about those ideas in the new sociobiology theories," said Karen. "Too theoretical. Doesn't help me here."

Ion rubbed his hands, "Look, *E. coli* bacteria inherit metabolic pathways. Well established fact. It's not too far to extrapolate from that that behavior can be inherited, too."

Theodora lifted her eyebrows and beamed. "Why, yes, the variety of our responses to environmental stimuli are pre-determined. Genetically, that is. We respond with a range of responses determined by our genetic make-up. Ergo ... " she smiled all around, "we can control human behaviour by merely selecting appropriate stimuli that would be 'self-enhancing' for the individual. Don't you see how this could open up all our understanding of human existence? How we could avoid conflicts? Bring every human being to his full potential? Why, it's marvelous!"

"What's that got to do with what Stan and Karen are talking about?" said Frances. "They are talking about 'feelings' about a place. Not Pavlovian reflexes."

"Feelings are responses to specific responses," replied Theodora. "In this case, Stan's and Karen's feelings are responses to the sights of ancient Thera and Akrotiri. Startling, I agree, that those places going back four thousand years ago could do that. But the blueprint is there, the DNA memory bank recognizes the stimulus."

"I don't get the connection between 'feelings' and a molecular reaction," said Stan. "If culture can be defined as behaviour that is socially transmitted, I'd say our reaction was no more than a cultural identification."

At that moment, the Letoites saw the captain move back into the galley where Takis stood. He had been watching his passengers, not understanding their discussion, but observing their body language. They were squirmy and their eye movements at each other were intense. They sweated. He directed Takis to help him wet down some towels. He sprinkled them with rose water from a tin shaker and passed them around.

The Letoites wiped their faces and arms appreciatively.

" 'Feelings' might have a molecular basis," said Ion. "Neurochemicals in the brain, dopamines, DNA-directed production of certain neurotransmitters that elicit pleasant or unpleasant autonomic nervous system reactions."

"Exactly," said Theodora. "You can appreciate that possibility, can't you, Stan?"

Stan groaned.

Ion to my defense, thought Theodora. *Bonds were forming. Predictable. Their scientific predilections, their sensitivities to things 'Greek.' What a probe!*

Ion played with his towel, wrapped it around his neck and burbled, "Excuse me. I didn't mean to go too far. Excuse me."

They all looked at him. Paul said, "You don't acknowledge a biochemical basis for the tremendous feelings we have about these marvelous ancient sites? Beside the DNA supposition, you know, you are evoking some very old classical ideas of the Atomists. Democritus believed that a unique assortment of what he called the four basic 'atoms' encircle our souls. Souls, he claimed, were composed of material atoms, fine, mobile, floating around ones, that determine the individuals life. Then, you see, Stan's 'feelings' have a molecular basis, and as we were saying, the Minoan sights are stimuli to remind us of our inherent, chemical compositions. It's really quite simple, don't you think?"

"That would connote that whatever we feel and think is a result of atoms," Ion said. "Who knows for sure about that! I mean, the human mind makes choices, we make moral judgments, have a conscience. No, it's not so simple as atoms. Memory and learning theories are arguable. All those philosophical notions—the Atomists, Pythagoreans and Epicureans—asked those big questions, but none of them, and no scientist, yet, has given answers. What is pre-determination anyway? No, I'm thinking now that Stan is on the right track. It's simply cultural identity, and we'll have to leave it at that."

Theodora slapped her towel across a handrail. The *Leto* made a slurping sound from the backwash of ferryboat breaking anchor. *Whose side is he on anyhow? How incorrigible!*

"Right on, old boy," said Stan. "What the hell do we know about human conscience? Skinner and Watson, Theodora, should have sat down with those Atomists and thrashed out how and where exactly those busy-bee atoms jerk off our souls."

Theodora bit her lip. The Letoites guffawed and picked at some melons. Takis passed around more paper napkins.

Frances stretched out her arms. "Well gang, we're all fabulating aren't we? And I'm enjoying it. Santorini is magnificent, no matter what we say."

Karen: "Did I start all this? Sorry. What I really want to say is that today, and tomorrow, and maybe forever—because of these Cyclades—I feel so, so very sensual. Whoeee!"

She wrapped her arms around her shoulders, hugged herself and then pouched her lips at Takis.

Too much, too much, thought Theodora. *What next? Out of control, everything.* She sulked.

The Letoites noticed. They had learned that Theodora's facial expressions were transparently Greek. They could "read" her easily by now. However, they all felt a loyalty towards their overly intellectual, overly solicitous colleague. She was like a stray retriever needing some petting. Paul offered her a juicy hunk of melon on his fork. "Bite on that. You'll love it."

"Tomorrow, Mykonos, gang?" said Stan.

Theodora didn't exactly like that either. She was to be the organizer of this trip. But long ago they all had said that they wanted to see it and nearby Delos. She'd let that go, for the moment. But in the future there'd be no more Santorinis. She'd see to that.

"Mykonos, eh, Ion?" the captain said. "Tell them we leave early tomorrow. It's a long way and if we get there midday, we can avoid the Meltemi. *Och,* the meltemi around Delos are *friki.*"

By then, the caldera began to darken, the rainbow lights paled, and tiny specs of light blinked up the villages all around them. The heat did not let up, though, the cliffs released back the absorbed day's heat, and again they wiped themselves with rose-water scented towels.

They went below to the saloon, hoping to find some cool, and studied maps on the long side table lit with small lamps.

Sure enough, they would be doing some backtracking heading up north. But the captain, more than the Letoites realized, was planning the itinerary not by the shortest distance between two points, but by weather conditions and the Letoites' impetuosities.

Ion suspected as much. He had been listening to Takis and the captain talking and he understood some of the Greek on the marine band. He was resigned to that, and resigned to bringing up his bunk's little mattress pad to the deck. He would sleep under the stars, not under Stan's hulk. And he wanted to think whether he shouldn't say something to the Letoites. They ought not to aggravate Theodora. They should accept her one-sided views. Her professional biases might be unacceptable to some, but why try to reform her? Everyone in the University had pet ideas. Still, there was something very odd about her persistency. Her intellectual defenses girded more than pet theories. They had to do with something very personal in her life, beyond scientific objectivity. That polluted cloud of atoms around her was just making her talk a lot of gup.

11
Mykonos

For five hours the *Leto*'s hull absorbed a merciless slapping. The meltemi had whipped up the sea and made her passengers feel like they were so much flotsam. They sloshed around the saloon, stumbling across each other and furniture until, finally, they sought refuge in their bunks.

Except the Greeks. They stood on the bridge riding the swells as if they were in an amusement park. Despite the heavy seas, Zeus' bolts left the sky electric blue. Naxos and Paros passed close enough to touch, and the temple of Apollo on the little island outside the town of Naxos looked like an erector set that some kid had just begun to put up.

"*Kapitanios*," Theodora said, "do the Naxians today ever think of Ariadne?"

"*Po, po, po,*" the captain said. "What do you think? She is in their blood. Are we not Greeks? Why, how many bars and discos do you think are named after her?"

"And I bet you know all of them," Theodora said.

The captain winked. "Some day, *thespinis*, I'll take you to them."

Theodora shrugged and laughed at him. "I'm not going to be trapped like Ariadne on that island."

Ion said, "Would you consider this weather rough, *Kapitanios*?"

"*Po*, this is nothing, nothing. Poseidon splashing his toes a little, that's all."

"Amphitrite nagging her husband, eh? *Kapitanios.*" Theodora added.

Theodora, after her long day of rest at Santorini, and despite last night's encounters, was in a playful mood. She wasn't oiled that morning, and she had put on a little rouge and lipstick. And her cotton frock, low-cut, displayed a smooth caramel chest with gentle mounds. She chirped about the weather and the sights, and the men liked her more. She had a certain *charisma,* a resilence, no doubt about it, even Ion admitted that.

"Here, *thespinis,* take the wheel," said the captain. "Watch the compass, NNE, and no arguing with me about the itinerary. I'm the *Kapitanios.*"

"*Sto diavolo,*" she replied, pulling his moustache.

Takis, coming up from the hold, brought up some *kourabiethes,* almond cookies with powdered sugar. With the *Leto* bobbing and the cookies missing their mark, the sugar powdered their faces before they could eat them, and Takis, giggling, tied a napkin around his face, crossed his eyes, and played like a baby.

Takis hardly ever spoke but liked to clown. Ion and Theodora, try as they might, could not understand his dialectical Greek. "He's a good boy," the captain always said of him. "Smart, a born mechanic. He needs educating. What do you think, *thespinis,* do you think the Jewess can teach him anything? She owes him something for his services, don't you think?"

Theodora and Ion exchanged embarrassed looks. Then, Theodora, turning away from the captain, said to Ion in English, "It's happened before, hasn't it, Ion, that the woman can lead the man."

Oh, here we go again, the feminist thing, thought Ion. "Disparities of educational levels are very apparent in academe, I do believe. I know a college president, female, married to a salmon fisherman." But what surprised Ion more was the tacit knowledge among the Letoites that Karen and Takis were having at it. He didn't want to talk about it, though, and he went below to the saloon to read.

Mid-afternoon, the harbor of Mykonos came into view. The seasick Letoites emerged from their cabins, slowly recovering as the engines decelerated and the *Leto* found its dock. They decided to wait until sunset to explore the town.

What a sight was presented them. The labyrinth lanes, arched passageways, colorful cubistic buildings and little flowered squares were charming, and the shops and boutiques gave the whole place a feeling of precious chic. It resembled Paros and then some, with red domed chapels instead of blue and green, but its uniqueness could be attributed to something else.

The town was blatantly gay, opulently gay, jet set type. Many of the "boys" wore jewelry and make-up, and not a few dykes walked around in patent leather boots and white blue jeans. Streets were crowded and much cruising was going on. Ion, only, of all the Letoites, garnered many glances.

"This beats the Castro any day. Look at 'em. They're dressed to kill," said Stan.

"Not a scruffy one among them," said Karen. "Why, it's all one big drag show. Better than anything I could stage, my dears!"

Eyes popped, they wandered up to high ground beyond some windmills with their spars flapping in the breeze near the Paraportian Church, four chapels cobbled into one weirdly shaped church. Along the way, they had picked up English language newspapers, and Karen purchased a large English-Greek phrase book. The view down to the harbor and the town's esplanades was panoramic, but they decided they'd find a quiet, out of the way bar and restaurant.

Below and away from the harbor, lay Alefkandra, the "Venetian Quarter," jumbled houses with overhanging balconies piled up on the sea's edge. Theodora sniffed out a bar where classical music was being played and the crowd seemed sedate. Prices were outrageous, and they ordered only ouzo and roasted nuts. They read their newspapers, talked little, then began to think of finding a taverna.

"Down the way," the waiter said was a good fish place. They got up to leave, but Stan said he'd join them a little later, meaning, Karen was quite sure, that he wanted to do some cruising. Ion hesitated for a moment, sat back down, and told the rest that he'd sit with Stan a while. He wanted to clear the air about that quarry episode.

The two remained mum, wiping the condensations off their ouzo glasses. The ice made the drinks opaque, white, and they became engrossed with why that should be.

"You're the chemist. You explain," said Stan.

"There are some oils in ouzo, and when the concentration of water reaches a certain level, a phase change.... Never mind, I'm not sure. Let's clear up something else, if you don't mind, Stan."

Stan folded his hands. "Shoot."

"You were the one who groped me in the quarries, weren't you?"

"You were groped? How shocking? *Moi?* How do you know it wasn't one of our horny women?"

"Because I saw how forward you can be. With that German boy, I mean. Fess up."

Stan smiled broadly, showing his teeth through his beard and moustache. Then he gave Ion a hard look. But said nothing.

"You do have teeth," said Ion. "I'm surprised. With all that hair, you cover up yourself. What are you hiding from? Your gayness? I don't give a shit if you're queer, Stan. Know that." His voice was completely unmodulated.

"So... Therefore, you think I was making a pass at you."

"What else can I think?"

"I'm not sure what I was doing. It was an impetuous act. My batteries weren't dead. I just thought I'd pull a prank. Sometimes doing something outrageous, you make discoveries. It's a trick of the trade with us anthropologists. Learn about mores and taboos."

"And what did you expect to find out from me? You expected me to fondle back? Or were you aware that you might have risked a sock in the face?" His voice still was in lower registeries.

"Hold on now, Ion. Don't make too much of this. I didn't have rape on my mind. It's no fun that way for me."

"You were just feeling me out, huh? See if I might not be gay?"

"As a matter of fact, I think it was something else. For all you know, you may not be my type anyway."

"What is your type?" He could have been asking a student to balance a chemical equation.

"Never mind. Listen. Subconsciously, I did it for a deeper reason. Can I level with you? I don't mean to be insulting. But do you know, what a prick you can be? You live in your own little world and don't dare let anyone else in it. Forget about Theodora's prying. Forget about how you treat all of us. If you don't like us, that's OK. But in the name of common courtesy and decency, can't you show just a little enthusiasm or a little sociability? Are you that contained in your test tubes? Open up man, be yourself. You need more than a groping. You need a good goose."

Ion frowned. His fists tightened. He caught himself before rising to leave. "You don't know me, Stan. We've been on the *Leto* for nine days, that's all. How can you possibly know what I'm like?"

"That's the point. We're in a unique situation on this cruise. We're encapsulated. We can't escape our personae. Look what we already know about each other. Karen and Takis. Theodora planning to hook you. Paul and Frances getting it on. You all know I'm gay. We share clothes pins. Karen's bloomers flap on the halyards. The captain has a steely eye on all of us. We know what he's thinking, and we know that he might very well score with Theodora, whether she knows that yet or not. But you? What do we know about you? Why, I don't even know if you like girls or not?"

"That's my business."

"You've certainly shown no interest in them so far. Heh, we've seen plenty of good looking gals around. You never turn a head. I've watched you. I've watched you starring at Takis in the engine room. He's very cute, I agree, wonderful features and muscle definition. He's straight, can't you tell that? See why I ask the question? OK, I'm intruding." Stan stopped for a minute to look at the dark sea. There was a luminescence coming off it, from moon beams or critters in the sea, he wasn't sure.

Ion didn't take the opening. He was thinking about whether Theodora really was out to hook him.

Stan continued. "As for myself, well, I'm not afraid of examining myself. You can call it intellectual honesty if you like. I'm not afraid of revealing it to you or anyone. Long time ago, I came out of the closet. I had to. I was going mad keeping things inside myself. And I'm telling you—that's all—that it's all right to let us know whatever you are or whatever you're thinking. Girls or boys. We don't care."

"Theodora certainly seems to."

"What's wrong with telling her?"

"What?"

"That you like her or don't. That you like boys. That you like certain girls, but not her. Just the truth."

"I don't want to hurt her."

"Theodora is a strong woman. She knows what she's about. You don't, that's apparent. Now that I think of it, I'm not sure that you don't harbor some secret desire that with time you two could . . ."

"It's crossed my mind."

"Good. We're making progress. Talk to me. What do you feel for Theodora?"

"She's admirable. A little conniving. Controlling. We're both chemists, or at least she was once. We're Greek. We share certain cultural values. My family would jump hoops if I told them I was marrying a Greek girl. And a PhD at that. There's logic to it."

"So, whoopee. How can we get the 'chemistry' going between you? Do you have an inkling of desire in your testicles for her? I'm not a bad operator. I could give you some tips of how to romance her. The game is the same, homo or hetero."

Ion grimaced. Back to the sex thing. He looked down the waterfront, hoping to see the others at an outdoor taverna. They should join the party, he'd say, and drop the whole subject. Yet, he didn't want to tell Stan that Theodora didn't arouse him. He'd think . . .

Stan grabbed his arm. "Have you had a woman? Tell me truthfully."

"One and a half."

"Tell me about the one. Who was she? How did it go?"

Reluctantly, clearing his throat often, he told him certain things of Sonja. How she had seduced him. How he hardly ever was the initiator.

"You weren't crazy for her. That's it?" Stan said.

"I liked her very much. A fine person. Smart, amusing. It's only that . . ."

"No spark. Let's talk man to man. How did you get it off with her? Was the sex complete? Reciprocal? Did she have big tits? Juicy cunt?"

Ion puffed some air out his mouth, disgusted. How crude of Stan.

"Don't put me off that way, Ion. We're human beings, sexual animals, you're a biochemist. You know enough biology. Just be honest with yourself."

"She had a great body. It was just that . . ." He struggled to find the words. "It was so much work. So many calories expended to get to the climax. She kept pulsating away while I chugged along for what was like hours."

"Wow. Multiple orgasms for her, but not for you. And it never got better? How long were you together?"

"A year or so. We'd sleep together maybe once a week."

"What happened to her?"

"She flunked out of grad school. Left town."

"How did you feel?"

"Not unhappy. I was rather relieved that I didn't have to perform. The convulsions were exhausting."

"Hmm. Do you masturbate a lot?"

"What are you, a sex therapist or something?"

"We're just chewing the rag here. Don't get worked up. I'll tell you what I think about when I jerk off."

"I'm not interested."

"Oh come on, tell me. Maybe we can work up some desire for Theodora."

"I don't think of a person, if that's what you mean."

"What then?"

Ion pinched his nose, looking away from Stan. He saw lanterns on fishing boats out in the dark sea. How was he to answer a question he had never been asked before?

"Something lubricious, that's all."

"Lubricious? What a two-bit word. Where did you get that? What kind of lubricious? A pussy? An ass hole? A mouth?"

Ion was feeling the ouzo. He was getting dreamy, light-headed, and told Stan that maybe they should head for supper.

"What kind of dreams do you have? What are your sexual fantasies?" Stan said.

He tried to tell Stan about his dreams, but he couldn't recall who were in them. But they were very lubricious and they didn't require an expenditure of calories.

"Very interesting, indeed," said Stan. "Pardon me if I'm acting like Sigmund. Are you ready for my diagnosis? You're either a severely repressed homosexual or a truly asexual person. We must analyze this. There are such asexual types, I hear, but I really doubt it. More like some psychopathy or a hormonal problem. No, not hormonal, kid, it can't be. You're plenty fit, hot to trot, I'd say. Furthermore, the fact that you have good dreams means that the apparatus functions OK. No, I think you've got to get to the bottom of this. Find yourself a good analyst and figure it out. Back home, it might take some time and money. It would be worth it in the long run. You can't just try to talk yourself into marriage with Theodora. You can't try to make yourself perform better mechanically with a woman. Learning jiu jitsu won't help, neither will lifting weights with your cock. It has to come from the heart, you know what I mean? Otherwise, it wouldn't be fair to her. Don't you agree?"

Ion nodded and said, "As for your first alternative . . . Mind you, I've never entertained the possibility, but how did you know you were gay, 'in your heart' as you say?"

"I knew it always. My first sexual thoughts were about men. I remember how I liked my dad when he would put me in the bathtub with him, back then. Incestuous little bastard that I was. Sleeping with women was more like what you describe with Sonja. I had to get skunked out of my mind and prove to the boys I was a man. Had to pretend an orgasm. Or I'd fake a premature ejaculation. What self-deceit. Somewhere around twenty, I could say to myself. I'm Stan Kruszenski and I'm queer."

"You blabbed it around?"

"I didn't attach a sign, but to friends and family, yes, I did."

"If you came from a Greek family you wouldn't."

"Are they stupid or something? They should understand. Hell, their ancestors invented it, didn't they?"

"They're so strong on family values. An offspring that couldn't procreate would destroy their purpose for living."

"Is that your problem then?"

"I value my parents. I wouldn't want to hurt them in any way."

"It's your life, Ion. They'll be gone soon enough and what will you do with the rest of your life? Why not hide it from them and go on with your sexual tastes, whatever they are? Maybe you'd like those hairless Oriental boys. Maybe you'll discover that you are a rice queen."

"Don't be absurd. A minute ago you were preaching about the evils of deception. Now you're telling me to lead a double life with my parents. For the record, Oriental boys don't interest me one iota. For that matter, fags don't interest me either. They are all such sissies. So swish and nellie. Like women."

"Aha, like women, you said it. So you don't like women. So what do you really like?"

They reached an impasse and their voices faded in the wind. Neither wanted to continue, and they were famished, only a few *kourabiethes* and some fruit all day long. The ouzo had served its aperitif purpose, and one minute more, they'd be on their faces. As they rose, Stan said, "If you want, you can come with me to a gay bar after dinner. There must be dozens of them in this berg. Have you ever been to one?" They settled the reckoning and walked towards the quay.

"Inadvertently. It didn't seem very gay at all. Everyone was skulking like hungry animals. I felt very self-conscious."

"You would. All eyes were on you, I'd be sure of it. Didn't you feel flattered?"

"Flattered to be considered a piece of meat?"

"There is that aspect." They stopped for a minute to contemplate the Milky Way, so distinct in the sky's blackness. "But you don't know about gay life because of one little inadvertent encounter. Do you know that there is such a thing as gay love?"

"No. I always thought when two men who lived together they only had an understanding, like sisters. Not liked a married, sexual couple."

"Well, there'd be no harm us looking around. Come with me after dinner. You might very well find some 'Ion types' there. Or . . . you might once and for all, get out of your mind that there might be even a smidgen of a chance that you might be gay."

"I doubt that there is. I never took baths with my father. I knew how to repulse advances of older boys. Or being groped in a marble quarry."

"Just offering, that's all. Take it or leave it."

They walked along the waterfront with their hands behind their backs. Ion noticed how much taller Stan was. His gait was much longer, too, and that meant that he must have very long legs.

"What would you look like without a beard? Why do you wear one?"

"I have a slight harelip scar. It's hardly noticeable, but I'm sensitive about it. Can't figure out why. You're not the only one with problems. Besides, to shock you, I'll tell you this: some bisexuals like blow jobs from hairy mouths. Makes them think it's a beaver burger. A rationalization, of course."

"Bisexuals. We didn't talk of them. What do you know of them?"

They spotted the Letoites ahead, just beginning to order their dinners. Stan, in a quick aside said, "My experience is that bisexuals are another example of repressed homosexuals. They might live their whole lives that way, frustrated I suspect, because the ones I've had are the greatest lovers. So pent up that getting it off with a guy is like paradise. So, are you coming with me afterwards to the bars?"

"We'll see."

❊   ❊   ❊

This time at the taverna, there was consensus, Ion told them about how delicious the fried smelt were in Greece. A different species from the one in California, smaller and crunchier. Great with eggplant salad and *tarama* caviar. At first, Karen cringed when Ion ate the first one, head, tall and all, with lots of lemon. But they ate dozens, and Paul and Francis ate their share so there was no bickering about the reckoning. Everything got divided evenly and everyone agreed that tomorrow would a great day to spend on the nearby island of Delos, their reason in the first place for coming to Mykonos.

The Letoites were developing cohesion, accepting even Ion's frequent reclusiveness. They were coming to that realization slowly, and they felt proud and protected. Group allegiance was not their normal mode of operation, but here, in this place and time, it fitted well. So well that Ion decided he'd keep Stan company for a nightcap at a bar.

Neither expected great revelations. They were a bit tired, and Stan was pretty spent by the high-jinks of the German boy. As for Ion, what he saw at the gay bar was completely unenlightening. The bar was very dark, the music some kind of Euro-soft rock, and the clientele too busy buzzing among themselves to pay much attention to the older Americans.

Off in a corner, though, sat four middle-aged queens who invited them as fellow Americans to their table. One of them with a green silk ascot said, "Mykonos is not too different from the Castro or Polkstrasse on Halloween really, is it?"

A few yawned at that comment and began to watch a couple of sturdy young boys in lederhosen glide by.

Another queen said, "Well, you'd think, at least, here we'd see a couple of Greek boys in tutus and pom-pom shoes and tassle caps. Oh heck, anyhow."

Ion frowned. "Those would be Evzones. The Royal Guard. You wouldn't expect to see them in this kind of place."

"Where then? Back in the barracks bumping pussies?"

"I'm certain women would not be allowed in the barracks," Ion said.

The queens laughed, and one of them said, "Where did you say you're from, honey?"

Ion turned to Stan seeing him shrug his shoulders and holding back a chortle. "This place is boring," he said. "Let's head back to the harbor."

12
Delos

Delos was to be a high point, and Paul had prepared the Letoites for it. At every chance he had prefaced his erudite travelogues with "when we get to Delos, you'll see . . ."

The next morning at breakfast, they saw the captain arguing with the Harbor Police farther down the dock. Many yachts were moored around, and the island's pelican mascot, Petros, was posing for the tourists' cameras. But the captain was not composed. He was agitated, flailing his arms around, shouting. He slapped his thighs and reboarded the *Leto*.

"Ach, those mule-heads. They say there are few moorings on Delos. We might not be able to dock with all the boats going across. What do you think? They want some drachmas underneath. What shall we do, *thespinis*? Kyrie Ion, what do you say?"

Theodora calmly said, "Let's not worry about it. We can take the public caique. It won't cost much." The Leoites agreed.

"Under the circumstances," Paul huffed, "we'll have to share with the riffraff. There's nothing else for it."

Karen said, "Oh, the depths to which we must sink to acquire the benefits of culture. Suffer, suffer." She took out her phrase book and translated to Takis the Greek word for suffer, *ipofero*. She clutched her heart and pointed out towards Delos. *Pame*, she said, she had heard the captain use it many times.

Takis raised his eyebrows and touched her shoulder. He tried to look sad, and then he tilted his head against clasped hands and smiled. *"Ipno,"* he said. Ion translated, Karen checked it in her phrase book.

"Maybe that's what I should do, sleep away the day." Then she shook her head. "No, I guess not. Let the poor boy sleep. He needs the rest. I really should see Delos, shouldn't I, gang?"

The crossing in a caique holding thirty *atomoi,* was not uneventful, however. Either the Mykonos passengers had shed their gay costumes or were of a different species, they seemed more like serious tourists with backpacks, cameras and bottled water, ready to spend almost an entire day for the excursion.

The thirty-minute crossing once more challenged the sea legs of the Letoites. The caique, like a roller coaster car, rose and fell in endless amplitudes, the passengers bucking the peaks and valleys like rodeo cowboys. Two Catholic nuns gripped their seats with prayerful looks. Several times they vomited delicately into Kleenex tissues which they wrapped in linen handkerchiefs and layered carefully in leather satchels embossed with crosses and acanthus leaves.

They landed at the Sanctuary harbor and began their visit to the Sacred Isle of Apollo. With their maps unfurling in strong gusts, the Letoites began yard by yard their survey. The entire island had an area of only one square mile, but much of it had been excavated. Only broad hints of its importance from the ancient days of Mycenae to the time of Roman conquests remained. The island's base of granite and gneiss resembled a nuked Manhattan. A few pillars and columns stood upright, but mostly outlines only remained, templates of a glorious past—foundations for giant monuments and statues, sanctuaries, exedras, agora, stoas, marble porticos, and an amphitheater.

"Its smallness belies its importance," said Paul as they stood for a few minutes in the shade of one of the five archaic lions carved of Naxian marble. "Geographically, it was the center of the Aegean and certainly it had commercial significance, but it became important because it was sacred and no one dared to attack it. Back then, as we do today, people made pilgrimages here to honor Apollo and Artemis. They celebrated it with athletic games and theater. Homer invented the whole myth, but there you have it. Isn't it amazing?" said Paul spreading his arms around all the rubble. "Shall we begin the prosodion hymn to commemorate Leto's labor pains?"

Stan and Karen rolled their eyes. Theodora smiled sheepishly. Ion merely grimaced. *Paul doing his schtick again,* everyone was thinking.

Theodora said, "I'm trying to imagine all the festivities. It must have been very grand."

Stan said, "It was like Disney Land, Fort Knox, and the Super Bowl all rolled into one."

"Hmm . . . yes," said Paul. "Great beauty was the final results. It speaks, don't you think, to what man can do when his spirituality becomes ignited?"

Frances said, "And it's amazing that we are making pilgrimage to their pilgrimages."

"Justly so," said Karen. She rose and asked the direction of the museum. They could cool off there. Then said, "It's no accident that *we* made the pilgrimage. We travel on the seas with her namesake. Ah, poor Leto! You can imagine that we are rather doing the same thing she was doing. Looking for a place to light, fulfill our destiny perhaps."

"Old Zeus knocked her up, and Hera was out to get her," said Stan. "Here she found a safe place to hatch. And voila, all this springs up. Marvelous story. Love it."

"What are we trying to hatch?" said Ion.

"Oh, Ion," said Theodora. "Don't be so literal," she said in an irritated tone she had never used before on him.

"Good question, nevertheless," said Frances. "One could ask what we are seeking on this journey. And perhaps it's not mere coincidence we travel on a vessel named the *Leto.*"

"Meaningful, meaningful observation," added Paul.

"I thought we were supposed to be just having fun," said Ion.

Now they all stood up and stretched. Dried thistles and reeds hissed in the wind. Rye grass burned imperceptibly in the sun. They could mull over it in the cool Museum, they decided, so they folded their maps and marched towards it.

"I wonder about the logistics of how they transported on their little triremes all the marble from Naxos and Eleussis," said Ion.

"Poseidon pitched them chunks with his Trident. Use your imagination, man," said Stan.

"Miraculous, miraculous," said Paul. "What the ancients could do."

✿ ✿ ✿

An hour and half remained before they would reboard the caique for Mykonos. But after more than four hours playing amateur archaelogists, they were exhausted. In the shade of the museum building, they spread jackets to lunch on what Takis had packed for them.

Afterwards, beginning to drowse, the Delian impresions seeped into their subconscious, but they could not pinpoint its exact form, could not deny that all the fragmented extravagances around them bore a hidden message. It tugged at them, as if some lifeline had been thrown out to them. But they were reticent to catch it. Why? That if they grasped for it, a frightening, all-powerful Divinity would haul them into a reality too incomprehensible, surreal?

No matter from what their reference point, whatever way each reasoned—anthropological, psychological, physico-chemical—the cryptic message was speaking to them about their past and their ancestors. But what to make of it? Here we are now, we know presumably from whence we came, but why we are the way we are, what about the future? How does this place guide us for that? Or does it only predict ultimate decay and hopelessness?"

The cicadas' songs and the cracklings of parched vegatation kept them from deep sleep. They fidgeted, lying on their jackets on gravelly ground, slapping at gnats buzzing around. There was no resolution, the cryptic message only repeated itself over and over, and like trying to wake from a bad dream they'd shift sides, trying to wake into the known.

Finally, Stan jerked himself up in a cold sweat and roused the rest. "I'm thirsty," he said. "This place is spooky."

The water supply from their plastic bottles was depleting, but, without qualm, they passed around the remaining one for each to drink from its lip. The cool water revived them like a sip from a communion cup. One by one, wiping their lips, they lay back down and covered their eyes from the glare. "Someone watch the time," said Theodora.

The other tourists had either departed on earlier caiques—or had expired, they joked, melted down on the granite rocks by the Delian scorch. Somehow, despite their agitations, they felt secure in their suspended states. They had strength in numbers, unified in knowing they were all searching, together, for nebulous past and future, an hour and a half from the real world of Mykonos. All they had to do was wait for the caique.

❂ ❂ ❂

The wind whistled around the edges of the museum. Karen, lying on her jacket and dozing off, began thinking of Leto and her daughter, Artemis, born on this very island. Ah, Artemis, as Paul's mythology book described her, "The tall and the beautiful, of the golden bow and the showering arrow, goddess, huntress, of unstained purity. . . ." Ah, to be her stalking, chasing in the forests with the wild animals. Chasing after *something*.

Love? Well, she couldn't be Artemis. But she was hunting for something. At one time she thought she knew. Her husband was an idyll to intelligence and male beauty. So she thought, but he turned into a yellow-centered flower with white petals. Her fluff dyke could just as well have been one of Artemis' loyal Oceanides who worshiped her and swore to her purity. That turned out all wrong too. Pure sex and pure love got all mixed up, and the Olympians never got it right either.

She began to fan herself, thinking about how hot she was, yet how strange the feeling of the air evaporating her sweat and leaving her almost to shiver. It was like the something she was hunting for, a quite indescribable pleasure keeping her riled and ready. And it pleased her to think that the Olympians had struggled between themselves and with mankind over the dichotomy of sex and love. How luscious that struggle could be!

She turned on her side and looked at Stan lying there mute, saliva dripping from the side of his mouth. Stan, a good guy, not unlike Mel. Strange that she started to think of him now. As an undergraduate, he had courted her and almost won her. She had almost forgotten about Mel, almost twenty years ago. Their families wanted them together, but Mel saw her as someone more than a person to love. She was to be his partner for his lofty ambitions of becoming prominent in business and the Jewish community of Dallas. Nothing wrong with that, but somehow, something was missing.

She tried to remember how she explained it. She remembered the "speech" she gave her parents (it was, in fact, what made her decide to study speech-making and communication).

"Folks, Mel is a platefull of the best gefilte fish gone bad. He bloats me, makes me schmaltz. I need 'purity.'"

So that's where the "purity" thing of Artemi comes in! She grinned to herself. The lusciousness of "purity."

Here in this Greek Light it had come to her, all around her, for every day of the *Leto*'s journey. And when Takis came to her cabin—how clever of him to know when Frances would sneak off to Paul—the abstraction of "something" manifest itself in a sensuality in its purest form, deep and to the core of her being.

He was so good. Without words, his whole body became a communicating machine that spoke to her like she had never been spoken to. She thought and thought about their evenings in the bunk, but she really couldn't identify his particular gestures or her particular responses. It wasn't only the way he could bury his soft-as-lamb's-wool hair in her thighs, the rose petal taste of his lips, the gentle scraping of his beard on her inflamed breasts. There was more, much more, all one seemless unity with that "something." Oh, bliss.

A gnat lighted on her eyelid. She blinked and saw for a moment Theodora lying next to her. She was onto her, she was sure, but how could she try to explain it to her? This passion for Takis? Would she understand? Could she bare her soul to her, would Theodora's psychological compassion help her to understand herself? She owed it to Theodora, she had become fond of the woman, even felt sympathetic for her almost too naive flirtations with Ion. If only she could experience the same passion and free herself from her constant cerebral masturbations. How could she find the right words? She was the expert on communication, there had to be a way.

It will come to her, she thought, the right words and way. *In my sleep perhaps,* she sighed, and she closed her eyes again and tried to drift off. Someone would wake her to catch the caique back to her kouros, who by now was well rested. And ready. And that's what she dreamed of.

❁ ❁ ❁

Only a yard away, Frances shuddered and rose from her reveries for a second and looked around for Paul. He lay beside her. She whispered, "Come with me."

He didn't respond at first, but when she pulled on his hand, he felt her urgency.

She led him to the trail up to Mt. Kynthos, the 370 feet high point of the island. Theodora, through slitted eyes, watched them depart. She was happy for them. They had lost their pinkness. Their skin took on the tones of their khaki shorts and their hair had bleached in the sun. From a distance, they could have been taken for sturdy athletes. They were not cute anymore, they were—that word her mother used to describe complete, shaped, handsome people—*morphosmeni*.

A mission was on Frances's mind. Her uphill pace was resolute and Paul, close behind, marveled at the tensions in her legs. Frances, tawny, had some of the patina of the koure in the museum, and Paul delighted in her smells, the rivulets of sweat pouring off her body. They stopped for breath at the Sacred Cave, the Heraion, and the Shrine of the Syrian gods, where orgiastic mysteries were performed. They embraced, feeling each other's slippery bodies, speechless, but knowing what each was thinking.

At the summit, they held each other's waist and gazed out to the Cycladic spectacle. Below spread Delos, in its heyday, five centuries of human wonder.

Frances waited for Paul to speak, but he didn't. She waited for the propitious moment and waited. She saw him brush his brow and frown.

"What's wrong, *Pavlo*?"

"I don't know, exactly. You know me. I get exalted at such moments. But at this moment, I'm not."

"Are you saturated with the Classic wonders?"

"Perhaps I'm tired."

"Perhaps there is something else. Talk."

They stood against a dilapidated wall, its granite stone amazingly cool in the sun. "I don't know. There's something inside I can't express."

"Is it joy you can't express? Are the goose pimples puckered in?"

He leaned into her shoulder. "No, it's more like sadness."

"For what?"

"Oh, Frances, look down there. Look at that waste. After all those centuries, what's left? It's not beautiful. It's only what we think was beautiful. I wish I didn't know its history. I'd see it only as a lot of rubbish and not moan its decline."

"But we do know. And we know what it has given us today. Certainly, you know the value of studying the Classics."

"To us, in general, yes. To the 'advancement of human knowledge.' That's the party line. But to me, personally? I look at all that and think, what if I had been a Delian? After all is said and done, I'd feel it was all for nought. For *me,* you understand. Death and decay, that's where it all leads. Nothing's permanent. That's all."

"What is this, darling? A Delorama?" She pulled him close to her face. "You miss the point. The point is perpetuation. Think of that."

"Oh, the art, architecture, philosophies, they all march on and evolve. But for me, a Delian, it's a dead end."

Frances took his face in her hands, licked the salt on his cheek. "You are so wonderful to talk to me this way. About yourself and your deep feelings. I'm so happy to share your doubts. I'm so happy you're not a leaden scholar. I'm glad I brought you here to this sacred spot."

"I don't want you to think me a weakling for having self-doubts. I know I cover up so many things. But I'm so grateful . . ."

She didn't let him finish. She slid one hand down his waist and into his khaki shorts. With the other she unzipped him. Quickly, she then put both hands on his smooth, firm little buttocks and freed his genitals to the cooling breeze. He shuddered and pulled down her shorts, dropping to his knees, running his tongue on her pubis. She stepped out of her shorts and pressed herself close.

"Oh, my Zeus," she groaned.

"My Leto, my Leto."

Their salivas and salt mingled all over their sun-scalded bodies. She inserted him and they rocked in quick thrusts of their loins.

"I'll bring you forth an Apollo," she said.

"And I, an Artemis."

"Apollo."

"Artemis."

"Apollo."

"Artemis."

Their knees trembled until finally a mighty simultaneous gush of passion soaked them.

They held each other, and Paul in his imagination thought that the insemination was consecrated to the gods. Frances knew otherwise. Then, under a scrawny cedar, they lay down on their jackets, arms covering their faces.

Finally, she whispered, "I lied to you. I'm not on the pill. It is my fertile time. Don't call me scheming. But I've solved your problem of perpetuity. Procreation, it's the essence of life."

His mouth gaped. He was about to yell, "What?" when from a distance, they heard the horn of the caique in the harbor.

"My god, we've got to run," Frances said. "It's the last boat. There are no overnight accommodations on the island."

They ran down. The horn kept blasting. They yelled "Wait! Wait!" They could see the Letoites on board waving them on. The captain was angry, and just as the crew began to untie the moorings, Paul and Frances leaped on board, Paul's fly still open, Frances's shoe strings undone and her face in ecstasy.

❈ ❈ ❈

After a swim and a quick dinner on the harbor's esplanades of cold, greasy *mousaka,* which they all detested, the Letoites retired to their cabins.

There was no need for the captain to tuck each of them in. In any case, that would be futile because by now, they would not remain tucked in for long. Somewhere about an hour or two after lights were out, Frances would tip-toe across to Paul's cabin. Takis, his sensitive ears picking up every vibration of the wooden boards of the boat, would sneak to Karen's cabin. He remained there only an hour or so, despite the fact that he knew that Frances would return to Karen's cabin at dawn. He would not risk being noticed, and sign language was difficult in the dark.

Theodora, a sound sleeper, thought at times of going up on the deck to gaze at the stars, but she wasn't quite sure if the captain wouldn't see her and misinterpret her motives. Yet, she would try, one of these nights, perhaps when they were on a quieter island where the stars might be brighter.

Only Stan and Ion remained in place, but Stan, that night, stayed a longer time in the W.C. before returning to the cabin he shared with Ion. "What do you think?" Stan said.

"Of what?"

"Look at me. What do you think?"

Ion saw something ghoulish in the dim cabin lamp. Stan's face had a whiteness around his jowls and upper lips. His moustache and beard were gone. His hair and pony tail were dripping wet. He turned on his reading light and asked Stan to come closer.

"Well, at closer inspection—better, much better," Ion said. "You look cleaner. I don't see any hare lip. Keep it that way." He turned off the light and pulled a sheet over himself.

To himself he thought that Stan was not bad looking at all. With a little more grooming, he might even be considered handsome, by someone.

❉   ❉   ❉

Later that night, in Paul's bunk, Frances cuddled up to Paul.

"Are you mad at me?" Frances said.

He whispered in her ear. "I don't know what to make of it. I don't know what a father is. Me? I cannot imagine. Will we call it Apollo or Artemis? We should have consulted the Oracle on Delos."

"Don't worry," she whispered back in his ear. "I may not have conceived. There are such things as abortions."

"How? You know of abortions?"

"I've had one. You need to know more about me. Before we decide."

They hugged more. In the dark, they tried to look into each other's eyes. A light from the quay barely shone through the porthole. What they saw in each other's face was not joy, not sorrow. Only wonderment.

13
Samos

No more quibbling. No more committee meetings. "Reckonings" had smoothed out into the honor system. If the drachmas in the pot were insufficient to pay the restaurant bills, Theodora asked for contributions. Even Ion's aloofness and wry comments went ignored and long-winded discussions about itinerary vaporized. It had taken eleven days for the skittish academics to accept carte blanche the captain's recommendations. No longer was there reason to argue among themselves, from real or false premises, by deductive or inductive reasoning, why they should visit particular islands. No need to question the captain's motivation. He knew his way around, and wherever they went in the Aegean, they knew he'd provide them well with sights and *glendi*—a party among beautiful settings.

Also, it was better to rely on the captain, because, though the Letoites didn't mistrust Theodora, they really did not want to rely on her either. Academic obedience to authority (for how else could they have earned their PhDs?) paradoxically didn't extend to some academics such as the Letoites, who, now independent and on their way up in academe, challenged paradigms and current theories; Theodora, acting as a presumptive leader, simply had to be challenged. That could lead only to more quibbling. To hell with it, they had all subconsciously decided, this was a holiday. So, when the captain stepped in as arbiter they felt freed, and, thankfully, Theodora most of all was the happiest for it. She could relax and work more effectively on the goals set in her Addenda.

For all those reasons, when the captain said the next morning, "We go to the Dodecanese, to a green island," everyone acquiesced. He commanded them to find provisions in the markets of Mykonos—beer, wine, snacks and fruit—while he and Takis went off to refuel the diesels and the electric generator.

It was to be about a seven hour sail, and the captain had plotted his course by the usual Greek way, by the seat of his *pantalonia*. The Aegean overnight had become silvery smooth, and the farther east they progressed towards Turkey ("No!" he shouted. "Not Turkey. Ionia. It was Greek and will always be.") the more placid the settings. Colors in a haze became more pastel, the blues more like a Maxwell Parrish painting.

The Letoites lolled. Ion and Stan studied marine maps. They wondered why the captain hardly ever consulted them. He told them, "I know the waters. I know depths near the cliffs. How do you think the Ancients knew? No sonar devices, sextons, no anemometers, no radio. We have all that on this ship, but we don't need them. The radio, yes, but I, like the Ancients, read the eddies."

Eddies? thought Stan and Ion. *No wonder Odysseus got lost.*

In the engine room, they watched Takis lubricating and polishing. He bounced around singing a ballad:

Samos maiden, Samos maiden,
when will I go to Samos.

Roses I'll throw on the beach
Rose blooms on the sand.

And on the boat you'll be going on,
I'll set my golden sails

And rich golden oars, Samos maiden,
so I can come take you.

Ion had heard the love song before, but Takis' rendition sounded particularly moving. The boy leered, smirked and winced, and it was true, as Ion had heard from his father, that the island of Samos had a reputation for beautiful girls. He told Stan about it, but Stan said, "Will the boys swim out to meet us?"

Frances, Paul, and Karen read, did laundry, and dozed.

Theodora played *koltsina* with the captain while Ion and Stan took the wheel. After the captain's seven consecutive winning hands, Theodora threw the cards in his face. He guffawed. She rose to get a beer in the galley, and as she passed by him, he gave her a little whack on the butt.

She took no umbrage. It was something Sammy might have done, and after all, they were in Greece where a *levendes,* a handsome and brave man, might have that right. Provided she regarded him so, which, without any contrary evidence, she could grant.

In the afternoon, the diesels humming softly and the *Leto* slicing through blue mirrors, Theodora retired to her cabin and her Addenda. Behind a locked door, she opened her notebook and tried to read what she had written. She stared at her scribbles, unable to piece them together. They were dry and pedantic, filled with ifs and peripherals. She turned to an empty page, beginning to fill it with other ramblings, about how her enthusiasm for her plans was waning. Why? She made a list—one by one, of each of the Letoites of their behaviors, predictable and unpredictable, the loose variables of the crew and their impact on the rest of them, the serendipitous events, the Ios party, seasicknesses, the sexual shenanigans of some. Whatever it was, the sum effect on her, she concluded, was an inexplicable feeling of—(shock) disinterest!

Why? She scribbled frantically. This was not normal. Failure of her research protocols ordinarily motivated her. This, however, was not altogether a defeat. Paul and Frances had proceeded to plan, Stan was behaving accordingly, even though Karen had introduced a chaotic element.

Then, clunk, there was Ion. He was the cause, like a fire extinguisher smothering her vim. Why was he so incorrigible? Her panderings and gentle coaxings had been rebuffed, not with hostility, true, but with a gentle disdain. She couldn't even discern what his likes and dislikes were in food and drink, what causes he espoused or renounced. He was, by all her descriptions of his behavior, unreactive. He was stone, *petra*.

Without one-way glass to observe continuously her experimental subject, without the "therapeutic atmosphere" of her office, without the reinforcing props, the "field testing" of her operant conditioning model was failing. Now she was beginning to admit it. To make matters worse, Ion's condescensions towards her had built him a Thermopylean defense. He was unassailable, remote from everyone, more interested in talking Greek with the captain, and with fisherman and shopkeepers at harbors.

One of the protocols in her Addenda, written down in the earlier pages, was to break down his defenses by being more Greek herself. She worked on improving her Greek, and she befriended, flirted a little even, with the captain to show Ion how wholly Greek she was, how desirable she might be as a life's companion. That didn't work either. (Whether the captain was aware of what she was doing, she wasn't certain.)

Another doubt rose to her conscious thoughts. This was something between the lines of the Addenda. Something she had better address immediately. Now it came to her, the source of this vague feeling of disinterest. Was it really right for her to use her ideas of operant conditioning on something so personal? Was there too much bias in the experimental design? It was one thing to help her patients and counselees overcome some of life's irritants, but wasn't it brazen to extrapolate those techniques to—could she dare use the words?—trap a mate? Who, in fact, was the therapist, who the counselee?

This really alarmed her. Was she becoming—oh God, a sociopath? Was she that desperate, that frustrated in her life?

She let the words flow onto the page. Then, she lay down to think. Forget all the psychological theories. Forget about professional goals. *Think, think,* she kept telling herself, *about ME, what I wanted.* Her science was too soft, no matter that she would like it to be hard like chemistry where experiments could be performed with reasonable predictability. What she wanted perhaps could not be designed. It had to be felt, not intellectualized. Oh, that old dichotomy again about the nature of man, the split between the rational and the sensual, the right/left side. What to do? Which road? Or was her life to be some undiscovered palindrome, a two-way street, leading nowhere?

She was about to close the book when in a flash she wrote, "All I want is to get get close to Ion."

She hesitated zipping up the notebook. Really? Was that it?

And that was another factor in her faltering determination. When she was selecting people for the cruise, his University picture was like a pin-up, a beautiful male hunk. In the flesh, that first evening in California, he was even more alluring. But now, after eleven days of living with his nonchalance and grumpiness and the strong Greek Light, Adonis was growing pimples. She'd look at him and think that immobile, yes, he would photograph well for a men's fashion magazine. Then as soon as he moved a little, facial muscles breaking alabaster smoothness, eyes wrinkling, skin ruffling and sun-blistering, his godliness vanished. Just another man.

She wrote all those thoughts down and then admitted to herself that regardless—from a scientific viewpoint—she still wanted to know what made him tick.

Only one person seemed to have penetrated his defenses. That was Stan. There was that night when the two seemed to be in a tete-a-tete at the Venetian Quarter in Mykonos. From the taverna, she could see their heads bent in the dim lighting of their table on the quay, and she saw Ion shrugging his shoulders, sometimes gesturing with his hands. What were they talking about? Knowing Stan, he was probably teasing him about something.

What? Ion only wanted to be left alone. He actually wasn't annoying anyone. Obviously, Stan wanted something from Ion, but Ion's tense and stiff body language intimated a rejection.

Of what? She flashed for a second. She knew, of course, that Stan was openly gay. Was he putting the make on Ion? And was Ion rejecting him?

Or only hesitating? *Oh no,* she thought. She knew Ion didn't go that way. The grapevine told her. There was the woman in New York, what's her name? Sonja. There was someone else.

Well, in any case, she had to change tactics. She began to write furiously. When experiments fail, the hypotheses must be restructured. The notion that Ion was a gentle and passive person, a little pusillanimous, and therefore not amenable to overt advances could be wrong—an illusion of deeper pinings. Perhaps, in fact, he was the aggressive type, the type slow to arouse, the type responsive only to strong stimuli. Some of her counselees were like that. She couldn't lead them to drink, but if she shoved their faces in it, they would drink copiously and gratefully.

She knew how to play that game; in a way, she had been doing it with the captain, and look how reactive he was. Conclusion: Don't be delicate. Forget subtitles. Make the connection. Boldly. That was it. She recorded all that, and closed her Addenda.

✿   ✿   ✿

They made port late in the afternoon at the town of Pythagorio, a small port very un-Cycladic with tile roofs and umber and ochre buildings. The captain directed them to a pebbly beach and after the swim, walking back, Ion said, "Theodora, I want to talk to you about something."

Ah, she thought. *Eleven days of kowtowing to him had made no impression on him.* Now, he was responding, wanted to talk, perhaps wanted to start a "meaningful relationship," a euphemism she detested.

Over dinner, Paul, leading the conversation, talked about Samos' history about Polycrates and Eupalinos, and about the island's intrigues with ancient Athens. Theodora wasn't paying much attention. Sitting at the end of the table, she kept her head turned mostly away from Paul and towards Ion sitting beside her. And she waited and waited. Finally, settling up the reckoning, they began to walk back to the *Leto*.

Ion, beside her, said, "Theodora, do you realize that Pythagoras, who was a Samian, and that he and Euclid set back the advancement of Greek science?"

"Is that so?" she said, not realizing the bathos in her tone.

"They had no concept of infinity. Zeno had confused them with his paradoxes and Aristotle took the bait. As a consequence, they couldn't begin to think of things such as rates and acceleration. Space and time became static. Can you imagine doing chemistry without thinking of rates of reactions?"

"You need the calculus for that," Theodora said.

"Why, of course! Why didn't they see that?"

Theodora gritted her teeth, and said nothing.

"We had to wait until the seventeenth century and Newton and Leibniz," Ion said.

"Well, we couldn't expect the ancient Greeks to do everything, now could we? said Theodora.

"It was in their grasp. They could have listened to Plato more and his ideas of the transcendental. Think about it."

With that, Ion crossed the gangplank, leaving Theodora to cross alone. But the captain quickly came to her aid, taking her arm and letting her light on the deck effortlessly. She went straight to her cabin, slightly exhilarated. It wasn't exactly an intimate conversation with Ion, but for the first time, the very first, he had initiated a conversation with her. *Malista, yes,* she thought. *It was time to make the bold move, the connection, the* sinthesis, *the tying together as the Greeks would say. Po, po,* her Greek was improving so!

※　　※　　※

The captain hired them two taxis for the next day, and they toured the island, seeing its lush pine and chestnut forests, vineyards, high mountains and the archeological sites, the giant Temple of Hera, and the ancient theater and aqueduct.

Ion took Paul and Frances in a taxi, Theodora took Karen and Stan. The drivers were very accommodating, and the other Letoites marveled at the rapport Ion and Theodora had with them. "What do you expect?" said Ion. "We're Greek, aren't we?"

Theodora, though, made a deeper association. During the whole day, she found herself being less the Experimental Psychologist, less the titular head of the Letoites, and more a Greek tourist who had returned at last to her homeland. The feeling surprised her, even though it was her first trip to Greece. Perhaps it had to do with her thoughts of her family, perhaps she wanted to be more Greek, to be more like Ion. Whatever it was, it made her think more about those mysterious intangibles of human behaviour. When the driver, Savas, spoke to her— "Look there, *thespinis,* that village on the mountainside, do you see the house with a balcony under the *platano* tree? That is my ancestral home." And her first thought was, *"Why, yes, it could be mine, too.*

She felt as if she had been here before in a—how ridiculous—previous life. Was it because her folks, from the nearby island of Chios, had spoken so often of their lives on the Greek soil? The olive presses, the orchards, the smell of wild herbs, they were all here, just the way they had talked of them. It was language, too. The intimacy in Savas' tone warmed her. "We live as best we can here in Samos, *thespinis.* God willing. What else can we do? The sea and the sky. Ah, our grapes, our oil. Why don't you come back to Greece where you belong? What a curse. So many Greeks leave, they all want to come back, and they wait too long. They die in foreign lands. Their bones should dissolve in their native soil. *Po, po, po.* Don't let that happen to you, *Thespinis.* Two months, you speak Greek as well as me. I swear to you. Come, get the group. I want to show you my cousin's goat herd. The angels tune their bells."

Near the high point of the island, 4,700 feet Mt. Kerketeas, they could look off to the nearby island of Icaria, named for Icarus, and she felt that she, too, could soar infinitely. Everything from that vantage point made everything in life crystal clear, and all around her was this nurturing panoply. *Ellas* had reclaimed her, and her identity had fused with the One of Parmenides.

She couldn't shake the mystical feeling. All day long, she hardly spoke to Stan and Karen, she gaped and ogled, from time to time lifting her shoulders, shivering. She belonged to this place, this centuries-old place, haunted by history and ideals. Then Savas would speak and she'd have to translate to Stan and Karen, and for a brief second, she'd return from her reveries and wonder whether she was succumbing to pre-menstrual cramps. Again, she'd return to her *fantasias,* and back and forth, all day long, she alternated those *schizo* moods.

So it was that at the end of the day, when they gathered at a little café where two by two they sat at three round tables, she sat herself with Ion, and shared their experiences with the taxis.

"My driver, *Sokratis* was a keen man," said Ion. "Got along well with him. He is a high-school teacher and in the summer is a guide for tourists. Knew lots about Pythagoras. One-upped Paul, believe it or not. Would like to have spent more time with him. How about yours?"

She could not relate her deep feelings about the day. It would require too many words, and Ion did not like too many words. Instead, she began to talk of the aqueduct.

"The Ancients, regardless of what we were saying about Pythagoras, had stupendous engineering skills. Can you imagine how Eupalinos was able to dig that tunnel through the mountain, coming from opposite sides, yet meeting in the middle? Can you figure how they made that connection?"

Ion pondered a moment and said, "Yes, a real accomplishment. I'll have to think about it. Maybe some scholar has figured it out."

They were quiet for a while, pensive, thinking of the tunnel, Ion about the calculations, Theodora about the moment the connection was breeched. Then, Theodora began to think about how today Ion had been more communicative than usual. They both obviously seemed relaxed. The time had come.

They were drinking *frappes,* foamed iced coffee. *Sotto voce,* so the others at their tables would not hear, she said, "I may have asked you this before, but do you plan ever to get married, Ion?"

Ion, lifted his head, looked around stiffly and said, "Probably, some day."

"And have children?"
"Probably."
"Why?"

Ion was taken back with her bluntness. He half-laughed and said, "Because my parents want grandchildren."

"What about *you*?" she said.

He looked at her quickly and then away and said nothing.

"I know why I want children," she said. Her tone was different from the one she had used with him before. It was didactic.

"Because we Greeks believe in family and continuity. We have a conceit about it. I do and so do you. Our bloodlines go way back and must continue to go on. Don't you know that, being here in Greece? Don't you see your importance?"

"To prove every Greek's importance would be a daunting task."

The antithesis. She had learned to expect it from him. "I'm speaking of *you*. You are a man of accomplishment. So would your children. It's your duty, don't you see?"

"Duty to have little Nobelers? It doesn't work that easily. I haven't control of that," he said. "It's a matter of chance. How those genes line up on the meiotic plane and how much chromosomal crossover occurs after fertilization. I can't take the responsibility."

"Well, I will, and let's not get bogged down on probability theory here. You can be willy-nilly about it but I'm not. Look me in the eye, Ion."

She grabbed his arm and held it tight to the table.

"I'll be to the point. I'll be logical and you weigh what I say carefully. *We* should get married. To each other, I mean."

Ion's eyes opened wide, his pupils dilated. He froze.

"Our families married that way. Choices were made. Marriages were arranged. Some were just expedient, but most of the time, they hoped, were for the long-term good of the gene pool. We needn't start a marriage with sacrosanct ideas of romantic love. We must examine only the logic of it. You understand?"

He could not believe his ears. The audacity! "What a logic?" he almost shouted.

Theodora stayed her course. There was no flinching now. "That we are both pure Greeks. Look at our physiognomy. Olive-skinned, black-haired, strong profiles, not a hint of the Slavic or God forbid, Turkish. Our ancestors practiced no out-breeding. They stayed within themselves. None of that hybrid vigour stuff. You follow me?"

He gave a slight nod, an incredulous one.

"And all the other determinants. Shall I list them? Age, educational level, professional positions in nearby institutions, no health problems, inquisitive minds, clean personal habits, no obvious psychopathies, no closet skeletons, a common background in chemistry, same religion, and a love of Greece. What matchmaker wouldn't see the compatibility?"

Ion stammered. "I . . . I . . . I can't abruptly start living with a stranger."

"I'm not a stranger. I'd be a stranger to your bed, that's all."

"That a humungous factor. I don't hop into bed with anyone."

"You mean 'desire' is lacking. That's a trivial matter. I've done marriage counseling. All that sexual electricity gets short-circuited very soon in newlyweds. Compatibility is the dominant factor. The sex can follow or not. And, sometimes it starts meaningfully at zero and accelerates with time. Those things we can't predict initially. But I earnestly believe that I, myself, can handle the sexual foment. Leave it to me, I'm a trained behaviorist. And think how delighted your family would be. You, married at last, to a good Greek girl. Back in the fold. You'd have status, a support community, and a sense of belonging. Life would be so much easier with a partner. You wouldn't have to be the odd man out at faculty socials. And an academic wife at that. Think what weight that would carry with your colleagues. All you have to do is (a) be your natural Greek self, (b) zip up your pants around cute coeds, and (c) enjoy my cooking." She grinned wide, a little twitch returning to her lips.

They stared at each other. He winced, she had the confident look of Athene meteing out justice.

Finally, she said, "That's not asking too much of you, is it? What do you say?"

Ion folded his hands in his lap and looked at the remains of his frappe. The foam on the side of the glass was drying to an ugly smudge. Sonja had physically seduced him by putting her hands in his pocket walking down the cold sidewalks of New York. She snaked her hand around his cock and before he knew it they would be in the sack at her apartment. But this seduction of Theodora's was another thing. It was an intellectual coercion. His eyes were wide open, there was complete awareness. And yet, he could find no way to answer her. He stared at her as if she were insane, frowning, his lips quivering to find the words. But every time he was about to say something, the membranes of all his neurons locked tight all their ionic gates. No electricity could flow, no thought could emerge. Her logic had with one fell swoop mummified his brain, stopping all protests dead in their tracks.

She held him in her vise for what seemed an interminable time. He searched the sky for an escape, but her hypnotic gaze brought him back to her.

Finally, bending forward, holding his forehead, he struggled to say, "I'll talk to Stan about this." Abruptly, he rose from the table and walked towards the interior of the town.

✻   ✻   ✻

He had to get away from that woman. The unmitigated gall. She was worse than those old maid aunts back home who were always demanding attention and favors. How he hated them, how, even when he was adult, they'd kiss him on the cheek with wide open, drooling mouths. "My darling little Ion, my sweetie." They'd exclaim and clutch him to their bosoms. And all he could think of were oozing vulvas.

He kept walking, past shops and people milling around, gossiping, and talking—loud. Greeks were always loud, flailing arms, and unless you understood the language you'd think the men were about to fist fight, and the women, screeching at each other so that even simple declarations like, "My son didn't come home for lunch," sounded like a murder scene.

He felt his mouth tighten more and more. *Get away from that woman!*

He turned a corner and found silence. Along a row of tables, a group of men stood watching older men playing backgammon. Everyone's focus was on the boards, and the only sound came from inside a nearby coffee shop where a strange sounding harp softly strummed.

Ion entered the shop and ordered a Fanta lemonade. The young man playing the small three stringed instrument, a *lyra,* sat motionless, legs crossed. He picked at each string as if he were making intricate dissections, and he'd occasionally turn his head and smile at his harmonies. Ion observed him, thinking that he had rarely seen such concentration. It was if Pythagoras himself was just now discovering the mathematics of string lengths and concords. Only the night before, he had been reading Schrodinger's discussions of Pythagoras' mathematical contributions to western civilization. Out the door, a similar scene was being played out, men concentrating on backgammon, calculating geometric movements of chips on the board and probabilities.

Ion felt relieved, away from Theodora's craziness, bathed now in reason, washed clean of sexual threats. *This* was the sublime world he belonged to, not the sneaky, sensual world of Theodora and Stan. Here were people basking in pure reason, the clicking of the chips on the backgammon boards and the plucking of the *lyra's* string resonating pure harmonies in the brain, simple, straightforward pleasures. Intellectual. No sordid, lubricious things. Numbers produce harmonies.

There was no talking, and that, too was a relief from the loud Greeks around the corner. But that seemed to be how everything was registering with him on this trip—that startling contrast between opposites, cacophonies and silence, the starkness of the landscapes and the opulence of the churches. The colors, so vivid that they, in themselves, not buildings, flowers, sea, or sky, were the only primacy.

He had never quite felt something like this before. This strange union, this *synthesis*, this tying together. Yet, at the same time, this strange feeling of being disjointed from this world. This need to—what was it?—to elevate himself above the humdrum. Inexplicable. To ascend to a reality of pure thought.

The silence broke. "Eh, Kyrie Ion, here I find you."

It was Sokratis, the taxi man, clapping him hard on the shoulder and shaking his hand. "I'm glad to find you here. This is the real Samos. *Ella,* let me buy you a drink. A little *ouzaki*?"

Sokratis was Ion's father's age, but there were big differences. This man was not a café owner, he read books, taught in a *gymnasion,* and knew classical Greek history. And unlike his father, this man, Ion easily discerned, was a man at peace, somehow integrated into his surroundings. Moustached, reeking of tobacco and the smell of the woods and marble dust, just a little scruffy, he seemed too proud ever to wait on customers or tourists. He could have been Pythagoras himself, so self-assured, so admirable.

Everyone knew him. They came around to greet him, and Sokratis, in turn introduced Ion to them. Ion felt even more relieved. Away from the *Leto.* Here is where he belonged. Surrounded by human warmth and reason.

Conversations were about weather, fishing, relatives in America. Then all had another ouzaki.

"Your friend, the little American, he's educated, eh?" said Sokratis. "Wanted to know all about Pythagoras. You know, my friend, we have to laugh about the tourists and Pythagoras. He lived here five hundred years before Christ, and people come here as they expect to find the house he was born in and the very spot where he invented the so-called *theoria*. Not that easy. They need to look for something else."

"What? Other triangles?" said Ion.

"You joke. There are no other triangles. Triangles are triangles, sizes are only different. You mean, perhaps, the transcendental ones? Let's not get into the Einstein ideas. Tourists need to know the real history. Pythagoras spent most of his productive life in southern Italy. And, he left no writings. What we know of him is all secondary sources. They contradict themselves, too. He appreciated mathematics, but probably made no mathematical discoveries himself. His disciples, the Pythagoreans were his most important contribution."

"And who were they?" Ion said.

"We need to go to the scholars. Names you have never heard of. But this is what must be remembered: Pythagoras was a *polymathitikos,* knew and theorized about many things, not just mathematics. He believed in *metempsychosis*, the idea that the soul is reborn in other humans or animal and maxims, *acusmata,* things heard, and *symbola*, things to be interpreted. He and his disciples told people how they should live; they should not eat beans, put on the right shoe first, never sacrifice a white cock, and never bathe in public baths. Of course, his disciples also proclaimed that the natural world possessed pleasing mathematical relationships. What I'm telling you is that Pythagoras was not a simple, pure mathematician. He had cosmological notions, and his moral teachings, or rather his Pythagorean successors, made him a preceder of Socrates—Ha! My name—and Christ. Think about it: could his ideas have stimulated Plato to the invention of monotheism and the invention of Christianity?

Now, what do you say? Here in Samos, all those ideas originated in a man twenty-five hundred years ago? How does it affect you?"

Ion rubbed his lips. "Perhaps he tried to make too many *synapsis*. All things interrelated, philosophy, mathematics, faith, morality. I cannot comprehend . . ."

"Of course, who can? But why not try, my man? It's what makes life beautiful. To reach for the big view, the search for the beyond. *Oneirologia,* the interpretation and understanding of our dreams—I mean our hopes and fantasies, dreams, inspirations could be expressed by a mathematical formula. No, it could never happen. Thankful be to God. Our human brains are too full of potentials to reach out to the great beyond where absolutes and meanings beckon. The eternal search. How stupendous!"

"You mean we should play at those Pythagorean maxims? What does it gain us?"

"For example. Think of this. I'm Pythagoras re-born, named Socrates in the present. Socrates, no doubt, adapted Pythagorean ideas. Anyhow, I feel actually that I am Pythagoras. I think like him. I have worldly views and take great pleasure in theorizing about the unknowns. He is in me and I'm his extension. It's the nature of life. Just as your children are an extension of you. You have children, of course."

Ion bit his lip. *Goddamn. Theodora again.* "No, does that mean Pythagoras would dismiss me because I have not begat children the way I should have according to his maxims."

"You will yet, my son. You will. Merely leave yourself open to nature. Your name is Ion? A famous philosopher on the island of Chios was a Pythagorean. His name was Ion. Who knows? Maybe he's reborn in you? And isn't there a woman in your life?"

Ion flinched. All this time, all he was doing was trying to get away from Theodora's craziness. Now this!

He stumbled back to the *Leto* to prepare himself for dinner, prepare himself for another frontal assault from Theodora. He knew what he'd do though. He'd hide behind Stan and let his acerbity disarm her.

14
Kos

After the harsh brilliance of the Cyclades, the Letoites, in the soft effulgence of a Samos evening, sat in the cool air of an outdoor *estiatorion* dining on roast chicken and okra. The elements of Empedocles lay subsumed and unperturbed by sweet melons and wine, and no one dared to disturb the tranquility. After melons and sweet Samian wine the unperturbed elements of Empedocles—earth, air, water and fire—conjoined in tranquil harmony. And Ion felt no pain and Stan was in good form, telling amusing stories about pygmies and gypsies.

Nor was Ion going to be disquieted by Theodora's absurd propositions. She made them sound like edicts. But now, he had calmed himself, realizing that despite all her logic she had no authority over him. And despite Sokratis' blatherings urging him to fatherhood, as one Greek to another, noblesse oblige, he could respect Theodora's wishes, but not necessarily bend to them. Forget Pythagorean maxims. When and if the time came, he might discuss the issue with Stan, but this evening was too sublime for serious talk. He sat and listened to the owls, and somewhere around him he heard vaguely the Letoites discussing tomorrow's early departure for Kos.

❖ ❖ ❖

They glided to Kos and spent half of the day exploring the terraces of the Asklepion, the ruins of the ancient medical school and clinics of Hippocrates. They sat under the forty-five foot diameter plane tree where Hippocrates allegedly had lectured and heard Paul read historical accounts of the early beginnings of medical science:

> Wherever a doctor cannot do good, he must be kept from doing harm.

Ion watched Theodora's expression to see if the aphorism had registered on her. With her patients, clients, counselees—whatever she called them—he wondered whether she shouldn't heed that advice and keep her pointy nose out of other people's affairs.

The rest of the Letoites began talking of Hippocrates, and Ion quietly listened, taking everything in. They talked about how before Hippocrates, people's illnesses were the results of demons and they could only be exorcised by shamans, weird sacrificial offerings, and mythical gods. "A most unsavory state of affairs," said Paul.

And for the first time in recorded history, diseases in Kos were actually looked at. Gout, for example, was characterized by certain symptoms and as Theodora pointed out, personality types and psychological disorders were classified by four types, analogous to the four elements of nature described by Empedocles. And the oath, of course, was a well thought out ethical basis for medical practice.

"Truly wondrous," exuded Paul, "this almost sudden flowering of science. Why, it leads, you must all know, to the most fundamental tenet of science."

Stan smirked at Ion and baited Paul. "Ah, Professor, and what would that be?"

Karen took a deep breath, and lifted her bosom to the sky, waiting for the distinguished Professor's pronouncement.

A flock of sparrows in the giant plane tree tweeted as the wind rustled leaves. A luscious cool zephyr brushed by the Letoites tanned skins. And Frances, tilting her head toward Paul, said in a sweet voice, "Yes, yes, darling, tell us, tell us."

"It is obvious, isn't it?" asked Paul. "Scientific observation," shouted. "Obsevation, first. We all take that for granted now in the so-called scientific method. That's where we must start, data gathering, before all the hypothesizing and theorizing begin. Hail 'observations'."

They all applauded. Except Ion, thinking of Schrodinger again, that the profoundness of the idea of observation was a sacrosanct concept and should not be theatrically ridiculed. But what could he expect from these Letoites, these so-called scientist-scholars?

He looked around him, saw the archaeological site not as a tourist attraction, but as a giant ancient clinical laboratory. He tried to imagine how on these hard marbles, physicians and their assistants would scurry around, making observations, discussing with colleagues how their observations would concur, how they would proceed with treatments and concoct poultices. And always, the beginning was observation. Such a simple concept, it seemed to him. But he tried to imagine how revolutionary it was back then. It had to lead to a whole new way of looking at life. That individuals are not victims of nature or the gods, that they could take command of their world, manipulate it to their advantage, improve the quality of their lives. Simply by making observations. Observing first would put the human brain on a track to logical outcomes, lead him to places that would innately lead to enhancements of his being.

Observation. One's own observations (or at least corroboration of others') would negate anyone's enticements and collusions. First, personal observations had to be made and evaluated. No extraneous distractions from pure cerebral processes. Following along that way, no stupidities or regrets would ever torture an individual. He would always be conscious of choices and no delusions would ever arise.

So simple. Yet so profound. He must remember that always. Not let the seductions of Sonja and Theodora lead him astray from the simple visual commandment.

✿   ✿   ✿

By now the Letoites, cooled and refreshed, began gathering themselves for the walk back to the harbor. There they reboarded and sailed a few miles down to the coast to Tangaki, a small fishing village with a fine beach. They dropped anchor in the bay and swam ashore, all except Theodora. Later in the afternoon, in the skiff, the captain and Takis brought Theodora to a fish taverna where they were to have supper.

They selected *astakos* lobster for supper, preceded by *mezes* of broiled octopus. Karen ate heartily, her squeamish stomach calmed apparently by the presence of Takis, who popped tentacles in her mouth, hunks of them, suckers and all.

They sat at a large table on a concrete apron by the taverna covered by bamboo. Observing them in the shade, Ion saw his shipmates differently that night. They seemed very different. He was observing them now very objectively. These were not Californian professors anymore. They were a dark breed of people, all barefooted. They all wore some white and some had lips smeared with zinc oxide, and the contrast to their dark skins made them look vaudevillian. They were loud, talking all at once, drinking lots of beer, saying nothing of importance. Only that life was good.

He preferred to watch the other boats in the harbor and the wind surfers, but before the sun went down, he began to observe their feet. They were covered with sand and made gritty sounds on the concrete. They made him bristle, and he began to study them.

They were of different types. The women's were not only smaller but the toes, proportionally, were tinier. Karen had red nail polish and the way she crossed and uncrossed her legs frequently made her feet seem like a bunch of bobbing little corks. Theodora's were delicate, thin boned, the skin taut like fine-fitted gloves. Frances' were a little stubby, child-like. The captain's were enormous, and black strings adorned their dorsal aspect. Takis', on the other hand, were sleek and muscular with toes that looked like they might be prehensile. He curled and uncurled them often. Hardly noticeable was their flaw: the underside was heavily padded because Takis on board never wore shoes.

Another thing he noticed, Takis' toes curled from time to time over Karen's, and one of Paul's feet and one of Frances' fused under the table, one on top of the other.

All feet were dark, as dark as their arms and faces, except Stan's.

His were curious. Ion didn't know quite what to make of them. They were long, as expected, but they didn't match the color of his face which was, after only being recently shaved, red. His feet were prettier than his face, and though they moved from time to time, they had a steadfast honest look, feet that made a statement about the one to whom they belonged.

Fruit and *gravieri* cheese ended their meal and the captain announced that tomorrow they would head north to the island of Patmos, "An island every Christian must visit." The island of St. John the Divine, everyone knew of it, and everyone was enthusiastic. The skiff made two round-trips to get everyone back on board for an early bed and a long sail the next day.

❂   ❂   ❂

The *Leto* sat on the dark bay gently rocking to the occasional wash of other yachts passing and gentle swells of the sea.

The only light coming through the portholes of Stan's and Ion's cabin was coming from a buoy about thirty feet from them. The lapping sea caressed the *Leto,* and Ion expected he would doze off immediately.

In the lower bunk, though, he observed that one of Stan's legs had dangled over the side of his bunk above. The cabin was stuffy, probably because the still air had not dissipated the heat from the engine room. Ion lay naked and he thought Stan did too. Stan had probably spread his legs out for cooling, just as Ion had, and one of Stan's feet in his sleep had drooped down above Ion's bunk.

It was not an annoyance. Ion, instead of dozing off, became amused at the small oscillations the foot would make when the boat rocked sporadically. He had never seen a foot dangling quite that way. The closest approximation to it was perhaps his own foot when the doctor had him on the edge of an examining table performing the hammer reflex tests. His feet would jerk, and he remembered why he might have over-reacted to the taps because of how he dreaded what was to come, the insertion of the doctor's fingers up his anus to palpate the prostate.

In the semi-darkness, he couldn't make out any sores or blisters on the foot. It seemed a thing quite self-possessed and confident of its form. No matter the translational forces applied, whether the vectors were two dimensional or three, whether the foot swung or swirled, it maintained its integrity. It just hung there, a thing suspended, a thing that clamored for recognition.

Ion raised himself to his elbows to study it more. He tried to remember the anatomical names. The tarsus, calcaneus, tarsals, metatarsals, phalanges. They were all in there, barely outlined by a smooth epidermis like polished light tan leather. The nails seemed pearly, even opalescent in the diffuse light. He wondered whether they had been manicured that way so they could protrude handsomely from a Gucci sandal in a fashion magazine.

Sometimes, with a stronger swell in the bay, the foot became more pendulous, and its motion could not be so easily described. Its gross motion, and all its little recoiling motions, its fractals, appeared chaotic. He suspected that all its traverses could not be easily mapped or mathematically defined, and it seemed as if it was responding to some internal drummer with a mind of its own. When the boat lurched sometimes, it hardly reacted at all, yet at other times it seemed to fling itself around almost spontaneously. All that made it even more appealing to Ion. He wanted to observe it, understand it, possess it, figure it out; but that would be impossible, of course. However, he could admire it.

More and more, it became enthralling. He sat fully up on his bunk. He put his face up close to it, tried to feel its heat. It smelled of sea sand and wood decking, of lime and resin. He liked that, and he liked that it wasn't sheathed in white athletic socks which would create a totally different illusion. Naked, it showed all its true character, unadorned by artifact and pretension. Then he strained to see it up closer, and he imagined he might have seen tiny violet vessels near the heel. On the arch he saw a whiteness, as if someone, (Narcissus?) had dusted it with talc.

Then, he noticed another amazing thing. At that close vantage point, he thought he could perceive tiny twinges in the minuscule muscles on the lateral surfaces, as if the whole thing was quivering, ever so slightly—proof of its livingness, proof of its willingness to respond to anything and everything around it.

Then he leaned against the bulwark and tried to compose its image in a different way. He had realized it, subconsciously at first, that it was in reality a piece of art. Not a Rodin piece like those statues at the Stanford Museum. It was not a Romantic object either. It was part of something more bold and real—yes, that was it, it was the carefully construed foundation of a Greek statuary or a model for one, for the bronze foot of

Poseidon, Hermes with the infant Dionysos, a foot supporting a mass, an extension of something above it of great beauty. But like the feet of great statuary, its form fitting its function, it was posed for whatever demand would be made of it—for the impetus to the thrust of a bolt of lighting, a trident, or a discus.

He studied its tensions, how the cabling of all the sinews linked to what surely was a massive source of energy above it. The mighty Achilles tendon lay suspended there, guy wire to the living force, its clean lines a marvel of engineering.

And what if he tickled it? Could he induce perhaps a subliminal response that would preclude an ecstatic motion? Something short of a orgiastic contraction that would ripple the whole apparatus, the whole being and essence of the thing and the thing to what it was attached? Just a little tickle, a little preview of its potential. That would be all.

With his little finger he feather-touched the arch as if it were a butterfly and lo! The big toe curled, ever so slightly. He repeated it, each time the stimuli summating until all the toes, Babinski-like, folded in. Wow. He mustn't go too far.

He desisted for a while. Waited to see what the rest of the foot would do. It continued its gentle oscillations, its slight quivering, and he leaned back again to observe it from a distance. The *Leto* had circled around slightly from its anchoring and now the buoy light projected a shadow of the foot on passageway's wall. The shadow image, magnified, clearly showed a vibration, the pulsations of the foot at rest and the foot in motion. He could play a game of shadow puppets and watch, as he teased and tickled its arch, how the foot could at one moment be a dinosaur at rest, the next a dolphin breaking the ocean's surface in a mighty plunge.

But he must be careful. He mustn't disturb it too much. Leave a sleeping satyr be. Now his eyes were wide open. What other game to play?

He put his face closer to it again, and blew on the bony tubercles—nothing. Then he blew farther up on the ankle, perhaps where sun-bleached hairs could be prickled. The shadow moved perceptibly. The tiniest fluttering, maybe little goose bumps popping up.

Then another curious thought came to him, a dreamlike thought, sort of a reverie. What did it taste like? Would it be salty? Or did it have have like the mouth, areas of different sensitivities—to sweet, sour, acid? But that made no sense. A foot doesn't have taste buds.

His touched his tongue ever so gently to the heel, to the arch, to the little toe, to the planar surface. It tasted luscious, rich, like bone marrow. Then he licked the big toe and had to hold himself back from wanting to suck it.

Was he dreaming all this? He must have been, because the next thing he did was not what he could have thought he would want to do. But he did it anyhow. Some muse, some incubus egged him on. He sat on the edge of the bed and pressed the entire foot to his face. He kissed it everywhere. He ran his tongue between the toes, pressed his teeth on the ball, sensed the gristle, dug his fingers around the tendon. His hands trembled and he clutched the ankle as if to grasp a haunch. He lifted his hands and clutched the bulging calf above him, worshipping it, feeling all its parts, its folds and ligaments. He reached higher for a thigh.

Then the rest became only a blur.

There was a wild commotion around the cabin, a furry hardness on top of him, and then some rhythmic surges of warm juices and soft inciting jabs enveloping his shaft, over and over again. Very soon, the passions subsided, but only for a brief time, very brief. Three times the sequence repeated.

By then, Ion knew it was not a dream.

❊   ❊   ❊

Early the next morning, he awoke thinking drowsily of his "observations" of the previous night. Some observations. Where had the logic gone? What was all that stuff about Hippocrates and observations? Observations were supposed to lead to new avenues, new hypothesis, new ways to lead one's life. What "new?" He could think of only one thing: Yes, he had told Theodora he would talk to Stan, but now the subject would be new and different as a result of what happened during the night.

Stan brought some fruit juice to his bunk and touched his face. Ion covered his body with a sheet a little embarrassed for his brazenness during the night but nevertheless he brushed the back of Stan's knee, feeling at the same time a little smug for his sexual prowess. They smiled at each other, but Ion knew that this was not the time to talk. There was much shuffling up on board and he knew that there was work to be done.

He and Stan helped raise the anchor and prepare the *Leto* for a long sail to Patmos. But they sensed an anxiety in the captain's manner. He was not his usual gracious self. He barely greeted everyone at breakfast, and he chain-smoked in the wheel house listening to a cracking radio. Takis, Ion noticed, didn't have Karen locked in his eyesight; he was below banging things around, stacking and tying things up.

Ion had no inkling. For their initial course out the bay of Tingaki and to the open sea the blue remained smooth and unruffled. Gradually, as the day progressed frothy egg whites began to pop up around them, and then Poseidon rattled the sea bed and whipped his domain into a maelstrom. Even Theodora retired to her cabin with the rest, and the captain and Takis spurred the *Leto* at full throttle to fight the Meltemi winds screaming down at them from the Dardanelles. Midday, the captain conscripted Ion and Stan to form a bucket brigade to cool down one of the diesel engines whose temperature had risen to alarming heights. Repairs would be in order when they docked in Patmos. If they made it to Patmos.

The women and Paul knew nothing of the *Leto*'s predicaments, but Ion and Stan felt a strange excitement, perhaps because they were asserting their manhood, battling the sea and sharing a fate, together. They heard the captain and Takis shouting at each other, the captain at the wheel. Takis below in the engine room, Ion couldn't understand their Greek, it could have been for all he knew ancient Greek, Homeric shouts of doom and desperation.

But the more they shouted, the more Stan and Ion became alarmed. They knew of Greek volatility, but the captain was usually sedate, not given to emotional or irrational behavior. But now, the look on his face was wild and as he growled like a lion at Takis, Takis skipped around like a wild goat, an *agrimi*, being hunted.

Ion pointed to the cabinet holding life jackets. He looked towards the captain, his palms open, questioning whether the Letoites should be alerted to the danger.

"*Ochi, ochi,*" he answered. "Wait, wait."

For hours, they thrashed their way north, each hour the boat tilting in every quadrant more violently. Ion and Stan ricocheted around the deck, hauling buckets of water and hanging on to whatever they could to keep from being washed overboard.

Ion, without realizing it, grabbed Stan whenever possible. And when he did, the feel of Stan's body gave him extra strength. Stan was tall, so strong, and Ion would hold on to him for longer than necessary; holding in an embrace, they'd laugh and squeeze each other like a couple of boys celebrating a touchdown. They were drenched, wearing only shorts, working as a team, their bodies straining against a howling wind, riding a lampooned whale. Ion had never felt such kinship, never fused his being into another's. Their bodies shared the supreme game: to survive—together.

Pausing for a moment to pass on a bucket to Takis at the ladder to the engine room, Ion wondered if anyone had noticed him and Stan embracing. Of course not, how could they? They were all below, and the captain and Takis were too preoccupied. Besides, everything that had transpired in the last twenty-four hours was due to peculiar conditions. If and when they survived the ordeal, Ion could address the issues. For right now, it was him and Stan against the world. And he remembered to resume his duties in the bucket brigade.

That's when Stan poured a bucket of water over his head and groped his crotch.

And that's when Ion dug into buttocks and it was no longer a pal thing. They clasped each other harder. What was Ion to do? Stop everything and let the *Leto* be swallowed by the sea? Go down to the deep in an eternal embrace? There might not be a tomorrow, hardly a time to analyze this passion that had seized him.

They couldn't talk. The wind howled and Ion wanted to hear what Stan was thinking. About him, about them. All he knew, the captain and Takis be damned if they were looking, was that something inevitable was happening to him. He and Stan were two giga molecular masses undergoing some profound reaction, catalyzed by the *meltemi* winds.

Out of control, that's what he was. Responding to stimuli beyond reason, to excitations beyond the mere orgiastic feelings that were so fleeting with Sonja. This was different. He knew.

The captain shouted. "Water, water, quick. More."

For hours, unabated, the *Leto* surged and plunged, Ion and Stan stroked and groped, the water pails filled and emptied. *It was unfathomable,* Ion thought, *this comedy of copping feels.* What was it about? Never, no never, had this prolonged "out of body" experience so consumed him.

He could not, between the buckets and the coppings, comprehend. All his life, events were more or less predictable and determinable. Now here was, since last night, a force possessing him he could not identify, classify, or place in the compendium of his life experiences. Was it real or was it a fantasy like last night? Or was that truly real?

By chance, when they were passing on buckets and not copping, Theodora came up to the deck from below. She was sallow and her expression was one of ghoul emerging from a grave. "Are we going to make it?" she screeched. *"Panayia mou, what does the captain say."*

She reeled on the deck, aiming to climb the ladder up to the bridge where the captain held the wheel like he was wrestling a wild beast. She was about to fall when Ion grabbed her. He felt her bony arms, her fleshy thighs bumping against his erection like pillows. "You must go down to your cabin. We'll tell you when to don a lifesaver." He was shouting in her ear.

"Oh, Ion. What have I done? Bringing you all on this disaster. Forgive me. Forget what I told you in Samos. I was out of my mind. Forgive me. Please. What are we going to do?" She tottered.

Ion held her for a moment, trying to steady her. For a moment, he felt protective of her, as if she were his sister. He saw her, for the first time, without her intellectual armor. She was better that way. Good enough that he might want to continue a discussion with her—not Stan—of her proposition and why it wouldn't work. Perhaps, even, perhaps—could she help explain this strange reaction he had been feeling since Samos about Stan?

It wasn't the time. He put his arms around her and guided her back down the stairs to the cabin. "Stay put. We'll weather it." He opened her cabin door and helped her lie down.

On the passageway, Paul's cabin door was banging open. He saw, for a second, Paul and Frances hugging each other, face to face, like children trading horror stories.

Back on the deck, Stan yelled at him; "Come on, get with it. Man, we've got a crisis here."

The coppings stopped. Now it was truly a matter of life or death.

15
Patmos

The *Leto* limped into Skala, the harbor of Patmos, with her decks crusted with sea water and her crew and passengers woozy. When she docked, the crew laid out her bumpers and hosed her down, but despite the protection of jetties to ward off the sea's wrath, the waters of the bay gave her no rest. She pitched nervously, and the wind crackled the Greek flag on her stern and flicked the ribbons on her halyards.

The Letoites, one by one, lurched from their cabin dungeons into the saloon. Karen was the first to speak.

"Jesus, here we are in the middle of the Aegean. How in the hell did we get here?"

"You should ask how in the hell will we ever make it back to Athens?" said Stan. He told them of the diesel problem, and they huddled to think over the crisis.

The *Leto* was theirs, by contract, for only six more days, but no one wanted more days of the Meltemi's batterings. No one expressed that dread, brave souls that they wanted to be. They hoped only for the captain's good guidance.

"*Po, po, po*, he groaned as he sat down with them. "I warned the doctor about the diesels. I must phone Athens. Where can we find parts? What do we do now? Maybe around here some place. *Po, po, po.*"

He shouted for Takis and the two of them went below to begin disassembling the bad diesel, pulling apart its flywheel and injectors.

But the diesel was not the only source of the Letoites' woe. They had been warned by the captain from the beginning that the Meltemi could last for days. That was why he had initially proposed a simpler journey around the Peloponnese. Now, there was threat of a long delay back to Athens, perhaps charges for extending the lease. Every day, they could see their paltry Assistant Professor salaries vanishing in a cesspool of drachmas.

The Letoites, though, by then had learned to displace anxieties with intellectual rationalizations, or failing that, with plain silliness. The captaina had called such Meltemi storms *foortooni*. They learned the word easily and it sounded funny to them, like a humorous apothegm. When Karen pronounced the word she pouched her cheeks and expelled fine droplets of spit. Stan made Harpo Marx faces, and Paul and Frances waddled around like drunk ducklings quacking "phooey, phooey, *foortooni*."

Ion was disgusted with that silliness. "We're quarantined. That's all there is to it."

Quarantined? And why, everyone thought, *did Ion have to be such a damn fatalist? As if everything in his world was destined to an inexorable entropic doom?*

"Oh hell," Stan said. "They'll get the diesel fixed. Not to worry." He squeezed Ion's biceps. Ion looked at him as if he were a stranger.

"Let's dress for supper," Theodora said brightly. "Bet we can find a good taverna in town."

That first night, the Letoites nourished themselves with a fish stew and afterwards, stretched their legs exploring the town. The next day, naively hoping that the weather would lift, they woke to howling winds, a sky of inkwell blue, and a blistering sun and a cool north air that brushed their skins to almost static ignition. It was a very strange type of quarantine, and Ion had already isolated himself.

❖ ❖ ❖

They decided to spend the day hiking up to the Monastery of St. John, and in desultory fashion, single file, women in skirts, men in long pants, they began the climb. Above them, they could see a circle of houses at the base of the medieval walls of the monastery, but by some strange inversion, instead of savoring the Cycladic brilliance, they felt the dread of climbing to the castle of Frankenstein.

The entrance to the monastery through the gateway into the central courtyard was the converse of classical Greece. It was, in fact, a fortress. They each purchased guide books and each went off like initiates, noses buried in descriptions of the various chapels, icons, and treasures filled with vestments, crosses, mitres, Bishop's staffs, candlesticks, censers, embroidered stoles, and frescoes. They paused in front of the Byzantine frescoes in the Chapel of the Virgin and studied the severe and threatening icon faces. They were like judges pronouncing terrible verdicts, sinister threats of hell, condemnations of misery and self-sacrifice.

Around them floated ghostly monks in black, and in the dark recesses the intrigues and warfares of a tragic past seemed ready at any moment to pounce on them. When they reached the Library, they found some relief. They studied the codices under glass, the catalogues of the monastery's immense collection of manuscripts, including classical texts of Homer, Lucian, Aristotle, Euripides, Sophocles and Plato (unfortunately the latter absconded by the Brit, Clarke, and housed in the London Museum). The archives impressed them, particularly the ancient sixth century fragments of the Gospel of St. Mark. They stood in awe, noses pressed against glass cases holding calligraphy and illuminations that ornamented the manuscripts. Eventually, blinded by the bright sun, they emerged from the Treasury onto the roof terraces of the Monastery. The battlements lay at different levels and as they clambered over them, looking down on the various domed chapels and courtyards from above, they found themselves congregated at the highest point, the western terrace.

There, referring to their guide books, they could see to the north, Samos, Korassiai, Phournia and Icaria, to the west, Mykonos, Naxos and the summits of Paros and Amorgos, to the south, Levithos Astypalaea, Leros, Kalymnos and Kos. Even the coast of Asia Minor could be made out. "The top of the world," they agreed, an incredible purple sight in the late afternoon.

"No wonder St. John chose the place, why he had the hallucinations he did," said Paul.

"Should we call the Revelations an hallucination?" said Stan.

"Have you read them? Gibberish. Scholars have a million interpretations to them."

"That's the whole point." The rest of the Letoites gathered around them to follow the exchange.

"The point being that Christianity is a myth. A glorious one at that," said Paul.

"The point being that mankind must invent those myths. His being demands something to hang a hat on," Stan countered.

Paul shrugged his little shoulders. "This character, the monk, Christodoulos, the founder of the monastery in the eleventh century, had a personal agenda. Or perhaps he was a paranoid schizophrenic who believed St. John's rubbish."

"What about that he might have had altruistic motives? Like, the people of Patmos were being slaughtered and persecuted by pirates, Turks, Saracens, Knights of Malta—whatever—and he found a 'cause.' Which rallied the islanders to defend themselves. For a 'holy' purpose. And then he enlisted lieutenants, monks, to help."

"Holy? I do not care for that rationalization. Why not say that he was a rabble rouser and could whip the people into a frenzy 'in the name of God'."

"Like Hitler, you would say?"

"Precisely," said Paul.

"Ah, one difference. This guy's 'cause' has lasted. Look around you. This monastery is proof. People from around the world come to it. They study its manuscripts. Why the whole place is a linchpin in the whole Christian enterprise."

"Its preservation, I say, has to do simply with its aesthetics."

"Whatever, aesthetics, in all cultures we need beliefs. Study some cultural anthropology, man, took at the most primitive ones—you'll find the same principle operating."

"Too bad," Paul sniffed, "that they didn't concentrate on preserving the Classics. Continued on with the glorious beginning of the Ancients in art, philosophy, and science."

"Pooh," said Frances, entering the fray. "If it weren't for Christianity and places like this and the great Italian Renaissance universities—supported by the popes, I might add—those Classics would never have been preserved. Galileo to the contrary. Christianity is really kind of extension of the Platonic ideas of monothesism. It isn't a matter of the beginning and end of human culture, it's all a continuum and must be viewed as such."

"Whatever you say, darling," he replied, giving her a smack on the cheek.

Theodora took center stage. "I prefer to see this place as another manifestation of human behavior in its most revealing form. Along comes this man, Christodoulos, with a keen mind who realized that he could make people do his bidding by rewarding them. The reward? Salvation, of course. Die by the Ottoman sword if God ordains it, believe in Jesus and St. John's piety, and you'll be sure to go to heaven. Simple psychology."

"If you can dupe the people thus," said Paul.

"That's not hard. Couch it with rhetoric, cloud it in incense, get the artists to make beautiful stuff, 'make a show,' and presto! You have people following you. That Christodoulos had it right."

They stopped to look out at the Aegean, the colors deepening every moment.

Karen now came forward, clearing her throat, and speaking loudly said: "This monk guy and all his monkeys. How can you seduce people, the way you say, Theodora, and expect them to give up sex?"

"Have you heard of sublimation?" Theodora said. "And anyhow, we don't know, do we, how celibate they really were. Maybe they needed little sex and got their jollies in prayers."

"We Californians don't believe that," said Stan. "We're for sex, right, gang?"

No one responded and conversation stopped for awhile, everyone trying to gulp down puritanical thoughts.

At last Ion, surprisingly, spoke up. "You all miss the point."

"Which is?" said Stan, giving him a little affectionate jab in the abdomen.

"The point is that Christodoulos was on the up and up. A true believer. And so were his followers. You people can't believe that validities outside your own little academic spheres can exist."

"Which is?" said Stan, this time putting an arm around his shoulder. Ion pulled away.

"That he and this place represent a spirituality. A humanity that cannot be rationalized. Only felt. A true faith. A true belief."

They turned their gaze again to the Aegean.

"Oh well," said Paul, "maybe you just need to be a Greek to understand this place."

"I'm Greek," said Theodora, "but I'm not sure what Ion is getting at."

Neither did anyone wish to continue the discussion.

Their Christian ordeal was not over, however. On their hike back down to Skala, they visited the Convent of the Apocalypse and the grotto where the Saint allegedly experienced his

Revelation. A shriveled old nun, murmuring "I am the Alpha and the Omega" . . . in badly memorized English related the legend and with bony fingers pointed to the cracks in the rock vault from which came the voice of God.

✡   ✡   ✡

Then, back in a rapidly setting sun and a dusty, abrasive wind they faced a thirty minute hike back to the harbor, two by two—Stan and Ion leading, Karen and Theodora bringing up the rear, descending like a chain gang shuffling after a day's hard labor.

"What are your rates, Theodora?" said Karen. "I mean for counseling therapy." She puffed and touched Theodora's elbow.

Theodora locked her arm into Karen's. "Oh, honey, for people like you, it's free."

"Seriously. Let's sit for a moment. I do want to talk to you about a problem. I was thinking about it when that old nun was giving us her spiel. Gal, I could use a revelation."

"Here, let's sit on this rock in the shade. Let the others go on. I'm all ears."

Theodora anticipated the subject and she went into the therapeutic mode, her hands gracefully folded, her expression one of complete acceptance. But she wasn't prepared for Karen's flip. "It's about Takis, of course." She paused to await approval.

"Certainly," said Theodora, "you two are having quite a fling. I'm happy for you."

"You're sweet to say that. I thought you might think I was some kind of femme fatale, that I'd vamped the poor boy."

"Oh, of course not. I'm sure your intentions were sincere. Obviously, he adores you."

The wind gusts made their voices alternately loud and soft, exaggerating their meanings. Karen related to Theodora the details of the affair, how they got started, how they managed their trysts in the cabin. The shenanigans going on in the cabins by now were not unknown to Theodora, or to anyone else, for that matter. What interested Theodora was how their romance could come to such fruition without a common language. Verbal communication was her main weapon in therapies of personality problems.

"I'm a speech therapist, too, you know, Theodora. What we have learned about human communication is that the voice is not a *sine qua non* for complete rapport. Whatever the cultural differences, there are ways that people find to communicate."

"Be specific. I mean with Takis. How do you read each other?"

"Easy. There's the tactile route, first of all. It's a cinch. All human beings know where their erogenous zones are. It comes naturally, and Takis is completely responsive. Then there are the auditory. I can place his fingers and mouth in the right places and groan or whatever. He gets the picture. Then there's a universal sign language, too, facial expressions for sorrow and pain. Just look at the masks in Sophoclean plays. His little idiosyncracies are easy to read. His body language, his little prancing ways. I'm not embarrassing you, am I? All I can say is that by all those means, our sex is the very ultimate. On top of that, there are times when sex and talk don't go well together anyhow. You'd agree with me on that, wouldn't you? We're in complete sync, believe me."

"So, what's the problem?" Theodora said, suspecting naturally that the subject was deeper than only matters of the flesh. The wind carried her words away, but she realized that it didn't matter to Karen. Karen was already ahead of her.

"Life may start in bed, but there's more to it than sex. Takis's gentleness begs for lots more. No matter how many orgasms there are. I know that he wants more than just my body. He shows it lots of little ways. His little favors. The frisky looks. The petting. The caressing and comforting. All that puppy love stuff. That's important in human relationships, too, don't you agree?" She looked dreamy, as if she were addressing a muse.

Theodora did not answer, only thought to herself that this was a part of Karen no Board of Trustees had ever seen, and never would if she was to maintain any authority as a college administrator. Nevertheless, she had to ask how Takis related *his* needs, apart from those directed towards satisfying *her* passions. But to that inquiry, Karen preferred to tell her about how her past affairs, the story of her marriage and of her Lesbian lover, had guided her, assured her even, to a full appreciation of the meaningfulness of the current affair. Takis, above all of them, was the real thing. And it was, "So amazing, that after only a couple of weeks I feel so sure of him. It's the Greek Light. It makes us see things so clearly, instantly!"

Theodora finally got a word in. "You've had a rich personal life, and your experiences must have taught you much. But, still . . ."

The wind whistled through the leafless limbs of fig trees and Karen hardly heard a word. But, as Theodora thought to herself, she wouldn't have listened anyhow.

"What do I do now, Theodora?"

"Now?" Of course, that was the crux. Only the previous night at dinner, they had talked very briefly about the end of the voyage and their return to their academic holes. The facts of Karen's attachments were not at issue, the "now" was.

"Should I take Takis back with me? Oh God, how do I do that?"

Theodora rubbed her chin. *Oh, this is juicy stuff,* she thought. Reality conditioning, right up her bailiwick. "Let's do some projections here. Think of your everyday life and think how Takis would fit into it."

Karen scowled. Then, hesitatingly, she talked of how she'd give him speech therapy, crash courses in English, teach him some American manners, buy him some shoes, teach him not to talk so much with his hands.

"In short, do the Pygmalion routine," said Theodora.

"In a way, yes. I know he's bright. He'd learn quickly. He'd have no trouble working on diesel engines in a Mercedes agency. I'm not planning on just keeping him or making him a sex toy."

"But how would he fit into your professional life? Do you see yourself presenting him at faculty functions?"

Karen was silent for awhile, then. "That would all take some time. I'll have to carefully plan it. I'm sure people will be intrigued by him. He's so clever with his pantomimes. Maybe he could fit into the Drama Department. And at my parties, he certainly could make superb omelettes."

"Sounds like a house boy. Is that what you want from him?"

"Oh, he'd be lots more than that. He has a soul, a very sensitive soul. His character would blossom. Look at all the advantages I could provide him."

She talked of getting him a car. His own television. A sharp wardrobe from Cable Car Clothiers. He'd be my "own little Adonis," she claimed. There was a Greek History Professor on the staff with his Greek wife he could make friends with. Greek churches abounded in the Bay Area so he wouldn't feel culturally cut off. She had figured everything out, she thought.

"Except, how do you know whether he wants to be in America?" Theodora said.

"Doesn't everyone? I mean, what kind of life does he have here, slaving on dinky yachts without a life of his own. I'd give him a house, creature comforts."

"Have you broached this to him?"

"Well, you know there is a sort of language problem. But have you noticed how he dotes on me? I feel he'd follow me anywhere, do anything I ask."

Theodora paused, took Karen's hand and said, "Tell me sincerely, how do you really know all that?"

"As I said, it's that non-verbal communication thing. So . . . this is what I'm asking: I wonder if you can't come to our cabin some night. After Frances has slipped off to Paul. I'd like you to observe first hand our intimacies. Be convinced that he really *is* mine."

"You mean for me to *watch*?"

"He wouldn't mind one bit. He's not shy. You can sit in the corner and watch, yes. Then if you could translate for me, we could get into the details of my taking him to America. I'd marry him, of course. In Greece, if he liked."

Theodora was stunned. She remained silent for minutes, turning away from Karen and watching the tiny white caps far out at sea. Finally, she said, "This needs some thought. I think you may be moving too quickly, Karen. I'm not sure I want to play the intermediary in this. I'm not sure he would want me to."

"Oh, he wouldn't care. He likes you. I can tell. Why, if you want to, you can play with him. He's awfully sexy. And I wouldn't be jealous."

Good Lord, Theodora thought. *What a bribe. What a . . ., could she dare say it? a psychopathy. She's deranged. She thinks of him as a play thing only. Her gigolo. Her dildo. She somehow doesn't realize that he is a human being.*

No, no, she said to herself. *I would never do such a thing, not in a million years. Karen has cracks in her head, bigger than the grotto's. She doesn't need a revelation, she needs a good full-time psychiatrist. I must keep calm.*

✿   ✿   ✿

Their walk back had other revelations. They caught up with Stan and Ion lying under an olive tree. Ion's head was turned away from Stan. Nothing struck Theodora as unusual about that (he was in his quarantine mode) except when the two men got up to leave and went on ahead on the trail, Karen said: "It's so nice to see those two getting it on."

Karen had to explain to Theodora what she meant, how Stan had told her of their cabin fling after she told him of hearing of the thrashing in their cabin. There it was, smack in Theodora's face. Karen, if nothing else, was outspoken and if she was a little crass, she wasn't a liar either. And it had come to this, this confirmation of Theodora's suspicions. It explained everything about Ion, his recalcitrance towards her and his general lack of interest in women.

Later, when she lay back on her bunk in her cabin, she thought of only one thing, throwing that stupid Addenda into the brink. But not here in the bay. Somewhere in the middle of the Aegean to add to the pile of all the other detritus of history. Someday they'd salvage it from the deep and think they'd discovered the writing of a Circe, a lovelorn American one.

Oh, how humiliating. What was Greece doing to them all?

✿   ✿   ✿

At the witching hour when the Letoites settled down into their love nests, Theodora, not thinking at all about "watching," tried to settle her troubled mind. She put on a robe and slipped out to the deck.

It was close to midnight. The sky was octopus ink, the stars twinkling for all the love birds below, but Theodora wanted only to shield herself from the wind and be alone. Behind the mast head, she found a place to bundle up.

Now, what was her new plan? What was to be her destiny? Ion had been a stupid fantasy, rationalized by all her academic paraphernalia and inculcated by her Greek peasant parents.

What a pity that this trip had taught her that Greece was not about simple virtues like marriage and family. Neither was it about application of murky behaviorist theory to husband hunting.

What was it about then? It creeped slowly into her thoughts. She had to elevate her plans to higher ideals, to what Greece really should represent for her: Thought, reason, and the glories thereof. That was the tradition of the Ancients, and she needed to emulate exactly that philosophy. A life of the mind, a search for meanings. *Agnos Sauton,* know thyself, that was her destiny.

She could take inspiration from her brother, Sammy. He always had that *charisma,* the Greek meaning of the word that had to do with talent and accomplishment and a little bravado thrown in. He was a "do it" kid, and he taught her that if the roller skate strap broke, you could mend it with some inner tube rubber. To hell with Ion if he didn't know how to skate. He was a bore anyhow. Let Stan have him. And we'll see how long that lasts. Stan was an OK kind of guy, honest with himself, like Sammy, and he could do better than Ion.

Her back straightened, and she thought more of Sammy. He knew himself. She knew that if he was with her at that moment, he'd encourage her to "take hold," "do something." They would have both seen that this trip to Greece, this return to their heritage had great meaning. It was a place to find inspiration, a place to find direction. She'd come again, often, seeking *her* revelation, a fulfillment not like Karen's sensual one, but one that had to do with deep discoveries of herself. And maybe in her intellectual pursuits, her desires for a man, a real, wholesome man, a man who . . .

Then imperceptibly, she began to notice an orange spot across the deck, and when the wind shifted she smelled tobacco.

"I wondered when you would notice me," said the captain. "Good evening, *thespinis.*" He touched his cap as usual.

She nodded, but thought not to speak. She wasn't in the mood for a game of cards.

"We will have the diesel fixed soon. Now, if only the winds stop we can see a few more islands. I was thinking of Andros. It's not a tourist island. It's for wealthy Greeks. Nevertheless, it has two fine museums, one for modern art. Does that appeal to you?"

"You're the *Kapitanios*. You know best."

To break a long silence she said, "Are you anxious to get home?"

"What home? This is my home, the sea. Two sons in Australia. Nothing else. But I will miss you Americans. You're all crazy. Real people."

Theodora accepted the compliment with a nod and said nothing.

"You are unhappy tonight, *thespinis*. Why? Because you think of going back to being a professor?"

"That. And how I will miss Greece. The sights we've seen."

"There are many more. You come back soon?"

"If I can. Could you bring me a beer?"

Back from the galley he pulled his deck chair closer and clinked their beer bottles.

"Let me ask you something, *Kapitanios*. I will try my best Greek. This boy, Takis. You say he is a good boy. You know he and Karen . . ."

"Ehhh . . . of course I know. I'm not stupid. Of course, he's a good boy. You disapprove what he does with the Jewess?"

"How do you know she's a Jew?"

"Never mind."

"*Oposthipote*, as you say. But there are some heavy things here. Karen wants to take the boy with her back to America. Marry him. What do you think?"

The captain laughed. "She may want to, but she should ask Takis first."

"She asked me to ask him. To translate for her. But I thought perhaps you would be the best for that matter. Would you?"

"Bah! How humorous! He with her? I would not insult the boy to ask such a question. *Christe mou.*" He crossed himself.

"You don't like Karen?"

"She's a fine woman, I think. But crazy. That's all. She doesn't know what she wants. A boy fifteen years younger. He's not even Jewish. He's a whole, complete Greek. What would he do with that 'old rag'?"

Theodora gulped. How quickly her Greek vocabulary was growing.

"He could benefit," she said. "Maybe, you think? Become an American husband. Make some money. Come back and buy his own yacht."

"What are you saying? Make such a sacrifice? Listen. In two weeks, he'd leave her. He's a simple boy, from a village and he believes that marriage is a sacrament. What in the name of God is wrong with all you foreign women? Excuse me, I speak not of you. The others. Greece is full of them in the summer. They come down here with their thighs open and what can a poor Greek man do but satisfy them. It is their duty as men, Kazantzakis says so himself. But marriage is another thing. What craziness with these Karens. They lose their minds and think because of a few nights in bed they own a Greek man. *Och, panaghia mou.* Excuse me. You are a doctor of the mind. Explain all that to Karen. And tell her to leave the boy alone."

He was right. Of course, Theodora knew that. The captain always showed a certain logic. Things were black and white, right or wrong, laws of nature had to be observed. His thoughts had the power of Newtonian logic. If he tried to abandon those German tourists on that island (a very moot question) that was only a momentary slip. He seemed to have regained an even keel, his principles unsullied. Yes, the captain was solid, in body and mind.

But his logic would be too good for Karen to ever understand. Theodora couldn't explain that to the captain and her Greek wasn't subtle enough to explain that simple, pure logic couldn't work on the convolutions in Karen's brain. She'd have to tell him that Karen needed a "cooling off" period. A good shrink in California could get her to talk more of Takis. They'd get around to subjects such as mutual needs, common interests, shared values, things that Karen already knew about but about which she was blinded by the passions of the flesh. Slowly, she'd come around to acknowledging the hopelessness of it, and her great fling of 1973 would dissipate into the folds of her memory banks.

For right now, those expositions wouldn't be understood by Karen. And there was no urgency, on Theodora's part, to hasten their understanding. Still, there would be the real problem of how Karen would take the brush-off from Takis. But Takis is a nice boy. She wouldn't have to say anything to him to blunt the shock. He'd be nice. Give her a little olive wood carving to remember him by and kiss her goodbye. Perhaps, in some kind of sign language, tell her that they'd meet again, next summer? Perhaps? (Perhaps not.) But he would let her off gently and wait for the next *tourista*.

The winds seemed to slacken a bit. "What do you think, *Kapitanios*, do we sail tomorrow?"

"We'll see what the radio says in the morning. But the machinist will not finish his work on the diesel until tomorrow afternoon. We stay in Patmos at least one more day."

It didn't matter to Theodora. There were some interesting knitting and embroidery shops in town she wanted to explore. Talking to the natives, too, was enjoyable. Perhaps because of her broken Greek, they took interest in her. And it was nice to be liked for no other reason than she was just another ordinary human being, not a professor, not an experimenter with devious goals on her mind.

Yes, so many things had happened so far on the trip. She needed to stop this posturing stuff about being a creative researcher. She'd be herself more now. She'd feel warm about herself, despite the embarrassments of her plan and the raging affairs around her. She could, at least, be at peace. And it pleased her that the captain was beside her. A mass of strength. A Newtonian example of laws of matter and motion. That's what he was. A solid mass. The thought made her feel strong and she sighed.

She heard the captain exhale his tobacco smoke and saw him flip the butt into the bay. She was thinking of retiring to her cabin when he suddenly asked:

"*Thespinis,* can you cook?"

"What do you think? Certainly! All Greek mothers teach their daughters to cook and sew. I make the best *skordolia* west of the Mississippi.

"Tell me how you make it, then I'll tell whether you are a Greek."

She told him how much garlic she used. "To where it almost burns the tongue," she said. How she boiled the potatoes. How she homogenized them with the finest olive oil and a touch of a fresh lemon. The pounder she used. The wooden bowl.

Then she told him how she fried the squash and eggplant with just the right batter and seasoning, with the right kind of pan, the right kind of oil.

And she told him of the other dishes she knew. The *loukoumathes* fritters that she drizzled with walnuts and fine honey, the stuffed peppers and the accolades from her American colleagues.

"You should get married, then, *thespinis.* You'd make a Greek man a fine wife."

As if she didn't know. She laughed, then almost wanted to cry. But how could she explain all in her limited Greek to this Greek *Kapitanios,* man of the world, a gigantic mass, a force to be reckoned with at rest or in motion.

She rose to bid him good night. "*Kallinichta, Kapitanios.* Some day I may cook for you, and you'll see how well Mother taught me."

He rose, too, and for a brief second face to face, they smiled weakly at each other. Then without warning *Meden Agan,* nothing in excess, he cupped his calloused hand on her cheek and kissed lightly the other. Then, like a mass coming to rest, his other hand dropped to her side and carefully feathered the side of her hip.

She said nothing more. Quickly, she stepped down into the saloon and down below to her cabin. Her skin felt flushed and as she lay on her bunk she tried to analyze what that touching was about. It couldn't be called a caress. It couldn't be called, certainly, a pass.

All she knew was that it made her feel good. No one had ever laid hands on her wide hips. Here was someone who had even mildly respected them or least acknowledged them. That was new and that was nice.

*   *   *

The next day stayed windy, but it didn't keep Stan, Ion, and Karen from snorkeling at *psilimo amos* beach. Paul and Frances were going to try to enter the inner sanctum of the monastery library. Paul's Fulbright credentials were supposed to allow him to look at the sixth century manuscripts. He was particularly interested in seeing the influence of late Hellenic calligraphy on the early Christian manuscripts. And Frances went along to play, as she put it, "As a sleuth of the secret Byzantine seraglios."

While the captain and Takis worked on the diesel, Theodora spent the day with an elderly woman, Kyria Irini, in her knitting shop and at her home for coffee. The patterns of the lady's embroidery were not dissimilar from her mother's, and like her own childhood home in Minnesota, the home had embroideries on almost all fabrics, napkins, tablecloths, arm rests, pillowcases, towels, and lamp shades. She liked the effect and decided that back home she would try decorating her house similarly. Besides, embroidering was good therapy, and it had an interesting intellectual appeal, too. The intricate decorative fringes seemed to imitate the patterns of nerve cell axons and dendrites. The spidery arrangements, in exquisite geometric order, were like neuronal networks of the brain. A little silly to make the comparison, she thought, but the verisimilitude had the queer effect of complementing her professional work. "Art imitating life," she ruminated.

Kyria Irini had another effect. The old lady touched her and addressed her like a child, and she smelled of incense and moth balls. "Come, my *koukla*, let us talk. Tell me." Her briki coffee and its foamy top and her little plate of *koulouraki* cookies top brought back memories of her mother and aunts, women of a household who would gather themselves away from the men and the outside world and confide in each other. She wanted to tell Kyria Irini everything, about her captain and Ion, her confusions about her future, but she really didn't need to. The old woman read her eyes, fussed over her.

"You be my daughter. Why don't you stay on the island? Let the rest go. I'll teach you everything about knitting." She smiled, knowing her empty offer was only a salve. Somehow, she knew, sensed like only a mother can, that Theodora was in crisis.

Theodora regressed twenty years. She was a helpless, forlorn adolescent, burying her fears in motherly warmth. She gabbled and giggled, goo-gooed and gibbered, about nonsense, about things like stray pussy cats, worry beads, baking and figs, about how the old lady got along with neighbors, about all the pompous priests. The old woman wouldn't respond to Theodora's questions about why she wore black, she played and touched Theodora, on her arms, the ringlets of hair on her brow, her flushed cheeks. Theodora became a doll, something to play with and make over, and Theodora relished all the attention she was starved for.

For more than three hours they visited, the old lady showing her everything in her house, from the wood-stoked stove to the roof veranda with its clusters of flower bushes and bird baths. Theodora spotted in the entranceway a parasol with red silk embroidered edges and spangles sewn into the cloth. She admired it, wanted to purchase it, but Kyria Irini would not hear of it, insisted she take it as a memento.

"Write me, my sweet one, you must return to Patmos, you hear?"

Theodora hurried down to the harbor in whimsical mood. *What a pleasant afternoon,* she thought. She really didn't want to dine with the Letoites.

All of which, at dinner, despite the disclosures about Ion, had put Theodora in an airy mood. Stan asked what had happened to her spunk, to which she replied, "Oh, so many things today I've had to debunk." Her tone had only a trace of sarcasm when she shot a quick look at Stan and Ion. Karen, Paul and Frances took no notice, being more interested in a discussion of the classical codices of Euripides and Sophocles in the monastery's library.

After supper, after the Letoites had retired to their respective rookeries, she thought to resume a tete-a-tete with captain up on board. She found him smoking and sprawled on a mat, staring at the sky. He seemed in a meditative mood but not unresponsive to her lightness. Briefly, they gabbed about how the diesel had been repaired, how they would sail for Andros.

They sipped beer from bottles and talked very little. He asked a few questions about California and Minnesota, and though she wasn't feeling lonely, she wanted to converse, express some interests in him. She asked about his life in Essen during the war.

"They treated us like dogs," he said. "Fed us well, gave us a clean bed and showers. But they had to keep us healthy to get the most work out of us. Germans know how work is to be done. I don't remember much of what I did in the factory. I pounded out steel and worked on the lathe. What military weapon parts I was making I had no idea. I was dried out. My spirit only dust. The day the Americans came was like the second coming. You cannot imagine our joy. And when they opened the gates of the factory, the first thing I looked for was one of the German guards. I wanted to break open his head. But they had run away like cowards before the Americans came."

"Did they beat you?"

"Only once they whacked me on the arm. Always they walked around with heavy sticks and guns and no one dared cross them. They bloodied one Greek because he spit in their face when he refused to say 'danke' in the food line. His face was broken. His family would never recognize him. But I was so lucky. Back home I heard worse stories of what happened in Arakhova."

"No wonder you hate Germans," Theodora said. "And no wonder you wanted to leave those German passengers on that islet."

As soon as she said that, she regretted it. There was no need to bring back his agonies. Damn.

Suddenly the captain banged his beer bottle on the anchor posts. "*Gamo, gamo,* those dirty pigs!"

She could figure the Greek. She became frightened. She had never seen him lose his temper, never seen him lose his composure. All that mass out of control. She had to calm him.

"It doesn't matter now, *Kapitanios*. Past things. Past things."

His lips and jaws tightened. She could see his whole body tense in the dim light from the quay. He reached out for her like a drowning man gasping for the last helping hand. "I suffer, I suffer so, *thespinis,* I cannot tell you."

"But you can. I am like a doctor. I know about grief and problems of the mind. Nothing you can say will be repeated by me. I offer you only a hand and sympathy. Tell me now. What bothers you?"

"Those German pigs. I don't care about them. But what if they had children? Beautiful, innocent blonde babies. All alone. God save me! God save me!"

"Orphans? You mean they are orphans now without their parents?"

"*Och, och, och.* He buried his face in his huge hands. Quickly he recovered though. "I mean, what if . . . I mean could have."

Theodora was quick to respond. "Could have left those Germans to die on the islet? But you didn't, you said. We must be careful about such things. We can become mad to think that all our evil thoughts and dreams might come true. Because we only *think* those things doesn't make them come true."

His fingers trembled in hers. "Yes, certainly. I only think that. You are so right. Such a good doctor." And he leaned over to kiss her cheek.

She felt the inertia of his mass all around her, buoying her, making her wanting to let it come to a floating rest. In her arms. Yes, in her arms. She realized that that was what was needed. Immediately. She rose, put her arms under his armpits, asking him to rise, to follow her to her cabin. She led the bull man to her bed, unbuttoned his shirt and buried her face in his brawn. He began to cry and she kissed his tears. He held her hips like sacks of gold, caressing them, rubbing the brush of his moustache all around them.

And thus, Theodora, for the first time in her life, at the age of thirty-five, authorized an ecstasy whose pleasure she could never have fathomed. And from a man who was beginning to show cracks in his Newtonian armor. *That* was the most thrilling part of it.

16
Nameless Island

The captain left Theodora's bunk early and by sunrise had freed the *Leto* from her moorings.

"*Kali mera,*" he greeted the Letoites, one by one coming on deck to the fresh but calm sea breezes. He told Theodora, with a twinkle in his eyes, "I will show you today a magnificent new island, Andros. Tell the rest. Tell them to read its history."

All morning they sailed, the captain and Takis for the first time unfurling a large trapezoid canvas to prove that the *Leto* was seaworthy even with decrepit diesels. In the galley, Theodora prepared Greek coffee with a *briki* and on a silver tray with a spoonful of rose petal preserves in a glass of cold water presented it to the captain on the bridge. He smiled, touched her shoulder and said, "You are a good woman, *thespinis.*"

She stood beside him for awhile, not talking, staring out to the horizon, an occasional islet here and there, and then back towards the lower deck where the Letoites lolled over their Nescafe and the usual eggs fried in olive oil. They were all coupled, their attentions only on each other. Takis was brushing back Karen's hair with lemon juice, to "highlight its reddish cast," she claimed. Paul and Frances, kneecaps rubbing, poured over their Hachette Guide, and Stan and Ion played chess on a pocket-size set. Coupled. All of them coupled, she, too, with a man twenty years older, a man she would never have thought could be a lover. Attraction of opposites, perhaps, she thought, but there was more to it: despite his strength, he was vulnerable and he needed her. And that was odd. She was the one to call the shots in her life, even Sammy gave her that prerogative. She devised the master plans of her life, the experimental protocols, the how, what, and when she would allow people into her life. And here was the *Kapitanios,* out of nowhere, directing her. She raised her face to the sail and grinned. Variables.

And how psychologically untraumatic was her evening with him. Despite all her knowledge of human sexuality and her counseling work, she had always harbored some trepidations about "when her day would come." The mere thought of vaginal intrusions, particularly from a man as large as her captain, she thought might cause malfunctions, obstructions, frictions, perhaps great pain. None of it happened, it came out naturally. She could have predicted it, she knew her physiology of the Autonomic Nervous System. She knew that the only requisite was "to let go," and that was what happened. In fact, she hardly remembered much of the mechanical aspects of the coitus. She remembered only embracing a hulk of flesh and hair that overwhelmed her in spasms of rapture. She didn't have to think about anything, she let him do the thinking, if he even had to think. He must have, the synchronization was so well tuned.

She watched the sail billow, then looked at the captain at the wheel. He gave her a sideways jaunty look and then shouted to Takis to tighten the lines. She studied him now and wondered whether last night he was that much "in command," or whether he had, like her, only "let go." She hoped the latter.

The thought surprised her. She rushed down to her cabin to make some notes in the Addenda. New protocols began permeating her thoughts, and she wrote about whether they were antithetical. Human passion to be studied? To what degree were there cerebral cortical involvements? Old problem. Maybe she could analyze it. How? By being more in a conscious mode the next time with the captain (surely there would be a next time).

She'd rather detach herself more, observe him, his nuances and body reactions. See to what extent they were instantaneous reflex or conditioned by previous experience.

Perhaps she could discuss that with him, about his other previous experiences with women. She bit her lip. No, she didn't want to know about his wife, his girls in port. Difficult, this new protocol. She wrote and wrote. Just what was the new emotion she was feeling? Did it have a intellectual basis?

The morning passed, and the *Leto* and her passengers sailed on resplendent. Time could stop, could reverse and leap ahead to eternity, but Theodora remained transfixed. There were so many analyses, rationalizations, teleological meanings to the moment. The rest of the Letoites must have been in the same state. Each, their heads pointing out to the sea, locked on one quadrant or another, and bearing vapid expressions, seemed to be taking stock of unknown unknowables.

Theodora mentioned in her Addenda that her "subjects" often displayed that stance. She described it differently at times, but it was not the gaze of a scholar or scientist. She'd had hardly ever seen it back home in her colleagues, and in fact, had not seen it in the Letoites until they had been at sea for several days. Now, it was common. She'd catch them at odd moments staring out, usually to a seascape, often with something on it, an island, a ship, an interesting cloud formation sieving sunlight into silvery shafts. And their expressions were indescribable; it was more like they were studying something with eyes out of focus. She compared it to the physiology of night vision where subjects are taught not to look directly at an object but to "defocus" so that peripheral rods in the retina could be brought into play. A curious phenomena, she noted, this use of night vision in the broad Aegean daylight.

The chess game between Stan and Ion faltered for that reason. They kept looking away from the board. Neither were the participants inclined to developing attacks on his opponent.

Stan, yawning, conceded and Ion, not exactly happy with the surrender, rose to stretch out his arms. "A swim would be nice, don't you think?"

He approached the captain on the bridge and suggested that they take a swim and lunch on a pretty beach. Theodora, beginning to tire of all her circular arguments she'd made that morning in the Addenda, agreed that a picnic lunch would be nice, for the real reason that with the Leto "parked," she and the captain might have more time together.

The captain, to Theodora's surprise, in an agitated manner said, "We'll see. We'll see. I must study the maps. Yes. Yes. There are lots of islets around. In about thirty minutes. We'll see. Magnificent waters. Tell Takis to come up. We'll have plenty of time to make port in Andros before sunset."

But the captain's mood now was definitely altered. He became imperious, shouting rough words at Takis, slapping around navigation maps and scanning wide arcs with binocs. Many little specs, mauve islets studded the blue, and he seemed confused until all at once he barked at Takis, "Prepare the skiff. Pack the lunches. Furl the sail. We head for there."

He pointed at a hilly islet, indistinct from the many others they had sailed by. It could not have been more than twenty square kilometers and seemed utterly lifeless. The captain maneuvered the *Leto* around to the leeward side, where he found anchorage by an escarpment separating two inlets. They tied up in shallow water and launched the skiff, which took the Americans around the opposite tip to a long deep bay with turquoise waters. Stan and Ion dove in immediately to swim ashore. The rest waded onto a sandy beach, its color ivory white and jeweled with tiny quartz crystals. On each side of the beach, slopes rose to the high points of the island, no higher than fifty meters.

They spread their beach towels and Theodora showed off her flashy parasol. In a hurry, though, they plunged into the amniotic sea, relishing its nourishing, cool fluids.

"Stop," Frances shouted. "Stop everything. Time, I command you."

"No, no, my dear," shouted Paul treading water nearby. "Tell it to reverse. Go back to the glory days when the ancients let the dawn shed its light on civilization."

Karen came dog-paddling by, Takis in her wake, saying "Time can be, whatever. Now, then, tomorrow. Let's enjoy it. Tra-la-la." Then she dunked Takis' head underwater, and he bobbed up to cradle her pendulous breasts.

Then all floated on their backs, some raising hands to the sun and letting droplets form cascading microprisms of rainbow colors. Ears immersed, they could hear only a faint rumble of the sea, sometimes a faint cymbal crash of the surf lapping the beach.

From a distance, louder and louder, they began hearing crashing sounds, and before their eardrums ached, they floated upright to see Stan and Ion, approaching them in long overhead arm strokes and foaming leg kicks.

All treading in a circle now, Stan, breathless said, "Can it ever get any better than this, I ask?"

Like children, they splashed their arms to make a spewing fountain of agreement. Ion, bronzed after almost three weeks, his teeth bleached white, his muscles like taut ropes shouted, "I'm starved. Let's go in."

Ashore, they unwrapped the baskets of *gravieri* cheese, *loukanika* sausages and rounds of crusty bread. Silently, in the shade of a cliff, but in hearing distance of the swirling turquoise waters around basalt outcroppings, they devoured their lunch and washed it down with Fanta lemon sodas.

Theodora began to notice the captain and Takis scouting around on the hill above them. The captain seemed to be unearthing dirt with a long stick, as if he were searching for a treasure. She became curious and rose to see what he was up to. She opened her parasol, its spangles jiggling as she climbed the hill.

About one hundred meters up she saw a small cave ahead of her and the captain furiously scraping away dirt and rocks. "*Kapitanios,*" she shouted, "what have you found?"

He didn't hear her perhaps, but shortly he whirled away from her and with Takis scurried down the slope towards where the skiff was anchored farther down the hillock.

How curious, she thought, and she wanted to know what they had found in the cave.

It took her a several minutes to reach the cave. Once, she fell on her knees on the rocky raw sienna soil, but her parasol helped her maintain balance. What she found when she reached the shade of the small cave shocked her. At first, they were indistinguishable from the splinty and curved white rocks. She pushed them lightly around with her sandals and realized that they were, yes, bones!

But of what? She could not tell. The spangles of her parasol jittered. They were badly distintegrated and a few roundish pieces might have been skulls . . . yes, they were smallish, perhaps of wild goats. But how could goats survive in such a barren place?

And then, the horror of the other possibility hit her. Oh God, were they human? German? Oh! She had to go tell the rest. Stan, surely knew something of physical anthropology. He could determine the bones' origin. She half-stumbled down to the beach.

But before she could reach them and tell them of her discovery another horror faced her: she saw the captain and Takis in the skiff, rowing hard back around the escarpment to where the *Leto* lay anchored.

The captain was leaving the Letoites, abandoning them, just as he had the Germans! This was incredible. The coincidence unbelievable. Deserted island, deep coves, torrid heat. But why? Why?

She rushed down the hill to the Letoites. The parasol gyrated madly, she shook, unable to utter a sound. Stan caught her in his arms as she fainted.

They sponged her down in the shade with cool sea-water. Slowly, she revived. Her eyes opened and she muttered, "It's true, it's true."

"What's true?" said Stan. "Tell us." The rest stood anxiously.

But she couldn't. She sat up and pinched the bridge of her nose. She had to think it all out. It didn't make sense. Why, after all these years would the captain want to come back to this cursed island? To find out whether the Germans had escaped or not? And he had told her that the islet was near Rhodes. They were far from Rhodes, or was that in his imagination, too? Could it be that until this very day, he thought he only imagined their murder? Had something clicked back deep in his subconscious to make him realize that *this* was the islet?

Oh my God, she thought. Was she the conduit, the means by which he could dredge up the grim truth—all because of her tender, loving, understandings of last night? That was the horrible consequence of their lovemaking? God. She thought of Kyria Irini and crossed herself.

She held her face in her hands. Frances tried to console her, but she made matters worse when she said, "Why has the captain gone back to the boat without telling us? It's time for us to head for Andros. Why didn't he take us with him?"

They began gathering their belongings, not knowing what else to do. Surely, the skiff would return. They helped Theodora up, but her agitated state made them even more anxious.

Theodora looked deep into Ion's eyes. "The islet, the islet," she said, "you remember the captain's story about the Germans." She spoke Greek to him.

"What did you see up there, Theodora?"

"Bones, bones, I don't know whose bones."

"Don't tell the rest about the German story. Let's wait and see."

Ion rubbed his face with shaky palms. "It doesn't make sense. If he found the Germans' bones, wouldn't he cover them up? Did he know you were coming up?"

"Maybe he panicked," Theodora said. "All these years, he was never sure they had expired. Now he knows. Don't you see? He knows we know, you and I, and he's afraid we might tell the authorities. Why else did he run away?"

"Oh, shit. What are we going to do?" He looked around the islet in the blazing heat. No drinking water, no food left. How long could they last? He stared up at the little cave. "What's the cave like?"

"Little cave. Shelter from the sun only. Those Germans must have died there, huddled and delirious."

"Let's not jump to conclusions. Should we go up and let Stan look at the bones?"

By then, the rest had gathered around them, demanding translations. "What the hell is going on here?" Karen asked. "Where has the captain gone?"

Theodora and Ion looked at each other, neither knowing what to say, where to begin. Theodora began to cry. Frances tried to console her. Stan grabbed Ion's shoulder. "Tell us. Has the captain abandoned us?"

Ion shrugged. Karen clenched her fists, looked around the islet and said, "What a godforsaken place," she groaned. Theodora and Frances clutched each other.

But it was Paul, looking out to the tip of the escarpment, who first saw the skiff coming around. He yelped and pointed to it. They all let out a cheer.

Then, the captain and Takis waded ashore as if nothing had happened. They were smiling and carrying two large melons.

Theodora, though, still could not comprehend. She kept looking at the captain for telltale signs. He avoided her, sliced the watermelon expertly and divided it among his passengers, reserving the reddest portion for her. Parched, she devoured the melon, all the time looking at the captain, spitting out seeds, until she finally caught his eye.

He read her concern, looked away at first, and then apologetically said, "I'll talk to you tonight, dear *Thespinis*. After dinner." But his voice was shaky, not at all the voice of a Greek captain.

❊   ❊   ❊

The sail to Andros was uneventful, the first time the Letoites stayed each to themselves. Paul and Frances were actually separated, he in the saloon reading *Modern Greek History* and she lay below in her bunk reading Seferis' poetry in translation. Karen sunbathed on the foredeck and Takis napped.

Theodora was in her bunk, mulling over what kind of explanations the captain would offer. Surely he'd have to explain the bones. And what were the possibilities? That he and Takis were searching for ancient treasures? Possible. No matter where one scratches in Greece, artifacts turn up. But why did they run away so quickly when they saw her approaching? Were the bones not human, just some kind of bones they accidently unearthed when they searched for—what? Maybe there was some kind of sea tale of abandoned treasures on the islet during the Turkish occupation? They were Turkish bones, perhaps—yes, that there might have been a legend about Turks being buried there by Greek patriots during the 1836 War of Freedom. But again, why would they want to hide that from her?

Perhaps they really didn't see her coming up the hillock. Perhaps they seemed to run away quickly because they suddenly realized that the time was getting late and they had to gather their passengers on board.

No, no. Her intuition was correct. Already she could read her lover's thoughts. His shaky voice told her everything, his avoidance of her searching looks. There *was* something to those bones and an explanation was needed. Would he be truthful to her tonight, or would she have to wheedle it of him? By her "open," "caring," psychological approach?

If those bones were actually the German ones he hallucinated about, then what? How was she to take that? Rebuke him? Turn him in to the Greek authorities? Forgive him, or, oh, God—make the most passionate, forgiving love to him humanly possible? A debased love of pure carnality. A fuck to end all fucks.

How could she think that way? What was happening to her? The same thing that had happened to Karen?

❖   ❖   ❖

Ion had found a space on the *Leto*, a place where only one person could crouch and think alone, under the shadows of the pointy bow. The captain's behaviour had unnerved him, too. There was no other explanation than Theodora's.

But he wasn't sure how far Theodora's relationship with the captain had gone. He suspected they had become lovers, if for no other reason that she spent more time with him and since Samos, had given up her solicitous behaviour towards him. And maybe he actually did hear noises, little sighs and grunts coming from her cabin the previous night.

Maybe not. He and Stan had ferociously played their sexual game for three nights now. That, too was something needing talking about. He could not explain it to himself, this sudden "coming out." To hell with "observations." His behavior could not be analyzed by any gathering of data that he could know about attaining. He needed professional help. He wished his shrink were on board, but the fact was he needed something now. Despite the libidinous pleasures, something was amiss. Whom could he talk to?

About—why he didn't want to talk to Stan about his feelings? About why his orgasms were so intense and why there were pangs of guilt. Why he would even care if people thought him queer. He didn't care that much about people anyhow. And wouldn't surrender to sensuality affect his clear thinking about science or—what was it, exactly?

Slinking his head on his knees, he began to think more clearly. He knew what he wanted to do. He wanted to talk to Theodora. Whether she'd been fucking the captain or not, she'd appreciate his dilemmas. After all, she no doubt had counseled many queers, and she could tell him whether three nights of same sex makes a guy queer.

He began thinking how he would tell her all that. She had bared herself to him with her ridiculous proposal of marriage, and that gave him the right to be just as open, ridiculous though it might sound. He never had been open that much with anyone else, not even himself perhaps.

That's where he had to start. With himself. To think about actually what sex with Stan really meant. Compare it to that with Sonja. The first night with Stan was almost the same as with Sonja. "Out of body" responses. But now it had become—how could he put it—more mechanical. A brief, very brief, "loss" of consciousness immediately before orgasm. But otherwise, the acts were more like—masturbation. Yes. And like masturbation, there was the afterthought of, "Glad that's over with." Relief. No more.

No, there was more. He could admit it. There were elements of disgust. Stan was ugly, period. Merely a machine. You can't truly love a machine. Sonja wasn't that way exactly. Afterwards, there might have been some tenderness. Maybe she was a machine he liked. Because she was a woman.

Then things got too complicated. He rose and went to his bunk to read Schrodinger. He was making lists of further reading when he got back. He had to get to that guy Nietzsche.

17
Andros

They docked on the east side of Andros Island and walked up terraced steps to Andros Town. The island was Cycladic but green and the town had overhanging balconies, marble paved streets, and neo-classical houses. At a taverna, they took a late dinner, and then on board, they turned in for the next morning's early exploration of the island.

Except for the captain and Theodora. They walked slowly through the town out to the promontory where a large steel modern sculpture to honor the Greek Unknown Soldier faced off to the Straits of Doro.

The captain had hooked Theodora's arm through his and with the other hand held her hand tight in his fist. Each waited for the other to speak. Then, sitting on a parapet staring out towards the twinkling lights of Euboia, the captain said, "How many warships have passed those straits. How much history. The ancients on their way to battle the Trojans in the Troad. The Ionian Greeks and their struggles with Athens and Persia. The same story. Wars breed more and more hate."

Theodora knew what he was getting at. "We can't erase our memories, can we?" she said.

The captain squeezed her hand, paused, and in a low deep voice said, "No. Now you know the truth of the Germans. Now I know the truth myself."

Theodora looked him in the face. "You mean you actually didn't know the truth before?"

His voice rose in pitch, became louder as he said, "You Americans are sheltered. You are unable to know the hatreds war brings to us common people. My family was slaughtered. Those German pigs insulted my ancestry. They said Greeks are nothing but Turkish Jew slime. Perhaps you think they are not the typical German? I saw they are more than typical. They are the type of German that rose to the top with Hitler and now are at the top again. With their deutsche marks to buy anything they want in this little country. The Aegean is only a swimming pool for them. Bastards!"

"That is the excuse for murdering them?"

"It is no excuse. It is the reason. I'm sorry, *Thespinis,* nevertheless. It is hard to explain. Listen. Have you ever, in a moment of anger, done something you regret?"

"Not murder."

"I answer you. You were not angry enough. Think: being insulted and spit on for more than two weeks by those drunkards. Those cows, bellies with hairs to their navels. I took so much. I went crazy. Yes, doctor, I went crazy. People can go crazy for awhile, can't they, doctor?"

Theodora barely nodded.

"My wife died because we poor Greeks after the war couldn't afford the Siemens X-ray machines and Bayer® drugs. But you are right. I cannot justify killing them. I was in a rage. I was out of my mind. Vasili, my crewman and I started telling each other that we had not left them. 'No, he said, we left them back in Rhodes, remember?' I told him, 'But didn't we forget them on that islet?' 'What islet? We let them swim on lots of islets.' I said, 'Of course, there were so many. Maybe we just forgot to pick them up on one of them.' Vasili laughed. We made play of it. 'Who knows?' he said. 'Who cares?' I replied and laughed. 'Who will miss those dirty pigs?'

"And we sailed on back to Piraeus like kids who have played a mischief and are tickled all over for it. Back home, I told my wife of the game Vasili and I had played on the Heinies. She didn't understand. She just thought it was funny. 'Someone will pick them up,' I remember her saying. I wanted to believe that. But inside me, a doubt ate at me.

"The years passed and every time I talked to Vasili about it, he made joke of it again. 'Forget it,' he said, and each time he said that, the whole thing began to become only a bad dream. Vasili thought it all a joke."

Theodora struggled to understand. "Are you blaming Vasili? What kind of man was he?"

"He was from Volos. An experienced seaman, but everyone said there was something was missing in his head. Too much *raki*, too many women. I don't know. His family were refugees from the Smyrna diaspora. He was a good man anyhow, and I trusted him. The last thing he said to me on his death bed was 'Count the passengers.'"

Indeed. Theodora thought to herself. *Counting the passengers was the right thing to do, always.* Her mind diverted, she couldn't grasp the reality before her. She thought about how she, actually, had selected the *Leto*'s passengers carefully, but if she had to count them now, where were they? They were not the same passengers. What had happened to them? Their personality profiles had vanished, replaced by sexual silhouettes. What had they come to?

She was too dazed to say more, her Greek tongue had turned to concrete. She waited for him to say something.

He was almost whispering. "No, *Thespinis*, I could not go on with my life doubting. Last night when we made love, I knew that my life was opening up again. No hiding anymore my agonies. I had to find the truth. And when Ion mentioned a swim on an islet, it was like a miracle. We were near that islet. I knew the time had come."

"Very well, then," said Theodora. "What are you going to do with the truth?"

His face contorted. He dropped her hand and lit a cigarette.

"I don't fear punishment. Whoever tells the authorities—you or Ion even—will not find an ear from the colonels. We could say, not even from any Greek. It would be difficult to prove that Vasili and I left the Germans. Most of all, you must know, Theodora, there is a great hatred in Greece for the Germans. Maybe ten more years it will be less, but by then the case will be closed. The bones will crumble. And do you think the CIA would want the Greeks and Germans to fight over this? They think of only keeping NATO together to fight the Russians.

"The problem is not the law. The problem is what stays in my soul. How I can ever find peace and know my evil. The shame. The guilt. Oh, what can I do, dear Dr. Theodora?"

Theodora's studied the marble slabs beneath her feet. He continued. "As the years passed, I become confused. Had dreams. It may have happened, the dreams told me. It was a miracle, as I said, when Ion suggested the picnic. It was time for me to find out. One way or the other."

Theodora lifted her head and glared at him. "And when you found the truth, you decided to abandon us, too, eh?"

The captain grabbed her shoulders. "What are you talking? Oh, no, *Thespinis,* that never crossed my mind. I ran away from you hoping you wouldn't climb on up to see the bones. I'm so sorry. Never would I leave you."

He pulled her head to chest and stroked her hair. "No, no, dear Theodora. Theodora, I will call your name from now on."

She felt herself vanishing, but when she finally found herself again she wanted to say something to console him. About how dissociative responses can derive from previous traumas, that human actions can take strange twists under duress. She knew, of course, that human behavior had many causations hidden by many factors, genetic, experiential, mere happenstance.

She knew, too, that they could be made predictive with careful study of the personalities and situations.

Or could they? The variables again. But his "madness" could not be classified as schizophrenic, not according to the APA's Diagnostic and Statistical Manual of Mental Disorders. She opened her mouth to speak, to say all this to the captain, to give him solace, but to translate it was too hard. She wasn't sure she could explain it all in English. Tonight, perhaps, she'd try to re-express her thoughts in the Addenda. But hadn't she pitched the Addenda into the brink?

Then, seized by some strange impulse, like a loving mother cupping the cheeks of her child with her hands, said "It doesn't matter now. I understand. You must do what you have to do. You've had your," she couldn't think of the Greek word for revenge, "debt paid off. Now you must proceed with your life. Be good."

"Certainly. Bravo. You are kind to say that. I will. I will, my *koukla* doctor." He stroked her hair again and again, and they both looked off to the straits. The wind had risen, and they knew they would stay another day in Andros. Another day or more together, neither wanting to think about what happened after Piraeus.

The *Leto* below in a not too sheltered harbor was bobbing, but sleep for them would be tranquil, in each other's arms, rocking away the night in consolation.

✯   ✯   ✯

Early the next morning, though, Theodora's bliss had taken a bathetic turn, from the exalted heights of passion to the very bottom, the *vathos,* the very depths of the common place. How could she be so forgiving of this criminal beside her? How could she be sure that his rage would not boil up again? All that strength and certainly of his was a Newtonian illusion replaced by something like the Uncertainty Principle in Nuclear Physics, and who is to say it doesn't prevail, too, in the new, scientific psychology? But that metaphor gave her no peace.

She quietly left their bed and went up on deck. The sea was glassy yet swirly, and the *Leto*'s timbers creaked louder than usual. She dangled her feet over the railing and contemplated the pewter sea in the early morning light. It never was the same, but why did it resonate so to her moods? All its undulations seemed driven by a giant subterranean centrifuge, stirring and stirring, gently enough though to avoid frothing. She watched its circularity; wondered whether something sinister could be brewing deep in the sea, just as her life had now deliquesced into confusion and randomness.

Disorder all around her. Hints of that had always confronted her in the past, but philosophically, scientifically she thought, with her precocious intellect she could make some order of it, make reality partially, even largely so, predictable. Now she was oppressed with doubts. Eros had undermined everything, she couldn't find a reference point from which to take her bearings. The giant captain had veered her off the course of her life's master plan. What was she to do with him? Treat him as a patient, a child, take him as a lover, marry him and make a home with children?

They hadn't talked at all about those possibilities. They had played, teased, screwed, and now comforted each other. But where were all these sinister, swarming currents taking them? Could she expect this man to fulfill her emotional needs? Could he admire her *baklava* and her PhD?

Sounds around the bay muffled in thin mist. Far off in the hills, she could barely hear a donkey bray. The sun on the horizon was coming up, lighting up an invisible mirror of the world, and she began to brush back her hair, imagining the sky reflecting her troubled soul. She opened her arms to the light and, at last, as the mist began to lift, to her great relief, so did her despair.

She whiffed the lavender of the captain's after shave. She could feel the heat of his body behind her, the sun rays in front of her. He wrapped his arms around her shoulder, holding her fast to his body. Then, he leaned down and kissed the crown of her head, holding his lips until she felt their warmth penetrate her cranium like an holy anointment.

"*Agape mou*, this will be our last night in the Cyclades," he said. He proposed the Letoites go off in taxis for sight-seeing while he and Takis brought the *Leto* around to a safer anchorage on the other side of the island at the port of Batsi. She didn't like the word "last," it had an ominous ring to it, but before she could retort, Ion joined them, coughing and embarrassed for his interruption.

✿ ✿ ✿

Plans for the day were set after a hurried breakfast. They engaged taxis to tour the inner valley of Mesaria, its mountains, orchards, and archeological sites. Paul was particularly anxious to photograph the Venetian dovecots and their tiles. Stan was interested in the stone field-walls and their triangular orthostats. "Anthropologists make much of how societies delineate their territories," he said, and Karen replied that was the job of administrators and politicians.

Ion disagreed with both of them and claimed that it had to do with how the geometric outlays followed the slopes of the terrain. "Fractals of nature," he said, "that's all there is to it, Stan." He touched Stan's shoulder as if to conciliate him, but Stan screwed up his mouth and said nothing.

They hiked through orange and lemon groves until they came upon a five stories high Hellenistic tower, probably Second ACE. Little was known about it, the books said, but, as usual, the Letoites delighted in theorizing about its function. "Actually," said Paul, "it was the same old thing the Tuscans did. Building high towers, feudal enclaves."

"Look out towers for enemy ships," said Karen.

"A round house for storing grain," said Stan.

"A dormitory for virginal goddesses," said Frances.

All that chatter of the Letoites was beginning to suffocate Theodora. She found shade under a big maple tree to cool off and be alone. Their jabbering went on and on and Theodora wished only to be with her captain, to talk things out about their future. If they had one. Things had happened so fast, too fast. She needed to recapitulate all the events, absorb them, interpret them, reason their outcomes.

Fifteen minutes passed before the Letoites decided it was time to head back to the road and the taxis. Theodora didn't rise, however. Ion approached her and sat beside her."

"You tired, Theodora?" he said.

After she answered him, he instructed the rest of the Letoites to go ahead and that he and Theodora would hold the one taxi. "They are getting on my nerves anyhow. Talk, talk, talk," he said.

He stretched out on his jacket beside Theodora and offered her some water from his canteen.

"*Yia mas,*" she said, as she drank deeply and sighed.

"Greeks are blunt, the ones I know back home," he said. "So excuse me when I ask, you're very sweet on the captain, aren't you?"

Theodora smirked in agreement but with a tinge of sarcasm too, because, without any prompting from her, he had shown some affection—a response that she had for almost three weeks tried to evoke with her psychological ploys. Now unprompted, it emerged in genuine form, but, alas, its origin was not for any *eros* for her.

She studied him for a moment. His face showed deep concern, his body, lying on one side, head almost on the ground, one leg bent in the air, reminded her of a fallen soldier in supplications to a god. She was touched, but how strange it was that now his handsomeness, the Hermes profile and bare thighs, looked no more than a advertisement for Abercrombie and Fitch hiking shorts.

She told him about how the captain was her first lover (she spoke in a mix of Greek and English), and how she couldn't quite analyze it.

"Don't analyze," he said, "let the love flow."

Theodora chuckled. Coming from Ion, this was fun for her, like talking to Sammy. She teased him about how he was out of character to say that, he, an analytical chemist. He had no defense except to accuse her of the same thing, she, an operant conditioner.

"We've learned something of ourselves," she said. The dappled sunlight through the maple leaves gave them a static look, like a painting drawn in pointillism—except for the moments when they slapped away the gnats.

"Perhaps," he said, "it's all just another step in self-discovery in this catenary series of events we call life."

"Hell, it may be simpler than that. Maybe we've lost our senses," she said.

"Not at all. Things stay hidden so long in us, but ultimately, they are expressed, inevitably like a line of dominoes falling. Genes and circumstances in our environment. I bet you think I'm a cold fish, just because I don't show much emotion. Insensitive to others. Conceited. Is that what you think of me?

"You come across that way at times," she replied without hesitation. "Perhaps too stoic."

"It's my shield. I'm not shy, though. It's more to the fact that I find my inner thoughts, my introspections, are a little too deep to find easy expression."

"Don't you try?"

"Most people I know—in the sciences I mean—would think me a little looney to talk of them. Colleagues want to talk about chemical equations and computations. I've always wanted to believe that I really do have a doctorate in philosophy. Biochemistry is the chemistry of life, and to know something about it gets you close to some basic questions like, what is life for, where is its beginning and end, conception and death, the whole problem of how each living thing fits into the cosmos. This is science with a capital S. But when I bring up the big, broad questions, those *ersatz* scientists, with their tunnel visions, think I'm some kind of *chimera*."

"I saw you reading Schrodinger. You're just too much of a crazy Greek, anyhow," she said. "Philosophy is always grumbling around in our guts. But philosophy only lets us formulate intelligent questions, never answers them, so how can we live in this 'do something quick' world? We gotta get grants. Impress students and colleagues. Be Americans, consumers, Greeks, philosophers, all together. Why, the stories of our lives are only big palimpsest. No wonder you're 'odd.' "

He grinned. "So are you. You impressed me from the beginning as someone wanting her way. As if you knew what was the right thing for others. You're naive, I'd say. Did you ever think that it might not have been the right thing for you or them?"

She rose up straight and looked down at him. "You refer to my play for you?" She laughed. "You're right. I'm sure people think me conniving. But I've learned a lot about myself. Actually, we're both victims of antiquated values. My narrow Greek-Minnesota background must have been inculcated with the idea that marriages are to be 'arranged.' I told you about it. By parents, other Greeks or whatever. Me. And you blather on about metaphysics and science—old-fashioned ideas that have been debated for centuries—all the time trying to cover up the fact that you're gay."

"That wasn't hard for you to figure, was it?" he said.

Deep silence, only the leaves rustling.

They looked up at the tower. "There are towers like that in the Mani on the Peloponnese," he said finally. "Defenses for the blood-feuds they waged. Greeks against Greeks. Part of human nature, I suppose. Bop someone on the head with a stone before you get bopped."

"We're not doing that, are we?" Theodora said laughing.

"This trip has been strange. Strange that we all started out sharing only one thing, we were all professors. Other than that, we are so different. It's a wonder we haven't stoned each other to death. How in the world could you have selected such a motley group?"

"I had my reasons. It was an experiment. All of you guys were supposed to fit neatly into my plan. We were to be thrown together, and ultimately, people develop a kind of cohesion, and with luck, something deeper. In a way, that's exactly what did happen. But not in a predictable way."

"Unpredictability," Ion sing-songed. "That's the nature of this world. How many scientists don't get that. They think with all their pat little theories they can make sense of it. Look, though, everything that really keeps us going is the unpredictable—that experiment or event that turns our pet theories topsy turvy. A little spot mutation here or there to keep evolution going. That one little receptor site that can pre-determines the metabolic pathways. Chaos, all the way, Theodora."

"Oh, shut up." Theodora screamed. "Must you go on so? Let's talk about people I don't want to hear any more about your all-encompassing world views. You sound like a dying duck waking up to the reality that life is not eternal. People, Ion that's what life is about. We must communicate with each other, try to understand each other. Forget God and truths. The moment, the now, the pleasures, whether you like Stan's penis. That's the issue."

"Do you like the captain's?"

She slapped him lightly on the thigh (how cool it was compared to the captain's hot loins!). Tussled his hair. She was playing with Sammy again.

They clasped each other for a second, and knocked heads, laughing hysterically.

"All right, then," Ion said. "What are you going to do with your captain?"

She turned serious. She talked about the intensity of her feelings for the captain, how she felt protective of him, her need to nurture him. Then about the logistics, the narcosis of love, guilt, and the rest. He wasn't married, professed his love to her, yet never mentioned how they could share their lives. He was expunging guilt, she said, for the murder of the Germans. He would need time to separate that realization from his affection (love?) for her. And in the meantime, what was she to do? She dared even to express the notion that if he really wanted her, she would forsake everything for him and come live in Greece. Make a home for him on an island, wait at the port when he would return from a tourist excursion. Provide him, if he wished, (and she hoped), children. But there was the age difference. No matter. She had self-reliance, too, if and when the day came when she would outlive him. Perhaps she could do some writing. Research the early psychiatric clinics in ancient Epidauros. There were many alternatives. And no certainties.

It was as if she were making notes in her Addenda, but when she finished talking into the canopy of leaves, she turned to look at Ion. He wa scratching the dirt with a twig, waiting for her to say more. She felt embarrassed, not because of him, but for herself, that she might be have been rambling incoherently.

"Well, all that doesn't matter," she almost whispered. "Time will tell. The fact is, and you would agree, that the trip has been sublime. Every place we've been—all the old stones and history and sea and mountains and morsels of food and sips of wine—makes me reflect, makes me want to forget 'I, my, mine', and lose myself to the cosmos. Zen Buddhists have the idea, but so did Plato. The oneness. That's what I really want to take away."

"I've felt some kind of elevation, myself," said Ion. "But I don't know what to make of it. I mean I don't know how it will play out in the future."

"My turn to be blunt, OK?" she said. "Where are you and Stan headed?"

Ion remained silent for more than a minute. Then, speaking Greek, carefully and slowly, he said, "He is nothing. A trial, that's all he meant. He is a fine man, but we don't mix. Prisoners resort to homosexuality. In that cabin, all of us imprisoned with each other my *eros* was bound to come out. And I was the one to instigate the erotic. That was a new thing for me, who is usually passive with other people. Sex was satisfying, pleasurable, like a *loukoumi*, sweet, yet cloying. But afterwards, I always felt thirsty for some clean mountain spring water to wash down the . . .

He stopped for a moment and cleared his throat. "What I mean to say is that Stan is not like you and me. He is not deep, worrisome, scratching out inner meanings to things. He wants for himself, self-gratification, no inquiring of feelings. Perhaps it's the gay way. Life is a big joke. Pricks only count. It has validity I suppose. But it doesn't take him anywhere. *Ta erotika* have their place, they do in the *Symposium* too, but for me, it cannot sustain me for long. I would as well move on to things like Platonic 'Forms, Ideas,' and such. If Eros seizes me again, why, I'll try someone else. Perhaps I've learned how. If that's really what I want. Anyhow, my readings in Schrodinger give me food for thought."

Theodora was not too surprised by Ion's soliloquy. Stan had the reputation for being predatory, she knew that from her "reserach" on him back in California. And she knew, too, of Ion's passivity. What was out of whack was her interpretations of his alleged affair with the female graduate student. He was seducible, that was a given, but it never crossed her mind that a man could seduce him, contrary to what Ion thought about his initiative in the affair with Stan. If he was truly AC/DC—and such personality types are well portrayed in the literature—he'd now have to work out which avenues he'd take in the future.

It didn't concern her, however. She had found a real man that was her type. Wishy-washy, confused men could become only case studies for her, and that was something she didn't want in her romantic life.

Still, the captain presented other problems, but those, like ephemeral obstacles, vanished in the heat of her passions for him. There was the truth. She had to admit it. Not logical, but the truth.

But what to say to Ion? She saw for him a long struggle, and for the moment, its discussion seemed futile. The day was getting late, and she wanted to get back to her captain. "Well," she said, "we've broached lots of topics. Our 'affairs of the heart' have many complications. This journey on the *Leto* sure has presented us with problems." She laughed, goofily. "Maybe it all has to do with our being Greek."

Ion rose to help her up, then he said, "*Panoyia mou*, is that what's wrong with us?"

On the way down to the taxi, they picked some capers off the bramble, and Theodora, seeing the wilted flowers around, remarked how beautiful the asphodels and orange poppies would be in the spring.

18
Aegina

From Andros, they sailed the next morning to Aegina, the island in the middle of the Saronic Gulf, not far from Piraeus where the *Leto*'s journey would end. The pastel sea and sky framed a grey-green island, more a cut-off hunk of the mainland than an island, and the Letoites, their sensualities blanched, looked at it like familiar territory. Even the magnificent Doric Temple of Aphaia failed to stir them. They trudged around the columns like pilgrims to a battleground or cemetery. No games this time, no ecstatic outbursts, only somber inspections, like sheep grazing for puny fodder.

The pistachio and olive orchards they passed on the mountain surrounded the ruins like giant wreaths, the silver of the foliage an implacable reminder that beauty is fleeting. And so were the joys of their three weeks. What lay ahead for them was one final dinner to honor the crew and a disembarkation the next day at the harbor of Piraeus. They were on schedule, to the day, for their three-week contract, and beyond that they had to scramble back to their academic holes.

They didn't talk about the ending, no one uttered the euphemism about the "best part of a trip is . . . home." Each, deep in their thoughts, tried to decide what to remember about the trip, but the memories were too dreamlike, segmented, impossible to piece together. Like the mythological Leto they had wandered the Aegean, island-hopping, searching for deliverance . . . from what? Even that, they were not sure. And how could they in only three weeks have found it when time had compressed everything into a ball of uncertainties?

At their last dinner at a garden taverna suffused with jasmine sweetness, they had ordered a whole lamb on a spit and perfunctorily presented to the crew their gratuities in a large brown envelope. There was some clapping, some congratulations and thank yous, but the spirits of the Letoites were reverting to primordial, ground states. Karen didn't beam, Stan scratched at the beginnings of a new moustache he was growing. Paul and Frances disjoined their appendages, Ion brooded, and Theodora moistened her mouth like she was contemplating an entry to her Addenda.

More and more retsina was ordered, and more and more the Letoites gradually began to deploy from their ground states. But gaiety was not the direction, it had to be something intellectual that would jumpstart them. So it was that Frances started to talk of Plato's account of Aristophanes' ideas on the real nature of man.

"The human race in the beginning," she said, "was divided into three sexes, he said: female, male, and male/female (we might call that third type hermaphroditic). The odd thing was that he postulated that these three types were globular, each with four arms and four legs, two faces, two sets of private parts, and whatever. Anyhow, these creatures offended Zeus, so he decided to punish and weaken them by cutting each in half! But this left each of the halved individuals yearning for its other half. Zeus took pity on them, so then he arranged their 'parts' so that they could have sex. Thus, LOVE was born. Imagine. So there are different types: male-female (from the hermaphroditic globular type), female-female, and male-male. And *voila*, we have an explanation of how heterosexual and homosexual love came about. The consequences, of course, of it all is to explain how our lives, to this date, we are looking for our other half—a search that can be pretty arduous."

Hearing her explanation, the Letoites looked around at each other frowning, wondering what had gotten into Frances. Why did she bring up *that* subject? It was embarrassing enough to each of them that for the last three weeks they had so overtly, so unabashedly, shamelessly, fornicated. In only three weeks, they had degraded themselves to that level? Were they animals? Where had their erudition, calmness gone? After so many years of study and contemplation, had they capitulated to unrestrained libidos? Yes, sometimes that could have happened in their pasts, but then it was a more controlled exploration—Frances with Victor, Theodora with her Swedish boy, Paul and Pia, Karen and her husband and dyke, Ion and Sonja.

Those couplings took some time to develop, these *Leto* ones were explosive. Stan was out of character in another way, going from anonymous sex to Ion. What had Greece done to them? Had they gone mad all of a sudden? Who was to blame? Theodora, because she planned the whole mess. Their own weaknesses and frustrations? Fate? The gods who imprisoned them on that *Love Boat*?

Now, here was Frances trying to justify the pairings of the "halves"—Karen–Takis, Stan–Ion, Theodora–Captain, Frances–Paul? Blame it on nature and Plato, she was saying?

"How neat," said Karen. Her tone was deprecating.

"Now, what happens?" said Stan. "Do 'halves' live happily ever after once they've found their other half?"

Ion held his brow and said, "How do you explain prostitutes, philandering, etc.?"

Stan clenched his fists. "Must you find every little exception to everything? Is your life nothing but re-examining beliefs so you can puncture them with critical scientific analyses? Damn. Get human, man."

Karen. "Yes, let yourself go. Be human. Things are not in your control."

Ion: "Well, I was just telling Theodora the other day about how she . . ."

Theodora: "Never mind, Ion."

Paul: "Back to what I was saying. Your postulates, Ion—philandering and stuff, are just failed attempts. I mean failure to find our true other halves. Real love . . ." His voice trailed off into almost whispers.

"And how in the world, does the 'half' know for sure when it's found its other half?" said Theodora.

"It's all myth," said Ion. "It can't be. Genetically, it wouldn't work. Must I remind you all that Plato didn't know about haploid and diploid chromosomes and dominant and recessive genes?"

"Horse shit," said Stan. "Of course you don't have to remind us. It's a metaphysical question, don't you see?"

Frances sighed, disgusted. "I believe that Aristophanes was trying to tell us that true love is very hard to find indeed. Our sins—think of the original one in Christianity—have made the gods punish us and we are doomed to struggle to find our true Love and gain our oneness again. It's the idea that life is tough, sure enough."

"And that part of the *Symposium* is wholly ontological," said Paul. "He was playing around with the meaning of LOVE," said Paul. "Besides, Plato had an absolutely delightful imagination." His giggles sounded like finch twitterings.

Meanwhile, their discussions didn't faze the captain and Takis. They were busy gnawing lamb bones and dipping bread into bowls of olive-oiled greens. Occasionally, the captain would lift his glass to the Letoites and say, *"Yia mas,"* to which they dutifully echoed, *"Yia mas."* But this final dinner was more like a formal banquet than the Dionysian feasts they had on the other islands.

Theodora still moped. She'd glance at the captain from time to time, but when she addressed him in Greek he seemed reserved. Of course, he always played that captain's role when he was in the presence of his passengers. But just this last time, couldn't he let his hair down and show the warmth he did in her bunk?

She turned to Ion, talking Greek so others wouldn't understand. "Where are *our* halves? Do you think I've found mine? Are you going to know where to look for yours?"

He looked down at his plate, and said nothing. *He was withdrawing again, into that private world of his,* she thought. Then she looked at Stan and damn if he wasn't gawking at Takis! The blatant faggot! Karen saw him and saw Takis giving Stan a faint smile. Daggers were in her eyes. Theodora watched the whole exchange. Then she looked at Paul and Frances and they were entwined again, holding hands under the table. Everything was back to where they started three weeks ago.

Or were they? Theodora's captain had changed her. Whatever the outcome of their romance, she could never go back to structuring her life. It didn't work, and she had written pages in the Addenda about it that morning. The gods were always thwarting, and she wasn't going to embroider her future with unattainable schemes. From here on, she was going to let things happen, and interpret them, if she wished after the fact. That was the best she could do with her new psychology. It was going to be some kind of "guessing" at the future of her patients with some knowledge of their pasts. Then, they could make the choices and she'd help if they wanted any. She needed to read up more about humanism and that new guy, Carl Rogers, who was making such a mark.

After all is said and done, she told herself that she did learn one big thing on the trip: the joys of sex. My, my, she wasn't going to stay in the corner anymore waiting for the perfect mate. She'd plunge—take a lesson from the flower children, not be such a huffy academic—right into all that sexual revolution stuff that was going on back in California. But how would she select a partner? Other than the captain, if that had to be?

Ion next to her was a reminder that Aristophanes' approach was poppycock. Carefully, she had selected, by Zeus' design what she thought would be an approximation of her other half, the true love. Congruence in age, ethnic background, education, profession, religion, private part complementarity (assuming they had been originally one of those hermaphroditic globs), etc. So what does she get? A confused bisexual. And conversely, what she ends up with is a "half" not at all reciprocal: twenty years older, no congruence except that they were both Greek. Such globs.

She watched the captain chew on a lamb bone. *Rather atavistic,* she thought. But there he was, imposing, romantic, the very antithesis to Aristophanes idea. Clearly he wouldn't qualify as the ideal love. Yet.

At that moment, he smiled at her, reached behind him and from another table placed in front of her a platter holding the sagitally sliced head of the lamb. "It is with great honor, *Thespinis,* that I present this head to you, you, the Queen of the *Leto.* You have ruled us well!" He raised his glass to the other Letoites.

They all clinked glasses, not exactly understanding the ritual. Theodora explained, but when they goggled at the head, floating in juices, the skin burned to a crisp, the bones charred, the ears crumpled, the teeth tinier than expected encrusted with burnt blood and slivers of singed fur, the brains a gray mess, they almost gagged. What was she to do with it?

She starred at the lamb's eyes, shrunken and burned down into their orbits. She steeled herself. She suddenly remembered what to do. Ion's eyes gave her assurance and they both grimaced, they were both Greek.

"*Yia sou, Kaptiani*! In your name I take the eyes."

She took a sharp knife that Takis handed her and carved out one of the eyes. The other one she spooned onto the captain's plate.

Both then, grinning at each other, popped the eyeballs into their mouths.

Everyone applauded, feeling greenish. "It tastes like marrow," Theodora said.

"We knew you had an eye out for us," said Stan.

✢ ✢ ✢

Making port in Piraeus the next morning was a *pandaemonium*. No sooner than they had tied up, they found themselves surrounded by taxis, shore police, hawkers, and tourists gawking at them. Their skins blackened leather, their hair stringy and bleached to orange streaks, they could have been bedraggled adventurers, perhaps refugees, perhaps derelicts. They stumbled over each other, pulling up their luggage to shore, sweating and scowling.

Smog and cacophonies surrounded them. Talk was impossible. The captain and Takis seemed to be almost scooting them off the gangplank, and they quickly began hosing and mopping down the *Leto* and getting things ship shape, coiling rope, sweeping decks, neatening up cushions in the saloon. It was if their passengers were strangers to them, that they were eager to be rid of them and be ready for the next cruise. Greek efficiency, such as in restaurants and discos, the Letoites had seen before, but this time the brusqueness, gracelessness seemed almost like demonic rudeness.

The Letoites stood dazed at the dock, the women in skirts, the men in long pants, wondering what, or if, a ceremony was called for. Perhaps, a sign-off of papers or at least some farewell embraces. Abruptly, the captain and Takis came ashore and shook their hands briskly, and proclaimed, loudly:

"*Kalo taxithi,*" have a good trip.

Taxis came around, and the Letoites still stood confused, uncertain of what to do next. They averted the taximen's entreaties, instead stared out to the Saronic Gulf. It was that curious reflex, they had learned to accept it, it was one that they had learned from being seafarers for three weeks. No matter where they had been, that's what they always did: they were always staring out to the sea, wondering. In that strange disconnect, standing by their luggage, staring again, thoughts fleeted by. Somewhere out there beyond the Saronic Gulf, way out in the Aegean—where was it, Paros, Samos, Patmos?—their lives had made a turn. It was too nebulous, though, it always had been, that reaction to the staring.

Now, turning themselves to the jumble of Piraeus, August, 1973, they had to find new ways in old California places, a daunting prospect they weren't ready for yet. They were alone again, the Platonic globs separated. Not even Paul and Frances held hands, they were beginning to lug their bags to separate taxis. Then each of the rest began to drag themselves to other taxis. For a second, they shouted at each other: "See you back home. Maybe we can have a reunion! Bye!" But their yells hardly resonated, the noise of ship diesels and motorcars throtted human voices.

Frances headed to the airport for a connecting flight to London. Paul was to be overnight in Athens before a flight back to San Francisco. Ion was to take a train to Munich for an International Meeting of Biochemistry. Stan said he was going to Rhodesia to do some field work. Karen kissed Takis on the cheek when he had presented her with another one of his wooden figures (another Priapic figurine) but she couldn't communicate with him that she was staying in Greece for a few days, nor did he give her any signs of how they could rendezvous.

Before entering their cabs, they took one last look at the *Leto*. She looked abandoned, squashed by large expensive yachts around her. Yet, she had been home, as much, perhaps more, than childhood ones. All the pictures of her would be treasured but they had no doubt that she was not long for this world. Like Leto herself, she was destined to become only mythical. She was Poseidon's property to do with as he pleased, and he would be storing her very soon in his briny locker.

And so, too, would she be stored deep in each of their subconscious. But how foolish of them to be so sentimental about an old tub that almost drowned them.

They slammed closed the taxi doors and didn't look back anymore. It was a good time with her, that's all.

"Take me to the Arakhove bus station," Theodora told her old, smelly, unshaven taxi man. Just before stepping ashore she had been told abruptly by the captain to meet him in the afternoon at the KTEL bus station. He had spoken of his wanting her to spend a few days in his village before she headed home, but the invitation was vague. Could she assume that they were to take a bus there together? But he wasn't explicit about where the bus station was or how to get there. Why hadn't they discussed this more, planned the details? Just why couldn't he be more predictable? And how long would she have to wait for him at the bus station?

And she had never, never seen him with rolled up pants and a mop.

19
California Redux

It took some time for all the Letoites to fully comprehend all the transformations incurred by their 1973 journey. Ten years after their return they held their first reunion, but not because they had promised to just "keep in touch." There was a tragic reason.

Each year, they had exchanged Christmas greetings with notes about "when will we do it again?" This time, Karen's message was urgent. She had heard about it from the Gay and Lesbian grapevine. They had to meet as a group and talk about Stan.

Paul and Frances had married, of course. On their return, Frances was pregnant by "Delian decree," and subsequently she had popped two more babies with Paul hardly realizing how it all happened. They had settled into a typical married academic life, leasing a house on campus, while Paul continued his scholarly work, which now could be effected with European and American CD ROMs of classical and archeological journals. Frances was happy as a mother, and occasionally taught creative writing in the Community College Extension programs. Travels back to the Aegean were infrequent, but along with their relentless researches of the classics, they remained to the core, Letoites. But their transformation to marriage and parenthood dependent on that trip in 1973? Well, surely it couldn't have happened at Chichen Itza. The screwing and all its consequences could only have happened in the middle of the Aegean on the *Leto*, so they believed.

Ion maintained some contact with Theodora, meeting for dinner in San Francisco for a Greek meal in the Tenderloin to reminisce and update their personal lives. He also kept in touch with Stan, attending a few 49ers games together. The butch thing.

But Karen's summons brought all of them together for a new purpose. Stan had contracted AIDS from his sojourns into Africa. His lust for the "dark boys" had not been quenched, and as he told Ion at one of their infrequent meetings, "I can't abide the Castro fairies anymore."

So, the Letoites made plans to help Stan who was alone and in a isolation ward in the Stanford hospital. Each promised weekly visits with him, and each month, they planned to meet at Karen's to review Stan's condition and commiserate.

At one of their earlier meetings, Ion related how he suffered the bitterness of not "coming through" for Stan. He wanted to think that had he, Stan might not have contracted the disease.

"You're not gay," Karen said to Ion, "and being his friend, unfortunately, could not have deterred him. It's a pity, a fact of fate, that Stan found the one man, you, he could truly love. But you couldn't be gay just for him. Let's be happy and celebrate that the *Leto* brought you together as friends."

"Damn shame, all the way around," said Theodora. "The way society condemns different lifestyles. His promiscuity was probably no worse than anyone else. Damn that virus."

"Yes," said Karen. "And another thing. You remember how he was always telling us about anthropological theories and the necessities of traditions and cultural myths? Yet, he couldn't abide many of them. Societies are so reticent to accept new values. Our world changes, populations change, it's a whole new ballgame each generation. Yet, we cling to the old antiquated beliefs. Such a pity. Gay activism is the right way to circumvent all those prejudices. He didn't have time to give much to that, did he?"

At Stan's bed, they heard him in delirium talk about "blue." "The blue, oh that blue—blue. And the white, the white-white marble, the white-whitewash, oh, how white." Then, in other moments, he'd say to Theodora, "Kubler-Ross. White tunnels. Will my tunnels be Cycladic white? I want some blue, too, please."

At his deathbed, they gathered as if in on board the *Leto* for the sunset. Stan's passing galvanized them, bonded them more. Afterwards, they talked of his sardonic wit, how he could puncture all their inflated pretenses. "In the picture we have of the *Leto*," Frances said, "he's always have the spot of the comic relief. So much fun, he was."

And more than that, as they remembered him, his acerbity, his iconoclasm, his *bon mots* (Paul declared). After his passing, they began their regular gatherings, their "Symposia," usually at Karen's with Paul and Theodora always facilitating their encounters. They'd bring old photos of the trip, of themselves young and bronzed posed against the Aegean brilliance of the *Leto*, of all the memorable places. They'd try to remember what had happened at each place and confessed everything, what they thought of each other, why they had spats. Over Karen's fireplace was a much enlarged, gold-framed picture of Takis, bare-footed and chested, pulling in the anchor line, every muscle taut and with the inimitable Archaic Smile. The most beautiful man, they all agreed, including Karen's husband, that ever existed. As for the captain, well . . . they would leave that to Theodora's rhapsodies.

At those long dinner parties, they bared their souls as they had learned to do on the *Leto*. Karen revealed what had happened when she returned to California. She was miserable pining for Takis, until during the Christmas holiday, unable to endure the separation, returned to a cold Piraeus where she found Takis working on the *Leto* diesels, grease up to his elbows. He was fully clothed in woolens and she didn't remember him being so small. He invited her to a nearby *cafeneion,* but their non-verbal communication flopped. At a nearby table, three foreign women watched them and Karen could not have mistaken Takis' smiles and nods toward them. Suddenly, everything became clear. Karen went home and into therapy. She "healed" quickly, if not miraculously, and she fell in love with the therapist, a huge overweight, jowly, rheumy-eyed man. She introduced him to fried squid, he provided her with the very best lox flown in from New York. They were destined to live happily ever after, trite but true, and spent summers in the Soprades Islands because they liked the grilled octopus there.

"I owe all to the *Leto,* to all of you," she said one night at one of their reunions. "I needed that detachment and all of you. We all cut loose that summer. What a catharsis. How wonderful the sensualities! However fleeting!"

"And to find how logic and rationality didn't always work," Ion said. "Remember us talking about Parmenides and what he said about the ου (the thing) and the νοεω (thinking)? And how Theodora was always arguing the Protagoras view? 'Man the measure of all things?' And me the opposite, Pythagoras, the worship of numbers. God, we were cocky. Look at us now. Humbled. Wiser."

They all nodded their heads. "Who is to know, 'us,' who are we?'" Paul replied, quoting Plotinus. "We became fused with the Eternal One, the union of body and soul in the vast universe."

Conversation stopped. All started looking out the huge plate glass windows of Karen's Douglas fir plywood home. Peeping behind the patio's philodendron, they could have sworn they saw Stan saying, "Oh, Paul, horse shit."

Ion's revelations about his own life at those dinners were sad for them, his transformations still in progress. After his parents died, his Greekness was no longer an impediment (or so he thought)—a Greek wife, kids, the Church. He should have felt free to find himself in a world of his choice, in California, far from his Greek confining roots in New York. But *Leto*'s voyage had made him dig only deeper into ancient philosophy and early science, particularly Aristotle and Archimedes and the Pythagoreans and Neo-Platonists. He brooded too much over his scotch, feeling that his own biochemical researches were trifling inquiries, lacking breadth of purpose or meaning. And he thought the same of much of the science around him. The DNA thing was simply a case of oversell. Science, as practiced by the run of the mill practitioner such as himself, simply lacked the gratification of grand philosophical meanings. It was supposed to, but in reality it was nothing more than solving little puzzles to gain research grants. Brick-laying. A business.

He talked, in serious veins to the Letoites, about how science, at least, didn't seem to be asking the big questions. Theoretical Physics and Mathematics seemed a more fruitful approach, but he hadn't the time or training to head in those directions. Nevertheless, he tried to broaden his scientific horizons, but in the process he lost ground in his own discipline Grants dried up, his teaching went to hell and many of his colleagues thought him spacey. At seminars and conferences, he seemed more an obstructionist, asking too many "big" questions, unable to stick to the immediate experimental problems at hand.

Worst of all, he told them that he daydreamed too much of the Greek Isles, those times on the *Leto* when he could take in those grand blue vistas, think big thoughts, and reminisce about Ideas, Forms and Plato. Everything in comparison, from the dingy lab benches to the dusty libraries and slovenly kids, seemed irrelevant.

He willingly told them that his depressions could not but help to contribute to his asexuality. (Now he could talk openly about that subject.) He had talked to Stan about his libido—he was grateful for that—and he could be frank to tell him that their playing around had no permanent effect on him. Occasionally, he'd noticed a pretty coed, and, surprisingly, because of his talks with Stan, he could remember his sexual dreams; they were, in fact, about females, but they could not animate his love life.

It was nice that he could be open to Stan about all that, he told the group, but it was nicer, too, that he could be open with Theodora, who seemed to understand him best. After their mini-reunions in restaurants in the Tenderloin, she began to invite him to her home for a *stifatho, arni so fourno,* or some pastries. And within the last few years, he spent a few weekends with her when she wasn't away in Greece with her captain. Besides their shared Greekness, they begin to share an antipathy to the modern world of science. As a result of *Leto*'s journey, they had both became more sentient about life and more doubtful of science's efficacy, he because of its piddling enquiries, and she because of how her behaviorists' notions betrayed her too often.

"Too much reductionists' crap," they agreed.

Meanwhile, Theodora's stories were about how her theoretical framework in psychology had shifted to the humanistic, Rogerian approaches. It was the vogue, anyhow, and it had its salubrious effect on her career. She became so caring and empathic that just about everybody loved her, students, colleagues, administrators. Her academic career prospered, and she basked in her popularity. And the Letoites loved her now even more.

She returned to Greece often. She and her *Kapitanios* worked out perfect schedules for the Christmas and Easter holidays. In the summer, on board bigger yachts than the *Leto*, she crewed for him as hostess and cooked for rich European (non-German) clientele. It was if everything that she had wanted in life had come true, like some miracle. And she hadn't planned any of it. The *Leto* be praised. The illusions of life, the "truths" revealed at last. Parmenides take a bow.

On rainy February weekends in Oakland with Ion, they'd talk of her bliss, and she, like a good sister, would listen and empathize with his laments, about everything from his science to his lonely existence. Ever so gently, she tried to coerce him to socialize more and in subtle ways even introduced him to potential mates at her small social gatherings. They didn't take. Ion's moods were like too much salt on the lamb.

✿   ✿   ✿

Stan's death, the seminal moment for all the Letoites, the *krisis* that made them all passengers on a becalmed ship of life, made them reach out to one another, clutch one another for rescue from the impending disaster that lay ahead for them all: the journey not across the Aegean enchantments but across the forboding Styx. It was as if to delay that journey they reached back into the past, to an imaginary *Leto* to transport them away from the gloom, to remind them of the joys of self-discovery, and to revel in the now and the evanescent future.

For this, their "Symposia" served another good purpose. They had discovered that the Letoite camaraderie became a permanent feature of their lives, and without planning it, they began at their bimonthly gatherings taking turns leading discussions on the Epicurean, the Stoics, the Atomists, the Neo-Platonists, the playwrightes. Those meetings, interrupting their usual academic praxis to broaden themselves with the Classics, had marvelous benefits for them all. Lamb was always served at dinner.

Unlike their earlier encounters on board when each bristled with self-importance, their discussions were congenial, largely due to Theodora's expert Rogerian skills. They listened to each other respectfully, tried to understand all different points of view, learning from each other the strengths and biases of their ways of thinking. For each, the enhancement benefited their professions, gave them broader views of their intellectual efforts, taught them humility. For some, they felt spurred on in their disciplines, for others it made them realize the shortcomings of narrow-viewed research. But for all, their philosophical examinations could not but make them more complete human beings.

Perhaps, as one of them had said early on, "Our degrees of Doctor of Philosophy" are misnomered. But as the years passed, their maturity and the voyage of the *Leto* and the "Symposia," they could refute that. With certain amount of conceit, they could claim to be bonafide "Doctors of Philosophy."

No more, thanks to Stan, the Great Debunker in their midst, were they prone to hide behind shields of pedantry, no more were they afraid to admit to their sensual, sexual needs, which now they could freely express to one another. Nevertheless, they were not immune to the sexual revolution that raged around them in their colleges and universities, and at times, it strained some of their personal relationships. Those temptations they freely revealed, and they found relief in the group therapy atmosphere of their meetings. Little, cute Paul seemed most vulnerable to coed seductions, and fat Karen day-dreamed too much of hot jocks. "Middle-aged satyrs make ridiculous colleagues," Ion reminded them.

Remembering their past licentiousness, their rallying call, "We need another trip," was met, at first with laughter, and then later, silence. Each, to themselves, would reflect and then admit the emptiness of the idea. They had turned a corner, there was no turning back to those young abandonments. And that saddened them. The *Leto* had landed, the goddess had given birth, and now, one would have thought, the only thing left was to celebrate.

However, celebrations play out in time and boredom replaces it. The only thing for them was to start another voyage, a different, quieter and internal one. Frances offered alternatives. They could find new challenges, students to nurture, children to raise, frontiers of knowledge to be opened. New experiences would need to be put into the context of old philosophical ideas; thus, journeys would always continue but now they would be more the "stay-at-home" variety. And, like the ancients when expounding their "travel myths," they could seek new "truths."

"Hmm," said Paul. "That is maybe what we must do. It seems we have been reduced to that kind of mundane intellectual exploration. I, however, would prefer something else than these quiet internal ones, some unexpected external event. Something that we would be forced to cope with, not of our choosing, something that would exhilarate us again to find new avenues of exploration."

"Some new sensual input?" said Karen.

Her husband closed his eyes and assumed an all-knowing Buddha pose. Obviously, he'd been through that recourse before, and all along, being a psychiatrist, he had long ago concluded that his wife's group were indulging themselves in some kind of effusive, mutual admiration society, a bit silly for a bunch of PhDs. But they seemed to be having fun and their "Symposia" topics were heuristic.

So patiently he listened while the Letoites sought "new avenues." They considered psychedelic drugs and talked of psycho-biology. The medical and legal aspects of that he easily torpedoed, and their ideas of transcendental meditation, which he did not object to, did not fit Paul's bill. Yet, they all agreed that what they needed was the intervention of some dramatic event in their lives that would put them on their heels and provoke some lively discussions.

"We talk too much theory," said Theodora. "Yes, you're right, Paul, it would be nice to put to the test some of our philosophical notions."

Then they argued whether to cause such a dramatic incursion. Frances perked up. "Let's go out and do something very anti-social—say, form a Society for the Promotion of Miscegenation, publish a journal. Have scholars submit papers on how to implement it. Think of the row in academe! Think of the fun we'd have to defend it psychologically and philosophically. Yes, Ion, and biologically too."

"Won't work," said Ion. "It sounds like a solution to the racial problem. But, we'd be thrown out on our asses. The wrath of the public."

"I should think," said Paul, pacing around the dining table, "we should put to test some of our experiences. Look, we've been talking about the Classics every since the *Leto*. We've been reading, discussing. My, we have become, in a sense, all Classicists. We know, from whichever our disciplines, the importance of the Classics foundation. I would propose we organize a massive, national grass root campaign to overhaul college curricula. Start, shall we say, with the first year studies to be devoted exclusively to reading the Eleatics all the way to the Neo-Platonists."

"We'd educate them, indeed, that way. But, my dear," said Frances, "you know what the feminists, Afros, New Age, MLA, PC people would say to that!"

Everyone shook their heads in agreement. They scratched their heads more.

"Well, look at us, gang," said Theodora. "None of us is exactly what you could call a 'revolutionary.' We're good at looking at Aegean sunsets and omphaloskepsis. No, I think you'd agree that Paul's idea can't be implemented by an active process on our parts. Seems to me that our best strategy would be to sit and wait, be on the lookout for that unexpected traumatic event. Then, we'll pounce on it and see whether our philosophical arsenals can ameliorate it."

They talked about the nature of such an event. Something geopolitical, something like a radical shift in scientific paradigms. They made lists—death of capitalism, global warming, anti-matter, string theories. Or some event that would affect them personally. Reincarnations (of Stan?). Their publication of a treatise, *Leto's Journey*, which would be a vague, conglomerate confession of their personal lives? But they weren't sure how or when such things might occur. Or whether any of the possibilities really had a collective purpose for a continuance of the "Symposia."

Karen's husband smiled at all their deliberations and thought, *At last, their little "games" were coming to an end. Impoverished, they'd soon disband, realizing all those years of nostalgia and philosophy were only illusions, Parmenidean ones.*

Epilogue

The unexpected event twelve years later reared like a Greek tragedy. The captain had begun to complain about his back. A severe vertebral dislocation coupled with hypertension decked him. Theodora, at every opportunity, flew to Athens to be with him, but his deterioration was rapid. When he decided to be with his family in Arakhova he told her—for the first time, in fact, commanded her—"Leave me," he told her, "go live."

Devastated, she again had to contend with Greek brusqueness. It was like accepting the horror of the Germans' massacre and having again to embrace his frailness and love him for it. She grieved and sought anodynes from the people who knew her best—the Letoites, who comforted her and tried to give her a rational, philosophical understanding for the tragedy—but, best of all, from Ion who understood her relationship with the captain best and who could make her accept its Greekness. By some godsent reversal or roles, Ion now became the counselor and she the counselee.

And he was good at it. Where that gift had welled up from surprised everyone. Perhaps it was no more than inherent *gnosis*, certainly not mere scientific logic. He would say things like, "You will have the eternal memory of him," "Remember his gifts," "How he taught you to love and be loved," cliches all, but they arose genuinely, and Theodora's pain each time subsided a little.

They spent more weekends together, and Theodora lavished him with ever more delectable dishes, *pastitso* and stuffed peppers with imported currants, *kouloura* bread with *masticha* from the island of Chios. And when summer came along, she discarded her black mourning dresses and decided that together they'd go back to the Aegean. "Recapture those glory days," she told him, "and not be sad for their passing."

In Athens, they would have impressed a stranger as brother and sister. Ion had not noticeably changed. There was gray in his hair, but his sturdiness and open, handsome face remained. She retained *kefi* joyfulness and the voluptuous contours of a hippy, mature woman.

But things changed by the time they got to their favorite Island of Paros. In the Baptistery of the Church of the Ekatontapiliani, in that lemony light with a service going on in the main church, they sat once again on the ledge of the marble font. Only this time, there was no conversation, no inane, feeble attempts of either of them to reach out to the other. No insipid comments about religious significances, meanings of birth and death, absurd biochemical metaphors. They sat there immobile for the longest time, barely hearing the chanting going in the nave next door. When it ended and a few straggling tourists came into the Baptistery, they rose and began to study the faded frescoes. Perhaps it was only that they wanted to maintain a connection against any intrusions, but they suddenly clutched each other's hands. They left that way, and when they reached the outside grounds of the monastery, they never let go.

Hello, Parmenides?

✻ ✻ ✻

Back home at "Symposia," the Theodora-Ion disclosure provided the grist for their philosophical mills, the "dramatic event" they sought.

Did Theodora, in fact, plan all along her union with Ion? Was the captain only an interlude in her quest? Were the Addenda proof of that? When they read excerpts at their meetings, they were all astonished at Theodora's acumen of them but a little embarrassed, too, at her arrogance and naivete.

Or, was it pure serendipity, the captain's demise and Stan's untimely death, that brought them together? Their closeness was long in developing and neither had ever alluded to any "plan."

Or, and this was the provocative notion, was there all along some very basic, inexorable force that sealed their union? Here, they argued, the profound concepts of ου and νοεω, the "being" and the "thinking," and of the more profound One of Parmenides, the "beyond Being," the ineffable force from which all else is derived.

"What the hell was in that baptismal font?" Karen said.

They never could comprehend that provocative notion completely, of course, and its relationship to the other intelligible divisions of the world, intellect and soul, left them to say what the Greeks would have said: *einai sto noein mas.*

"It is on our minds," ineluctably and indelibly, that's all.

And *that*, perhaps, could be the philosopher's meaning of the One, and why it propelled them on to another journey, the one that launched their penultimate travels to the realms of Kant, Hegel, Kierkegaard, and beyond.

Kalo taxithi, as the captain would have said.